WITHDRAWN

DARKBOUND

DARKBOUND

THE LEGACY OF MOONSET: BOOK TWO

SCOTT TRACEY

flux
®
Woodbury, Minnesota

First Edition
First Printing, 2014

Book design by Bob Gaul
Cover design by Kevin R. Brown
Cover illustration: Aaron Goodman

Flux, an imprint of Llewellyn Worldwide Ltd.

Library of Congress Cataloging-in-Publication Data
Tracey, Scott, 1979–
  Darkbound/Scott Tracey.
      pages cm.—(The legacy of Moonset; book 2)
  Summary: Malcolm Denton hates being a witch and is at odds with his four Moonset coven siblings, but an alternative offered by a demon comes with dire consequences for Carrow Mill's teens.
  ISBN 978-0-7387-3649-5
[1. Witches—Fiction. 2. Magic—Fiction. 3. Demonology—Fiction.
4. Orphans—Fiction.] I. Title.
  PZ7.T6815Dar 2014
  [Fic]—dc23

                                                              2013041665

Flux
Llewellyn Worldwide Ltd.
2143 Wooddale Drive
Woodbury, MN 55125-2989
www.fluxnow.com

Printed in the United States of America

ONE

It is 100 years since our children left.

....

Oldest Written Records from the
Hamelin Town Chronicles (1384 A.D.)

I was finally back in school, after a week of security proto-
cols and constant supervision, and now there was a sorority
girl trying desperately to piss me off. Now, instead of just
one blowoff class about magical theory, the five of us had
two: one before lunch and the other at the end of the day.

Kelly was barely older than us, a recent college graduate who split her time with the Witchers between teaching
and babysitting duties that came with being Cole and Bailey's
guardian. She smoothed her hair back every time she got nervous, until her hands spent more time in her hair than on the
podium she stood behind.

"Malcolm? What do you think about the Coven bond?"

Five pairs of eyes turned to me. I'd taken up a spot in the back of the room where I could slump down in my seat and work on the Civics essay that was due on Friday. Nobody but me was concerned about all the school we'd missed after nearly getting possessed or murdered a few weeks ago. The others were still riding high on this new curriculum.

Somehow Justin had talked the Congress into actually giving a damn about us. He had that way about him sometimes. It's the only reason I was here right now. He made me promise to show up, but he couldn't make me participate.

They waited. Jenna rolled her eyes. Bailey and Cole looked nervous, and Justin calm but worried.

Kelly seemed desperate to be the kind of teacher she thought we needed. I'd seen her in the halls that first day, the bottled blonde with the dark eyes and California tan. None of the guardians ever showed up at the school, so at first I didn't recognize her. She'd changed from the comfortable, casual look, opting instead for something better suited to a private school. Her discomfort was obvious.

If I was a nicer person, I'd smile at her. Give her a silent moment of reassurance. I knew that, aesthetically, she found me attractive. When guys checked out girls, they were obnoxious about it. Active. There was a running commentary, obvious gestures, or catcalls: ogling by the ignorant. But girls were sly predators of appreciation. They waited until they were unobserved before polite smiles turned hungry, and casual eyes devoured. Kelly always looked at me with hungry eyes.

Girls have looked at me like that since I was twelve or

thirteen. I'd become immune by this point. Kelly wasn't much of an authority figure, but she wouldn't have been the first to stare too long.

We were wrangled in a small classroom in the fringes of the school, a room that I was pretty sure had only been storage a few weeks ago. Whipping up a new class in the middle of the semester meant scraping the bottom of the barrel, I guessed. The walls were a stark, chipped gray, plaster grooved away by something small, like a screwdriver or a pair of scissors.

It was all such a joke. Didn't any of them realize it? The Congress, suddenly giving a crap about the five of us. Like they'd really just turned over a new leaf and now we were all besties. I couldn't believe I was the only one who was skeptical.

Justin wanted me to wake up and smell the magic. To give our latest fresh start a chance. Like it was okay that we'd been used as bait, that we could have *died,* all so the adults surrounding us could smoke out a warlock. In exchange, now we would be taught magic like the rest of the kids our age.

It was remarkable how quickly Justin and the others fell in line after that. All it took was a little attention, and all four of them were eager puppies who would do anything they were told.

I was the lone holdout. I didn't want anything to do with Illana Bryer's plans for us. But they didn't see it. All they saw was getting everything they'd ever wanted. Nevermind that it was the last thing I wanted. They didn't understand me. They never had.

How did I feel about the Coven bond? Or how did I feel about this *class*? Coven Bonds for Dummies. "I ... think this is a waste of time," I said finally. Jenna snorted, because of course she had to make her opinion known immediately. "Why does it even matter what I think?"

People fantasized about doing what I could do. About being able to bend the world to their whims. Witches. Magic. Power. I fantasized about a senior year unmarred by devastation and changing schools, where I spent all one hundred eighty days in the same building. With friends who preferred sneaking beers and watching the game to sneaking spells and toying with chaotic forces.

All I wanted was one day without magic. Was that really too much to ask?

I sat up, grunted when my knees slapped against the metal bar underneath my desk. *What do I think about the Coven bond?* A few weeks ago, it had been the Coven bond that had nearly gotten all of us killed. One of us had been infected by Maleficia, dark magic, and the infection had spread into all of us like we were a single organism being brought down by a virus.

Everyone knew the saying "a chain is only as strong as its weakest link." What we didn't know was that it had been a witch who had first coined that phrase. And she'd been talking about the Coven bond. The idea that our lives weren't really our own had never been more clear. I could live my entire life on the straight and narrow, and one of the others could destroy me in a matter of minutes. They were my biggest threat, and my biggest weakness rolled up into one.

They said that was how Moonset devolved. That when Justin and Jenna's dad snapped, his invocations to the Abyss corrupted his entire Coven. It took years to put them down, and along the way they'd murdered thousands of people, stolen grimoires and priceless artifacts that were never recovered, and committed acts of terrorism that had struck more than just the magical world. Moonset didn't care which terrorist groups took credit for their attacks, they encouraged it. The world was happy to speculate in its ignorance.

All because one member had been weak and succumbed to the dark power of Maleficia, of the Abyss itself. Now our parents were all dead—executed—and we lived in their shadows. One mistake was all we could afford. One mistake might even be too many.

Bailey turned away, ducked her head in shame. She'd been our weak link, but it wasn't her fault. The darkness slipped in while her guard was down, after exhausting herself trying to do the right thing and save innocents. She blamed herself. Our entire Coven could have been taken, and all that strain weighed heavily on her. Since we'd been saved, Bailey had withdrawn, prone to nerves and more apprehension than I'd ever seen out of her.

Being in a Coven meant you could do things other witches couldn't. You had strengths they didn't. And you had other people to rely on when there was trouble. But that's not all it meant. It meant that you were in the line of fire more often. You had no choice but to deal with the bickering between Coven mates. You were shackled to other people for the rest of your life. Their weaknesses were your weaknesses. Forever. They could manipulate your friends in order to manipulate you.

And those were just the *normal* problems I had to deal with.

"And why do you think that?" Kelly asked.

"Don't bother asking him." Jenna reclined back in her chair, hands tangled in her hair as she shook it out. "Malcolm hates everything."

No, I just hate the things you like. I decided not to say it. There was no point in fighting with Jenna. She and I never agreed on anything, but this was something we worked extra hard at disagreeing on. Jenna thought magic would solve all her problems. She hated the idea that anyone else had the authority to tell her what kinds of magic she could or couldn't use.

I could be honest. Tell them everything I was thinking. But what was the point? Jenna would play the wounded princess. Cole would sulk. Bailey would probably cry. Justin would get that constipated look he got when trying to mediate, even when he'd already chosen a side.

I chose to be silent. To wait it out. Kelly would get bored eventually, and she'd learn not to call on me soon enough. Focus on the others who *wanted* to be here.

She stared me down at first, probably assuming I'd crack sooner or later. "Malcolm?" she prompted. Like I'd forgotten to speak.

I pulled out my mp3 player and popped in one of the earbuds. Only one, to maintain the pretense that I cared about this class. Cared about Coven bonding.

"These lessons are only going to work if all of you are committed," Kelly continued. It was ironic that Kelly was pulling double duty. At home, she was both a guardian and a jailer. And now she filled the same role at school. Charged with putting us down if we gave them even a whiff of dark magic. "The Coven bond works by finding the common ground you all share, and tapping into it. Without that basis, these lessons won't do anything but waste your time."

I slowly, insolently, stared her down as I slid the second earbud in and let the rest of the class blur into a montage set to industrial rock. Jenna's shoulders squared in front of me, and even though she never once turned around, I knew that all her focus was on me.

I sighed. It had been a few weeks since our last big blow up. I guess we were due.

TWO

The Coven bond has been central to magic since the beginning. Covens are how we know we are meant for something more. That there is a grand design that we are all a part of.

....

Coventry in the 21st Century

Winter in New York was underrated I thought as I focused on the window instead of the lecture. Snow days were a luxury you didn't get in the far south, where it snowed once if you were lucky. This was the first time in a few years we'd gotten a real East Coast winter.

I didn't mind the snow at all. It might have been nice not to be the only one driving in it, since Justin and Jenna weren't allowed to drive, and Bailey and Cole were still too young. But there was still something to be said for the snowy, quaint town we called home. For now. Carrow Mill was the perfect small town nexus—tiny in itself, but ten minutes in any direction led to a city three times its size. Cities that held all the amenities Carrow Mill lacked.

I kept my focus on the outside because it was infinitely better than the brewing tension inside the classroom. I'm sure the others were eager and attentive, but even still I knew that I was a stone in their shoe they just couldn't shake. Even if they wanted to ignore me, I was there in the back of the room. Insolent. Ruining everything. I knew they were just biding their time until class was over.

Until the real lesson could begin.

I kept an eye on my watch, but otherwise let the rest of the room fade out around me. There was still too much going on today: one more class with Justin, then our afternoon lesson, and an excruciating ride home before I could escape them and be free for the rest of the day.

Ten minutes before the bell, movement in the corner of my eyes made me look up and freeze. The tension in the room was more apparent, even though we were one person short. Kelly was gone, and Cole had shut the door behind her.

The four of them watched me each in their own peculiar way. To Cole, I was like a science experiment he thought might explode. Jenna, like something she stepped in. Bailey, something that broke her heart. And Justin, like I was a showdown he was resigned to lose.

I sighed, pulled the music from my ears and stood up.

Of course Jenna was the first to start. She prowled across the room until she was on the other side of my desk, her dark eyes narrowed.

"It's simple," she said, tapping her nails against the laminated desktop. Her nail polish was royal purple, the exact shade of her top. How Jenna had been elected to lead the intervention, I didn't know. "If you screw this up, I'm going to kill you."

The other three alternated who looked at me, and who looked away. Justin shifted closer to the door, matching Cole on the other side. They acted like I was a wild animal, and any sudden movements might spook me out of the room entirely. If only it were that easy.

"Come on, Mal," Bailey said softly from my left, staring with the baby deer eyes that might have worked a few months ago. But not now. "We need this." Ever since Luca's attack, Bailey grew quieter, day by day, fading into the corners. Was I the only one who noticed?

Two weeks ago, the five of us were subdued and attacked. Luca had invoked Maleficia and painted the town with Moonset's symbol. A circle shaded except for a crescent moon of white, with six curving rays like a sun. It had been Moonset's marker during the war, and Luca's calling card fifteen years later. He'd brought us here and hoped to sacrifice us to his masters in the Abyss. Only Justin was able to fight back—we owed him our lives. Later that night had come a second attack, just as unexpected, and again Justin fought for the rest of us.

Part of me wished that he had lost. One of them. Maybe both. It was hard to say. He'd faced off against a warlock who had summoned a group of monsters straight from Hell—monsters who tried to possess us and take our magic for themselves. Then he fought the witches who were supposed to be looking out for us—the government that used us as bait, as sacrifices, as tools. They wanted to lock us up and throw away the key.

They thought we were dangerous. We were the children of Moonset. There wasn't a witch alive who didn't know about Moonset's crimes. Most couldn't help but wonder: how far had the apples fallen from the tree? My father had named me Malcolm, and in Spanish, "Mal" meant bad. It was a little on the nose as far as I was concerned. But no one had ever asked me what I thought.

"We *don't* need this," I snapped. Bailey winced at my tone. "Are you all *insane*? They used us as bait and hoped Luca would *kill us*. And now you want to cozy up to them because they're promising to teach you some scraps?"

"They want to teach us to protect ourselves," Cole chimed in, parroting words that Jenna had most likely repeated several times before. He even matched her tone—part disdain, part amusement. "So that what happened never happens again."

"And you're just going to trust that that's the truth?" I asked, arching an eyebrow at Jenna. This wasn't really four against one. It was Jenna versus me, the same as it always was. Justin might step up to her when she went over the edge, but when it came to magical power, they had the same hunger. Feast or famine, it put us all in danger either way.

She pursed her lips and shook her hair out again, the helmet before battle. "That doesn't matter," she said. "We protect ourselves. You know that's the only way."

There were certain rules we'd come to live by. Some were more important than others, but two were particularly sacrosanct. The first: we could only ever rely on ourselves. The second: adults couldn't be trusted. I agreed with the second wholeheartedly, but I was an island compared to the others: the only person I could rely on was me.

But now it seemed like the rules had changed, and all it had taken was for Jenna to fake a change of heart. The adults saw contrition and it had soothed away seventeen years of bad behavior and outrageous stunts. It really made me wonder who was more naïve: Jenna, who thought the adults were doing this to help us; or the adults, who thought that Jenna would use her power responsibly.

Either way, I wanted no part in it. But there was only so far I could go. The albatross was never far.

The issue at hand was the bond that chained all of us together.

Our coven bond was . . . unconventional. Most bonds form in high school, sometimes in college. Ours was prenatal, or something close to it. Moonset had learned ways of manipulating the Coven bond, and ours had peculiarities.

Normal covens could come together or move apart as they wished. Their bonds would stretch from one side of the planet to the other. But ours was not made out of elastic, it was forged out of steel chains.

The curse. Moonset wanted to make sure we were never separated. Anyone who tried to split us up was hurt, and catastrophes struck until we were reunited. It offered a measure of protection—like when Justin was attacked by the wraith last year, the bond activated and destroyed the creature.

"It's not the only way," I pointed out, "but it *is* the only way you get what you want. That's all this is. You want to be the baddest witch around, and if it gets the rest of us killed, oh well."

"Hey, that's not fair," Cole said, climbing to his feet. Justin grabbed him by the back of the shirt and yanked him back down, but Cole wasn't placated easily. "You're not any different," he continued. "You hate magic so you're punishing the rest of us by epoxy."

"Proxy," Justin corrected quietly.

Cole looked mystified. "But epoxy's that stuff that's like glue. And you're sticking it to someone, so you punish them by epoxy."

Justin shook his head, hiding a smile behind his hand. "Not exactly." But as he inhaled to explain the actual phrasing to Cole, Jenna cut him off.

"Cole's right. It's not like you're doing this out of some sort of evolved sense of morality. You're pouting, and you're screwing over the rest of us."

"Did you ever stop to think about what's going on around us?" I pointed out calmly, focusing on the other three and letting Jenna stew in her own juices. There would be no getting through to her. But the others . . . they had good sense. Some of the time. "The only reason we're in danger at all is because the Covens keep jerking us around on chains. And because we keep trying to use magic to make our problems go away."

Justin looked towards the windows, a flash of discomfort slipping across his face. *What's that about?* He shifted where he was, putting his weight on his right foot and toed the ground with his left.

"You can't blame the Covens for what Luca did," Bailey said quietly. It was like the volume in the room had been instantly muted. Her quiet acceptance of her role in Luca's plans had been hard on her. "He used me. And I turned on all of you. What happened was my fault."

"No, it wasn't, Bay," Jenna said, instantly all warmth and light. She shot me a dirty look as she crossed the room and crouched down in front of Bailey, clasping their hands together. "You're nothing like Luca. He chose to do everything he did. You didn't get a choice. You were infected. Just like the rest of us."

"But I should have been better," Bailey protested, and I could hear the building tears in her voice. "I couldn't do anything to stop it."

I hesitated, though it took me a second to figure out why. The self-loathing in Bailey's voice was just a little too pitch-perfect. That's when I realized that they'd worked this out in advance. When did Bailey get so manipulative? No, that wasn't it. When did Bailey start studying Jenna 101? It was a classic move, threading a moment of weakness into an argument she wanted to win.

Neither Justin nor Cole looked all that concerned, which cinched it. When reason and threats didn't work, they would move on to deception. Awesome. These were supposed to be the only people I could trust.

"Coven magic requires everyone working together," Jenna said, repeating the day's lesson. "We have to commit."

There was someone here who definitely needed to be committed. At least we agreed on that. "We don't work together," I pointed out. "Ever."

"Don't you think it's time we grew up?" Jenna asked, and that was the last straw. Jenna could pretend to be the bigger person, but I didn't have to play along with this. With any of it.

"So you're all buying this crap?" Silence from the other three. "You'd have to be. Glad to know the rules have changed. If one of us disagrees, we do whatever it takes to force him to do what we want? Manipulate him, control him, whatever. Good to know." Sure, I was always the counterpoint to whatever Jenna wanted to do, but usually Justin and Bailey could be made to see reason. But they had her back this time.

"Maybe she's doing it for the wrong reasons," Justin finally said, breaking a silence that had run as long as the intervention, "but she's not wrong about it being necessary. We can't protect ourselves the way things are going. Maybe if we'd been able to, Bailey could have fought off Luca's influence. Or you guys could have resisted Bailey's influence on *you*. Or...I don't know. A hundred other things. We don't *know* what the Coven bond can let us do. We need to learn."

"More magic," I said bitterly. "Because that always makes things better."

"Things are already worse, cupcake," Jenna said snidely. Immediately, Bailey and Cole jumped all over her, and she held up her hands in apology. "Sorry. But this..." she took a deep breath. "It's important, Malcolm. We're sitting ducks in the meantime."

"And who's going to save us, Jenna? You?" The snide disbelief in my voice comes naturally. She's not exactly the most magnanimous person I've ever known. She's a typical girl of privilege—her problems are always more serious and fascinating than anyone else's. "Thirty-one, by the way."

"Thirty-one what?" The attempts at sibling cohesion dropped from her face all at once.

"That's how many people you sent to the hospital the last time you played around with magic. Since I'm sure you never actually looked up what kind of damage you left behind." I skimmed my eyes over the other three, because I knew none of them probably had either. All three looked away.

It didn't faze Jenna. She stared me down, unblinking. "Do you even remember what it's like to have fun? You're such a buzzkill all the time. God forbid you let loose a little."

There was no point to any of this. I tried not to think about her words, about the accusation, but it rattled around inside my head and touched on things I didn't want to think about.

Jenna left first, pulling Cole along behind her. Justin tried to say something to me, but I turned my back to him and pretended that there was a sudden need to investigate the contents of my backpack.

Eventually, he left, and it was just me and Bailey. She hesitated at my side, a baby bird that was caught between a desperate fear of heights and the need to fly. "Mal? Are you okay?"

I grabbed a handful of the backpack's material, rough and slippery against my hand. Squeezed until some of the pressure left my head. "You're better than that," I said quietly.

"I know you think I am," she said, ghosting away from me. Her voice echoed from the door, weary and older than she had any right to be. "But I'm really not."

THREE

The Denton family was one of the first to settle in Carrow Mill. Always a haven for witches, the Dentons were known for their loyal and generous natures. But even the old bloodlines can go bad.

....

Moonset: A Dark Legacy

I was halfway down the hall on the way to my locker when the halls started to clear and the bell rang. So now on top of pissed off, I was going to be late for my next class.

I opened my locker just to slam it closed, and then repeated the process.

"Congratulations, I think you killed it," an amused boy said from behind me.

"I'm not waiting all day," a waspish voice added. "You're the one that wanted cheese fries, not me."

I turned to find Kevin and Maddy, friends but not really friends. At least not yet. But one thing was for certain—more witches. I couldn't get away from them.

They were two of the locals who'd been here before us. Kevin was cool, even if he was like our guardian Quinn: part of the magical elite. His great-great-someone-or-other had made a name for themselves years ago, and his family had been in the thick of magical politics ever since. He'd moved to Carrow Mill a few years ago for school.

Maddy, on the other hand, was a native. She'd grown up here, and her family had known the Moonset witches back before they were terrorists. As it happened, she wasn't my cup of tea, but she was Kevin's best friend, and where one went, the other invariably ended up. There was the whole rivalry she had with Justin—I had my suspicions as to why, but I kept them to myself—but in recent weeks she'd been almost pleasant. Until today.

Actually, all the witches of Carrow Mill had been incredibly tight before we arrived. Maddy's *other* best friend was Justin's current girlfriend, Ash. I hadn't seen much of her around though, ever since the farmhouse.

"We're heading out for food. You want to join?" Kevin asked, eyeing my locker. "Looks like you could use the break."

"You're just going to take off, and no one's going to notice?" I crossed my arms in front of me and leaned against the locker. "I've read the handbook. Students don't get off-campus privileges for lunch."

Maddy rolled her eyes. "Students, no. Witches? Yes." She waggled her fingers and then gestured both of us to follow her as she started back down the hall. Without anything better to do, I started to follow. "As long as we show up for our *real* lessons, no one's going to say anything. And as long as you're with us, no one's going to give you a hard time."

"You want to talk about it?" Kevin asked, as we shouldered our way out the side exit of the school and headed for Maddy's car.

Did I want to vent about Jenna and the others? Of course I did. "Not really," I grunted.

He nodded like that was the answer he expected. "You'll feel differently after the cheese fries, trust me."

"I don't know what you think is going to happen, but cheese fries aren't going to fix my problems." Maddy faked a gasp as she clicked the button on her keychain to unlock her doors. She drove a nondescript black sedan, the kind of car that looked more like it was for security than lunchtime jailbreaks.

"You haven't had Charming's, obviously," Kevin said, claiming the passenger seat for himself. I climbed into the back, half-wondering what I was doing here. Or why they'd been so interested in dragging me along.

"Charming's is this restaurant outside of town with seriously the most amazing food," Maddy said. "Trust me, it's the kind of thing only the locals know about. The first time I took Kevin there, I thought he was going to faint."

"I wasn't going to *faint*," he replied with a good-natured grin. There was a moment when it faltered, when he glanced in his visor mirror and our eyes met, before he snapped it shut and shifted in his seat until his back was to the door and he could look at both of us. "It was during two-a-days, and I had low blood sugar."

"You had a cheese fry addiction," Maddy laughed.

When she wasn't picking on my brother, she was actually almost ... pleasant. Who would have thought?

I listened to their back and forth for a while as Maddy drove us out of town. "But seriously," I asked during a lull in the conversation, "Charming's? That's really what they named their restaurant?"

Kevin shot a triumphant look at Maddy, who scowled in the rearview mirror. "I told you I'm not the only one who thinks it's stupid."

"It's not stupid," she said, turning her attention back to the road. "It's tradition. It all goes back to the Carrow family, the ones that helped settle the area. After a few generations, there was just old man Carrow and a few distant nieces and nephews who wanted nothing to do with him.

"Old man Carrow loved kids, but every time he tried to have some they died young. Influenza, croup, that sort of thing. So eventually, he was a rich old man who'd outlived everyone he knew. And he decided to take his fortune and do something useful with it. And what he ended up with was an amusement park for the children of the community. He called it the Enchanted Forest because he was obsessed with fairy tales."

An amusement park? Around here? *I think I would have noticed that.* "So where is it?"

Maddy waved a negligent hand. "Back there somewhere," she said, gesturing towards the woods on our left. "Most of it burned down a long time ago, but if you get past the fence, you can still see the main plaza. It's all that's left of the old park. A couple junked-up outhouses, a rusty old food truck, and a whole lot of garbage. Kids around here used to hike over there, but there's not really all that much to see."

After a few more minutes, we pulled into a parking lot for a run-down but thriving restaurant. The sides of the roof slanted in, like the wrong gust of wind would send the whole building tumbling down. One side of the building was taken up by a giant mural of a castle and a tower, but it had been in the sun so long that the entire thing was faded and washed out.

I looked back the way we had come, and tried to imagine it in the past. Maybe it wasn't so weird. An old-fashioned amusement park and a local business trying to capitalize on the theme. "So the park shut down and the restaurant survived?"

"Basically," Maddy nodded. "I'm telling you, you're really underestimating the cheese fries."

And it turned out she was right. The fries were thick with batter, crisp and golden, and scalding to the touch. And the cheese tasted like actual cheese made by angels, the kind of delicious that was terrible for you. I ate every bite, and as I did, the whole story started to spill out. Jenna, and the tension between us, and the new Coven class and everything.

"You need to find something for *you*," Kevin insisted. "I mean, I play sports and try to do the regular teenage thing because it's the only way to keep myself sane. Both of my older siblings were magical prodigies. A football scholarship won't impress my parents, but I do it because it's something I love. You just need to find that."

"Yes, Mal," Maddy added, in a monotone, "live your dreams. Be the ball. Jock out with your—"

"Alright!" I said hurriedly. "I get it." But I cracked a smile for the first time in hours.

"You just want him to join one of your six thousand teams," Maddy said, using a French fry to point at Kevin. "I see through this whole pep talk. What's next, anyway? Baseball?"

"It's not just about the team," Kevin said, but he ducked his head down and I saw through the lie. He looked down at the basket in front of him, empty except for a single French fry, which he then dipped in Maddy's cheese. "If Mal doesn't carve out a place for himself, it's not like the others are going to do it for him. He's got to stand his ground sometime."

Maddy sighed and leaned back in her chair. "I just think you're underestimating what his sister's going to do if he gets in the way of what she wants."

Kevin laughed. "How bad could it really get, though?"

As it turned out? Really bad.

FOUR

*Everyone knew the Denton boys. Cy and Charlie
went everywhere together. Before they got older,
before all the bad blood, all they had was each
other. Charlie adored his big brother.*

....

Elizabeth Holden-Carmichael
Carrow Mill, New York—
From a written account
about Moonset's development

Kevin's words rang in my ears when we got back to school.
He and Maddy took off for their own Magic 101 class, while
I headed in the opposite direction, towards the front of the
school. If nothing else, the long walk would allow me time to
figure out my next move.

After the morning's class, I didn't see any point in showing up for the second. It was just going to be the same BS all over again. It wasn't like the adults were forcing me to show up. I'm sure they would all sleep a little easier if there was one Moonset witch not being trained in volatile new magics.

Kevin suggested I find something else, something that gave me an outlet the way that he had football. A chance to laugh and tease and joke around with normal kids my age. Making friends at a new school had never been hard for me before, the hard part was keeping them from getting *too* attached. But after the wraith attack, and then everything that happened with our move to Carrow Mill, I'd forgotten how to be the easygoing friend.

The stories all said that Moonset had a disciple, a man they'd trained to continue all their works after they were gone. A man named Cullen Bridger. The name was whispered around for years, a phantom who laid claim to acts of terrorism that paled in comparison to Moonset's works. But when the wraith attacked, it had used Bridger's name. There was a psychopath out there looking for us, and the others weren't concerned at all.

Maybe Jenna and the others thought I was a pain in the ass, but they were all obsessed with magic and the Covens. It was all they ever wanted to talk about, all they ever seemed to *think* about. Justin and Bailey had always been a little more on my side, the ones who at least *attempted* to have an outside life. But Luca ruined that too. Now Justin's focus on magic was fevered, and Bailey was wilting away, and I didn't know how to deal with either of those things. Problems in the coven were Justin's area. He played mediator. He'd always been good at it.

As I hit the three-way junction that led to the main hall-way, I passed a wall of posters, advertisements for fundraisers, school clubs, and a couple of local advertisements. But one of them caught my eye.

The school didn't have a woodshop program, which had bummed me out when we first enrolled. I always liked the idea of working with my hands, of being able to see what you're actually creating. Unlike magic, which just forced change into the world whether it liked it or not.

There was a school play, however. And a school play meant sets. I instantly changed directions, heading for the auditorium where the drama classes were held. This could be my fresh start. No more witch drama. Just drama drama.

So of course I walked into the auditorium in the middle of a fight. Not just any fight, but a three-on-one beat-down. Because that was my life now.

At first glance, all I saw was three guys surrounding a younger, smaller guy. The three were obviously athletes, bas-ketball players if I wasn't mistaken. They certainly had the height for it, although a couple of them also had the width for football.

"What'd you say, you little shit?" one of them growled.

Two of them were just enforcers, I could tell even as I approached. They stood at either side to keep the kid from run-ning. It was the one in the middle, the sullen-looking kid with all-American hair and the viper eyes that was the ringleader.

Their victim wasn't such a wilting flower, though. First impressions weren't what they used to be. "Is there even a step below remedial?" he sassed. "Because I don't know how to dumb it down for you anymore. Get out of my face, Cauley. And take your goons with you."

"Is that right?" Viper boy smiled. "I saw you at lunch, Hamilton. You really think that's smart, flirting with my girl? I warned you before."

"How about I warn you?" I squared my shoulders and finished striding across the auditorium floor. The four of them were so engrossed in each other that they hadn't even noticed my approach. "Three on one? Those are shitty odds. Three on 'I'm going to kick your ass' is a whole lot better, don't you think?"

Viper barely inclined his head towards me, eyes flicking my way like a serpent's tongue. "And who the fuck are you?"

"The guy that benches two-twenty-five and *really* wouldn't mind making you bleed."

"What are you doing?" the kid at the center of it all asked, then bit down on his lip like he couldn't believe he'd spoken. The others turned their attention back to him, and that's when I got involved.

I grabbed Viper by the shoulder, and that was the move he'd been waiting for. He swung around the moment I touched him, fist arced towards my face. Only he must have expected a fragile flower, because the punch was sloppy and wide. I knocked his arm to the side, then swung the other one behind his back, shoving him forward until he slammed into the wall. Then the other two came at me.

Neither one of them was dumb enough to throw a punch, but one tried to shove me, only I didn't go anywhere. My feet were planted on the ground and I stayed exactly where I was.

The other got in my face, nose to nose, like he could force me back with just his forehead.

"What are you looking at?" the guy snarled.

"Your pretty mouth." And then I flashed a grin. "Hey there, sailor."

The guy growled and moved back, half in shock and half to reposition for the inevitable swing. But I didn't just go to the gym to work out. I'd done years of self-defense and martial arts training. I knew how to handle myself in a fight. I just didn't like to. So when he swung, I ducked, and then darted back out of his reach. He swung again, and I leaned back, his fist missing my chin by inches. Each failed attempt only made him growl louder in frustration. Each subsequent swing became more and more reckless, until I was barely doing any work at all.

"You think this is some kind of joke? You really that stupid?" Viper was back on his feet and stalking towards us. "I can have you expelled like *that*," he snapped his fingers. "Picking a fight with us, freak? Bad move."

"The worst," I agreed. "You want me out of your school so bad? Try it. Please. *Begging* you. But you lay a hand on this kid again, I'm going to hunt you down. And I'll definitely get expelled, but they'll have to follow it up with assault charges after I'm done with you. Understand?"

There was a stalemate then, three of them staring at one of me. Not that I was worried. Even in a three-on-one I figured I'd give at least as good as I got.

When they walked away a minute later, I made sure to blank my face while they muttered their threats. The other kid was still on the ground. I offered him a hand.

I wasn't expecting the murderous glare the boy turned my way. "Are you kidding me? Seriously, tell me that the three of those Neanderthals gave me a concussion and this is all some sort of fever dream." He lunged to his feet on his own, shoving past me hard enough that he managed to make me step back when the others didn't. Then again, I didn't expect quite that reaction out of *him*.

"You're welcome?"

He spun around like he'd been waiting for the opportunity. "For what? For reminding Zach Cauley that beating the crap out of me never goes out of style? Today might have been a one-off, but now that you're involved, he's going to be lurking around all the time. Just waiting to take it out on me. So thanks. I'm sure I, and my therapy bills, will be much more gracious about it in the future."

Now that I got a better look at him, I saw what had made him a target. High school was about conforming, about finding the lowest-common denominator and making sure you were in tune with it. This Hamilton kid wore a pair of maroon skinny jeans and a gray fitted cardigan, hipster black glasses, and hair that said he didn't give a shit.

I cleared my throat. "You know how people say ignore it and it'll go away? It doesn't. But what they should be saying is 'if you talk a lot of shit, then someone's going to take it out of your ass.' So maybe shut your mouth once or twice, and you won't *have* Neanderthals like that trying to kick the crap out of you."

There was a moment's pause before the kid started fighting a mocking smile. "Shit. Ass. Crap." The tension eased out of him like a squeezed sponge. "Someone's got an anal fixation."

The word had its desired effect on me, and I dropped my eyes, focusing on my irritation if only to suppress the flush I could feel spreading to my cheeks. "And again, about that whole 'shutting your mouth' thing," I growled.

"Nope," he said instead, fixing me with a surly expression and a slow gaze that started at my feet and worked all the way up to my head. "Go to hell. I'm not getting saved by someone that looks like *you*. With the face and the eyes and the ... Jesus, you know it's okay to have a little fat on your bones, right?" He shook his head like his thoughts needed to be restored to the factory settings. "Not happening, dickbag. Go be someone else's Disney prince."

"You're a little late with this epiphany. You realize that, right? Bullies gone?" I made a running gesture with my fingers, and then I opened my palm and swept it towards him like a silver platter. "Moron safe to run his mouth once more. Since it clearly bears repeating: you're welcome."

"I'm not thanking you," he insisted, his face going red with a frustrated energy he'd lacked in the face of a beatdown. "So go on and work your shitty good mood on someone who needs it. Because I don't."

This is the universe's way of punishing me, I realized. Avoiding the rest of my siblings should have given me some peace, but the universe couldn't have that. So it supplied me with a seventeen-year-old bottle of sarcasm, aged to condescension.

"Are you always this charming?" I asked through my teeth. We were quickly veering off into a scenario where a kid gets rescued from bullies only to make his rescuer so angry he becomes a bully himself. Because, seriously. I wanted to punch this kid if he said one more—

"—Are you always this egotistical? Who waits around after saving the day to be thanked? A dickbag, that's who."

"Stop calling me a dickbag!"

"Stop being a dick in a bag, dickbag!"

"I'm ... not." I gaped, momentarily floored by the way the conversation had devolved. "Just ... shut up. Listen for a minute. Are you here for the drama class or not?"

His sneer widened. "There *isn't* a drama class right now. But I want to start auditions this week, so I figured I'd start setting up. Those other dickbags interrupted first."

"Wait," I had a sinking feeling, "you're not in charge of the play, are you?" Because that would be *all of the luck.*

The kid rolled his eyes. "Of course not." I relaxed. "I'm the student director. Mr. Pollack is the man in charge. The school got tired of me playing the lead in everything, and it'll look good on my college apps."

"Oh," because I didn't have anything else to say.

The curtains at the edge of the stage fluttered, and I looked away from him, both feeling the charged moment surrounding us pass and wondering suddenly at the surge of paranoia deep in the way back parts of my brain. *Was someone there? Were we being watched?* Fingers in chitinous armor climbed up my spine, slow and precise.

I shook my head and willed the worry away. If anything, it was probably Justin or one of the others. No reason to act ridiculous.

"I'm Brice," he said finally. He looked a moment away from tapping his foot against the ground, and I was struck by the realization that he was an impatient college professor trapped in a high schooler's body. The fitted gray cardigan, the glasses, the mop of unruly hair like he'd been up late grading exams from idiot freshmen and didn't own a comb.

I looked away from the curtains, huffed out a breath that said I was going to regret this, and then said, "I wanted to see if you needed help with the stagehand stuff. Set building, construction, whatever. I was told to talk to you."

The words acted like a password, stripping away the acerbic exterior and revealing an actual, genuine smile. Or at least what I perceived as one. "Why didn't you say so?" Brice beamed in my direction. "There's a stage meeting here tonight at seven. We probably won't start any actual construction until after the cast is chosen, but you can help out in the meantime." The fact that he was basically commandeering my service didn't occur to him. The dark curve of his mouth returned. "Unless that interferes with practice or a game or something?"

"No," I said slowly, "I don't play any sports." He opened his mouth again, and I rushed to continue before he could elevate the sass levels higher than they already were. "I don't have a job, I'm not part of any clubs or activities, and I'm not dating anyone. So I can be there."

"Good," Brice said, his tone sharp. *Making my own path. Not a bad start,* I thought, chancing another look at the boy. Maybe this could work after all.

FIVE

It was strange to see little Cyrus in love. He and Savannah had hated each other at first sight, and then a few months later were groping in every dark corner of the school they could find. Everyone thought they'd be together forever.

....

Sara Bexington (S)
Personal Interview

I walked through my front door after school, only to find that I wasn't home alone. Illana Bryer was in my dining room.

You've got to be kidding me. I skipped through the room on my way to the kitchen, didn't even stop to acknowledge that I'd seen her.

It was hard to say how old Illana was, because even though she was a grandmother, her skin was nearly free of lines from a life lived hard. Iron-gray hair was knotted up in a bun, and even her wardrobe was hard to pin down. One day it was flowing skirts and jackets, and then today she was business professional. Suit, skirt, heels. There was a cup of tea tucked between her hands—a fancy piece of blue and gray china that I was pretty sure didn't come from our house.

She'd angled her chair away from its typical spot at the head of the table and I followed her eye-line to see what it was that she was looking for. With the wall at her back as it was now, Illana had a perfect view of both the front door, back door, and garage entrance to the house.

There was no sign of Nick, my guardian. I was the only one of us who had a guardian, and a house, to himself. Justin and Jenna shared, same as Cole and Bailey. But I liked the solitude, and Nick was the relaxed, unconcerned type. We got along more like roommates than warden and inmate.

Nick had a scholarship to play soccer for Indiana before he'd decided to go through D.C. and train to become a Witcher. We both understood the appeal of a normal life. We also understood how unlikely it was that we would ever have one.

No Nick meant Illana wasn't here to discuss Council business. She was here to see me.

My procrastination didn't bother her. She sipped at her tea and pretended to ignore me just as I was ignoring her. It was hard to recognize this woman with who she really was. What she really represented.

She was the leader of the Fallingbrook Coven.

She was part of the Invisible Congress, the governing body that kept all witches in line.

She killed my parents.

She might yet kill me.

"It's about time," she said, her tone sharp as knives. "I don't like to be kept waiting."

I feigned looking down at my watch and shrugged out of my coat. "Really? Hell must have frozen over ahead of schedule. Been happening an awful lot lately. You'd think they would get that fixed."

"Sarcasm," she murmured, a predator's smile on her face, "is the lowest form of wit, you know."

"I don't like to set the bar too high," I admitted. "Makes it harder for everyone else to keep up."

She studied me for a few seconds, her finger tapping a steady rhythm against the lip of the cup before she set it back down onto the matching saucer. "Quick-witted too. I don't think I like that much."

There was a tiny, sunflower seed–sized bit of hope that Illana simply had the wrong house. She always dealt with Justin—made sense, he was the group parent. If she controlled him, she could control us. "I'm not interested. Go ask Justin."

"Ahh, but this isn't a task suited to your brother's skills. This is something for you, and you alone."

Something Justin couldn't handle? I knew half of the Congress wasn't much impressed with him, but he *had* managed a victory against them recently. Justin was the reason our leashes had been loosened. So what did she need me for? I was no one. In spite of myself, I was curious. "What is it?"

"I want to know *why*."

She didn't follow it up. Didn't finish her thought. It took a few seconds to realize that was my cue. "'Why?'"

"Luca. Why him? Why Maleficia? How? Why now? He's at the center of the web, and I want to know *why*."

Oh. Curiosity soured in my chest. This wasn't about me at all. I was just a container for what Illana was really after. The Denton family tree was a disease-riddled monstrosity. First my father, Cyrus, turned out to be one of the deadliest warlocks around, and now his nephew was channeling the same black arts twenty years later.

"Orphan" was a word that chased us all growing up, one of the many legacies handed down to us by the monsters in our blood. Meeting Luca was a shock I hadn't wanted to deal with: finding relatives where I'd never expected them.

My father had a brother, and that brother had a son. A son who had grown up haunted by crimes that weren't his; punished for monstrosities that happened before his birth. No surprise that Luca wanted nothing to do with me. The feeling was mutual. It was easier to ignore him than it would have been to sort through something complicated and stressful.

"He won't talk to me," I said, wishing for a glass of water but reluctant to turn my back to her.

"More accurate to say that he *can't*. The boy is catatonic."

That was news. "Still? Since the night at the farmhouse?" A sharp nod. "Then I don't understand."

Illana produced a tiny spoon from somewhere and set to stirring her tea counterclockwise. "Charles Denton, like you, loathes the place he came from. He lost his first girlfriend, Savannah, because of your father. When Moonset revealed themselves, Charles stood up against his brother's actions, but Cyrus's crimes still took everything from him. His wife was weak, and ran, but Charles was stubborn. This was his home, and he would not be run off. But he did turn his back on our world, and gave up his magic completely. Now he's refusing to speak with us, or help us understand what happened to his son."

It was like someone had run their finger up my spine. *You could do that? Just walk away?* I licked my lips. "He didn't have a coven, though. Did he? He wasn't bound up with someone else's fate?"

Illana sat back, the spoon being swallowed up into her palm and spirited away like a magician's sleight of hand. Something in my expression made the tension in her mouth evaporate. "He's alone," she confirmed.

Then our situations weren't the same at all. It wasn't just the Coven bond, but the curse laid over the top of it that kept the five of us together. Splitting up only put other people in danger. The others would never let me go—even if they could.

"You have an opportunity here." Illana rose up with her teacup and saucer still in hand and walked into the kitchen. I got up and followed her, unsure of what else to do. She stood at the sink, carefully washing the cup out. "It's natural to have questions. But how many people really know what they were like before they were Moonset? The men behind the monsters. Aren't you curious?"

"And in exchange you want me to interrogate him about why Luca went psychotic?"

"Luca was in his right mind," Illana said, turning. She was tall enough that she could look down on almost anyone, but she had to lift her chin to look at me. I couldn't shake the feeling that my response had let her down in some way. I didn't owe the woman anything. She killed my parents. She'd played puppet master with my life since I was a kid. She wasn't the kindly grandmother.

"They're not my family," I pointed out. "We just share a last name."

"Family isn't about what's easy. It's about what you do with the hard moments. How you surmount them," Illana responded easily, like she expected my reticence all along. "You can try to run from this as long as you want, Malcolm, but you *are* one of them. It may be exactly the kind of shock that Charles needs to shake himself out of his . . . devolution."

I huffed out a breath, leaned against the counter and grunted. "What do you *want* from me? All your files and notes about me, and not one of them told you how much I hate all of this?"

Her face hardened into a dark mask of fury and ice. She could very well be the queen of the Courted Fae like this, pronouncing judgments from her throne of wrought shadows. "I *want* to know why. The boy didn't simply stumble upon a grimoire of Maleficia by accident. It was provided to him. Someone set all this into motion. And I will not allow history to repeat itself!"

"So I'm still bait," I said flatly. "You're still using us."

"What would you have me do?" she demanded. "Your brother fought for knowledge. Everything has a cost, my boy, and the cost of learning to defend yourselves is that you do something for *me*. You may hate me, Malcolm, and everything that I stand for, but I have been fighting for the five of you since you came into our care all those years ago."

"Do you even care about what I want?" I asked quietly.

She turned and dried the saucer with the blue terrycloth hanging over the edge of the sink. "It may not be what you want, Malcolm, but it is something only you can do. Someone exploited Luca, no doubt because of what his last name is. No one, not even you, hates our world the way his father does. Our window to find out what really happened here might not be open for long."

Nothing she said was an outright lie, I was sure. And there was no doubt that she was right about Luca. If someone had smuggled him the grimoire of Maleficia, they'd done it knowing exactly who he was. Which also explained why she needed me—if Luca's dad wouldn't talk to the Covens, maybe he would talk to me.

It was only moments after Illana left before Justin came surging through the front door. I wondered if he'd seen her car and had been lurking on the front porch waiting for her to leave.

"Why was she here?" he asked, barging in without knocking.

I grunted, but went back to making a protein shake. I'd skipped out on lunch and just needed something to tide me over until dinner. What I ate was one of the few things about my life I *could* control, and at least I knew the shake would be better than eating something heavy or bad for me. I pulled one of the frozen bananas out of the freezer and tossed it into the blender.

"Mal, what'd she want?"

Another grunt, but that wouldn't stave him off for long.

"I keep trying to get Quinn to let me talk to her, but he keeps saying she's too busy," Justin added. "But she shows up at your house? What's going on?"

He was acting like the meeting was my idea. All the earlier frustration came surging back. They couldn't ever just leave something alone. "She didn't come over looking for makeup tutorials," I said sharply. "She's looking into what happened with Luca. She thinks his dad might talk to me."

There was a weird look in Justin's eyes, something I didn't typically see turned my way. Normally, it was Jenna who got those flashes of hurt and betrayal. Which was insane, because we all knew that cooperating with the Covens was a terrible idea. The last time we'd tried, they wanted to frame us for what Luca had done.

"She didn't really leave me much of a choice," I said, thinking back over the conversation, "but I never exactly said I would either. She just assumed it was a done deal. That it's part of my 'destiny' or something."

Justin didn't like that either. His eyes narrowed and his stance shifted as he squared his shoulders. "Why would she go to *you*? You hate magic."

I expected contempt like that from Jenna, but not from Justin. He was usually a lot more levelheaded than that. "Because he's my cousin? What's your damage?"

Justin ducked his head and shrugged. "Nothing. It's fine. Just weird, that's all."

"Hey, I didn't ask for any of this," I snapped. "You want to play hero? Fine by me. But don't act like I'm somehow screwing you over by all this. She came to me. I didn't go to her."

39

Justin's face flushed, and he opened his mouth to protest, but kept sputtering out his words.

"Instead of running around all butt hurt, why don't you look at this from my perspective for once," I continued on, unable to stop now that I started. I could feel my body growing hot. "I don't want any of this shit, but the rest of you keep dragging me into it. I just want to graduate, maybe go to college, and forget that there's anything but a real life out there. I don't even bother making friends in these towns anymore because I know Jenna's just going to ruin it for the rest of us."

"Mal..." Justin looked ashamed of himself, which he should.

"No, screw that. Maybe the rest of you hate the fact that you've got monsters for parents, but I hate the fact that no matter what I do, I can't ever escape all of this. I'm locked up with all of you for the rest of my life, and all any of you care about is yourselves. Who cares if Malcolm has to sacrifice what he wants—again!—as long as we get to learn magic, or move out of the Midwest, or don't have to take finals."

My outburst had effectively shut down whatever had been building up behind Justin's eyes. His skin was white and splotchy, the way he got when he was horribly embarrassed or upset.

"Go home, Justin," I said, looking pointedly towards the front door. He tried to say something else, but I crossed my arms over my chest until he finally took the hint.

SIX

The children of Moonset have it hard enough. They are children, yet they are prisoners. They've already lost all semblance of a normal life, a normal family. You cannot lock them away for their parents' crimes too.

....

Illana Bryer
Speaking to the Congress

After Illana's visit, the house felt ... cluttered. Too many ghosts and not enough air. If I stayed in the house, Justin would probably send someone else in to bother me until I told them all what Illana had said. But I wasn't sure I wanted to talk about it at all, let alone with them. So I did what I always did, and tried to push her request, and the truth about my family, down where I couldn't dwell on it. Driving helped, sometimes, when I split my attention between the music on the radio and the traffic on the road.

It started snowing again the moment I turned the ignition, but I found the blanket of gray over my head to be comforting. Behind the dismal bank of clouds, the sun was already a distant memory, though it wouldn't set for hours.

There were lots of churches for a town supposedly full of witches. I passed three on my way out of town. The weights in my chest eased once I crossed the town line, and even though I knew I wasn't really getting away from all of them, it still made it easier to breathe. Carrow Mill was one of the towns where witches were gathered together and taught, there were dozens of them all across the country. But this one was notable because it was where our parents met, where the Moonset Coven bond first formed.

Illana had brought Fallingbrook, her coven, along with her when she relocated here. The addition of a Great Coven meant an armada of Witchers preceding them. Regular witches too. Teachers at school. One of the baristas at the coffee shop. A couple of the guys who went to my gym. There were witches everywhere, and they always *stared*.

At least I'd always had Justin and the others to rely on. People who understood what it was like to be watched, judged, or studied. Who did Luca have? Who made him feel like there was more to him than the judgments people stapled to his face? Anyone?

No. I wasn't going to do this. I wasn't going to fall under her sway just because she dropped someone else's problem in my lap. Luca made his own choice. He did that to himself. And if she wanted to know why so badly, she could do the legwork. It wasn't my fight.

I drove for hours, switching the satellite radio at random, barely allowing one song to finish before I cut out to something else. I found a measure of peace in the moments of jangled confusion between genres, as heavy industrial crashed into German pop then into Mozart until it ground to a halt by the heavy bass of dubstep. The threads of dissonance were a moment of relief, when Illana's words couldn't pierce my skull.

When I pulled back into my driveway, the porch light was on like a beacon, meaning Nick had beaten me home. I climbed out of the car and heard a sliding shuffle from behind. Cole was half-running, half-gliding like a skier across the snowy street, heading right for me.

"They sent *you*?" I asked, hearing the contempt in my voice but not caring for a moment. I knew Justin wouldn't let it lie for long—I could have a few hours to myself, but that was all they'd allow me.

"I can do things on my own." The sneer was new, the attitude not so much. Some of us had done well with the move, not exactly thriving, but learning to adapt. Cole had been the opposite. Carrow Mill had changed him back into the sullen, angry teenager that made him hard to like.

Suddenly, being a dick didn't seem so important anymore. I exhaled, trying to shake off the bad mood that Justin's visit had put me in. None of that was Cole's fault. And me getting pissed at him wasn't going to make anything easier. "Sorry, man. Bad day."

"Bad life," he muttered tonelessly, but after a few second's pause, his eyes flicked up to me and he smiled. Smirked.

I sat down next to him on the porch and rested my elbows on my knees. "So what's going on?" Justin's house was dark, no signs of life. That was odd in itself. There was always *someone* hanging around. Quinn was in charge of his own mighty Witcher militia, and lately there was always someone coming in or out. It surprised me that they got any sleep at all in that house.

Cole slid his phone out of a pocket and proceeded to let it waltz across his fingers and hands in a display of contact juggling that I hadn't seen in years. He could have had a golden career as a pickpocket, but instead he used it to make his phone do tricks. The movements had an almost ritualistic feel to them, something I could see him practicing over and over again until he could perform it flawlessly.

He stopped in the middle, raising one hand to cradle his head.

"Headache?" I asked.

He grunted, nodding after a few moments. I saw the tension in his face, in his eyes, but after a moment he let it dissipate. "I'll be fine," he said. "Been getting a lot of them lately." And then just like that, he went back to his brooding.

I let him go. He'd talk when he was ready. And in the meantime, the quiet was nice. Cole had always been a handful growing up, buzzing with energy from the moment he woke up until he abruptly powered down halfway through a story, or a game, or an activity. When we had to room together, those were always the best moments: Cole, slumped on the ground and dead to the world, and a drowning silence pouring in to balance out the hours of constant noise.

It had been a long time since I'd had to heft him up off the carpet and throw him into bed, though.

I ruffled his hair. Cole, predictably, scowled and batted my hand away. He started typing out a text, and still I waited. Finally, he started to tell me what was on his mind. "I know you think I'm stupid, but that's okay. Because I think you're stupid too."

Okay, that wasn't what I was expecting. "Cole, I don't think you're stupid."

"Well, I think *you* are. Justin said that Mrs. Bryer wants you to get to know Luca. You know how many nights I went to sleep wishing for something like that? That my dad wasn't..." Cole caught himself, shook his head once, and soldiered on. "You've got an uncle *and* a cousin. But you don't even care. Jenna's right. You hate everything."

I took a moment, let his frustration sink in. Each of us, in our own ways, had hoped for a way out. Cole used to think our *real* parents were in Witness Protection, and that we'd been kidnapped by Moonset. Bailey kept hoping for an adoptive family that actually *cared*. Each of us had something we wanted from the parents we were never going to have. They were nothing more than hopes and shame we didn't trust to anyone, kept buckled down under rib cages where they couldn't be used against us.

"I don't hate *you*," I said slowly, nudging him. Trying for a smile, and failing. Cole shook his head, like he knew what I was doing and it wasn't going to happen.

The hard way, then. My heart picked up its pace, and the familiar itch in my legs made me want to start running and keep going until I collapsed. "I'm..." I couldn't believe I was about to tell *Cole* out of everyone how I was feeling. Jenna would know before I even made it in the house. "I don't know what I'm going to find. If I did. Get to know them, I mean. Not knowing... it's easier."

"Are you afraid they're going to hate you?" Cole asked, the curiosity softening his mood until it was pliable and familiar. The little brother I remembered. "Nobody hates you, Mal. You know that."

"What if I hate them?" I asked, ignoring the fact that I was basically confirming his (and Jenna's) initial argument about all the things I hated. "Or worse, what if I start to care what they think at all? They're not my family. You all are." *Like it or not,* I added silently.

Cole nudged me back and leaned against my side, the way he'd always done when he was younger and knew how to be afraid. "I'm not Justin. You don't have to tell me what you think I want to hear."

The confessions were like falling dominoes—now that they'd started, I couldn't stop them. Even though it was Cole. Little Cole, who'd never been my ideal concept of a confidante. But maybe that was more my fault than his. Somewhere along the way, I'd forgotten that Cole was more than just Jenna's shadow. "Look what Luca did," I admitted. "Look who his father is. I don't... I know everything I need to know about my dad. I don't need that changing. I don't *want* that to change. But how can I possibly deal with either one of them without finding out stuff?"

Cole shrugged, looked up towards the sky. His ears poked out of his hat, and I reached out and tugged it down. "Maybe you're looking at it from the wrong direction," he said, even quieter now. I had to strain to hear him. "Don't you ever wonder what they were like?"

"Our parents?"

He shook his head, lips turning down. "Justin and Jenna have it easy. They know where they come from. But what about us? My dad was a monster, right? But what about my mom? They don't even know who she is. Or where she is. Same with you. What if they're out there somewhere. Waiting for us? Or what if they were just . . . pawns. Like we were to Luca. Don't you ever wonder?" He took a deep breath, and his lips moved, but no sound came out. *I do,* he admitted, even if he couldn't bring himself to voice it.

I do, too, came my soundless reply.

SEVEN

*Members of a Coven can draw upon the strength
of their bond mates, track them no matter how
far they've traveled, speak without words, and
summon collective magics far stronger than
anything they could invoke on their own.*

Coventry in the 21st Century

I decided to give Coven class one more try, for the sake of everyone else. The classroom desks had all been pushed against the wall, our cue to sit on the floor. If we started doing some sort of group share, emotional trust exercise, though, I was out. There was only so far I could be expected to bend.

The lights were off, and the overcast sky kept the room swathed in shadows. When we walked in the room, Kelly had us empty our pockets and leave everything on one of the desks lined up against the walls. *As few distractions as possible,* she said.

"I want you to close your eyes. Listen to your partner's breaths. Feel the connections that exist between you, lines of power that link you together by immaculate design."

Kelly leaned against the back of the teacher's desk, looking down on us. I was paired with Bailey *and* Cole, because "Justin and Jenna already have a blood connection." Which, to me, sounded like a reason *not* to put them together. Maybe she was afraid of not having any progress to report, though, since I had been holding back the rest of the group.

"Great. She's one of those 'God is magic' people." Even though I barely muttered it out loud, Bailey giggled so hard she snorted. Twice.

There wasn't anything wrong with witches who believed in magic as a higher power. I didn't have anything against them, I just didn't understand it. They believed that magic came with some sort of "intelligent design" because covens didn't form at random. Reality bent, sometimes, to make a coven form. Accidental meetings, weird coincidences—there was an element suspiciously like fate involved in the coven-building process.

The people who linked "fate" with "faith" took a relaxed view of magic. There was an Almighty out there somewhere, and magic was His gift, covens were the warriors who served at His pleasure. And bad things happened because...

Well, that was the part where they always lost me.

If God was magic, and Maleficia was magic's evil twin, did that make God schizophrenic? Or did it suggest that He, too, had a twin?

"Concentrate." Her voice was a boom from right behind

me. Did she hear what I'd said? Did I care? Obediently, I rolled my eyes before closing them, and focused on the nasal sounds of Cole's inhale. Focused on the spots where my knees brushed up against both of them.

"There is a bond that connects you, deeper than anything." If nothing else, Kelly's voice was hypnotic. Engaging. Against my better judgment I started to relax, to let her words direct my mind. "You are a wheel with five spokes. A star with five points. Your breath is theirs. Their hearts beat for you."

I could feel … *something.* Maybe not what she was saying, but what she said about a star triggered colors and shapes to burst forth behind my eyes. It was hazy and bright; words hidden behind clouds. Maybe not words, but lines. Black and red, pointed and sharp at the ends. A star made of knives. Sharp. Deadly. No, it wasn't knives exactly. Keys. Keys of silver and half-truths. Still not right. Blue fire, sparking gold at the tips. All. None. Something took shape behind the clouds, behind the mist. I could almost reach out. Almost touch it. Almost see it. Know it.

Her voice continued, a low and steady drum. "Stretch your mind, as far as you can. There, in the distance, can you feel it? You belong together. You will never be alone."

You will never be alone. The words snapped across the width of my mind like a shrill scream of thunder, and I bolted to my feet. There were too many walls, all of them huge and looming around me. The others hadn't noticed yet. They were focused. Under her spell. They couldn't see that there wasn't enough room. The air was almost gone. Everything was too close, pressing down and too *real.*

You will never be alone.

The calm I'd found cracked and shattered at my feet. I opened my mouth, saw and immediately dismissed Kelly's O-face of surprise, and couldn't catch a breath. My lungs failed to inflate, there was nothing there. The walls pressed in, reaching for me, collapsing inward faster and faster and there was nothing. Nothing but bodies pressed against each other like sardines, too many of us to fit in one space.

My feet did the work for me, running for the door without any of my things. Running and fleeing and escape now superseded everything. I ran before any of them could stop me, because they would try. Before the walls could press in any further, or the world could shrink down any smaller.

I didn't catch a breath until I made it to the parking lot. As soon as I inhaled, filling my lungs to the brink, I took off. Ran across the parking lot, hopped the gate that closed off the football field, and cut across to the empty lot on the other side. The faster I ran, the faster the walls behind me grew, gaining on me like a storm on the horizon. Inescapable.

I didn't look where I was going, just that once I found sidewalk I kept running until I was forced to turn down another street. The burn in my calves was a welcomed friend, the surge of blood carrying away...whatever that had been. Terror. Panic.

I was miles from school before the grip on my heart eased.

EIGHT

Cyrus Denton had it, y'know? The kind of presence that made people feel. He could make an angel weep. Everyone adored him. I heard he died young. What a loss. I always thought he would do great things.

....

Nathan Hartley
Classmate

I ended somewhere on the far side of Carrow Mill, where the divide between cities was hazy and swept up between rows of warehouses. I collapsed down on a stoop, my shirt clinging to my chest and back, chill with moisture even as my skin felt so hot it should be steaming.

There were no street signs nearby, not that I was in any shape to go looking for them. My phone was somewhere back at the school. My options were limited—if I could find a pay phone, I could call someone to come pick me up, but I'd need to find their number first. I barely even knew what my own cell number was.

Who would I call, anyway? There weren't a lot of options on that list at the moment.

It didn't take long to come to a decision, for me to turn back the way I'd come. Only this time, I walked. It took almost an hour of walking before I started to see things that looked familiar. I was heading in the right direction at least.

I wasn't sure how many classes I missed, walking through town. At the moment, my only thought was for the spare outfit I kept in the gym bag in the back of my car. I could get to school, change in one of the bathrooms, and then at least I wouldn't look like I'd spent the last two hours in a sauna.

The school parking lots were still full by the time I made the trek back across town. School might not be over yet, but it couldn't be going on for much longer. I had no idea how long I'd been gone, but it *had* to be almost time for class to let out for the day.

I grabbed my gym bag and headed for the closest entrance. I could have gone by the gym and changed in an actual locker room, but I'd take my chances with one of the normal bathrooms. I just wanted out of these clothes and into something that didn't smell like panic and fading deodorant.

The halls were empty when I came in, which I took for a good sign. The last thing I needed was to get stopped by someone looking for a hall pass I didn't have. I stripped in the bathroom, wiped myself down with paper towels as best I could, and changed into my gym clothes. Thankfully, I switched those out on a regular basis, so they were still freshly laundered.

There wasn't much I could do with my hair, which was still damp and prone to falling down into my eyes, but I scrubbed some towels through it anyway.

It took a minute for me to do the math and figure out where I was supposed to be. Last period would have started about ten minutes ago. Which meant that the rest of my family was in our new Magic for Morons class. It still got under my skin how much they couldn't see. Buying in to the magic classes was just the Congress's way of shutting us up. They were still manipulating us, they probably always would be.

There were a couple of people in the halls, not unusual for the end of the day. Study halls around this time were always lax with letting students roam around the halls. If someone skipped their last period of the day, would it really make a difference? No one seemed to think so.

I could go sit in the car and wait for the others to get out of school, but I decided against it. Someone was certainly going to start complaining that I skipped magic class, so I decided not to. I just wouldn't go to the one they expected me to.

The class that Kevin and Maddy had was separate from the rest of us. A month ago, Justin had been segregated in with them, along with Luca. But now Luca was gone, and the rest of us had been pooled together, like we were somehow easier to manage that way. I think Kelly would have disagreed on that one.

I headed down the side hall to Kevin's class, still in the same room it had been all year. When I pulled open the door, three sets of eyes peered up at me, but only the teacher was unfamiliar. He was young, Witcher-aged, probably one of the new recruits brought along with Illana.

"Room for one more?" I asked, but I closed the door behind me and headed for a seat before permission could be given.

"What are you doing here?" Kevin asked, shifting around in his seat.

I shrugged.

"Just get out of the shower?" Maddy's pinched face eased a bit, though her eyes were speculative on mine. Whatever falling out had happened between her and Justin, at least she wasn't taking it out on me.

"This isn't really appropriate," the teacher began. Like Kelly, he didn't seem like he'd been out of college for very long. But there was none of the shrewd awareness or perception in his eyes I'd come to expect from the Witchers. "But I don't see what it could hurt."

I took a closer look at him. Dark haired, just a little too long, and a strong jaw line didn't match with the thin, reedy voice. Nor did the blasé attitude about letting a Moonset kid sit in on his lesson.

"We're doing a history lesson," Maddy said, almost like she could read my mind. "No trade secrets."

I actually don't mind history. I mean, I don't enjoy learning about the secret truths behind modern mysteries, but history is full of lessons where power and magic have caused some sort of crisis. Learning more about covens in the old days armed me with more information. And my arguments against using magic became stronger.

But the class itself wasn't dealing with something helpful: like times in history when trusting the authorities had led to chaos. No, instead the teacher lectured on old threats. Monsters and creatures who lurked in the shadows of history. Creatures that many people believed magic was created expressly to fight.

I'd had a run in with one of those creatures already. The Abyssal Princes, creatures that had been bound into Hell for maybe the whole of recorded history. Some of them had tried to escape—and use Moonset's offspring as their hosts for a grave new world.

This wasn't my class, so there were no expectations. I liked that; it made the class almost enjoyable. Or at least as enjoyable as it was to discuss what happened when a wraith caught your soul between its finger bones, or how the old Aos Si could hide themselves inside newborn children, only to burst forth from their skulls once the children were full grown, like a monstrous Athena escaping Zeus's head. Only the humans never survived, of course.

"No, Justin, I'm done with him." One of the windows was cracked, and during a lull in the lesson, Jenna's piercing tones carried from the parking lot below.

"Jenna!" A frustrated Justin chimed in just as expected. "Jenna!" A little more frantic now.

I got to my feet, saw Maddy and Kevin doing the same, and approached the window. Jenna was still talking, but now that her voice had dropped down, it didn't carry enough for me to hear it. But from the finger jabbed into Justin's chest and the sour twist of her mouth, I knew exactly what she was going on about. The same thing she was always pissed off about.

"If I was a nicer person, I wouldn't say I told you so." At least Maddy didn't smirk at me when she said it. Though it was implied.

"What's she doing?" Kevin asked, forehead scrunching up. He leaned forward to get a better look, and I turned back to the view of my siblings to see Jenna... I don't know *what* she was doing. Her eyes were concentrated on the blacktop in front of her, and a small breeze rifled through her hair as her hands were dropped parallel to the ground.

"She's using magic," Maddy said, stating the obvious.

"I can't hear what she's saying, can you?" Kevin asked, but I shook my head.

The problem with magic was how hard it was to contain sometimes. Normal people saw things, and you couldn't always rely on them to rationalize away what they'd seen. My first concern was that Jenna was going to do something to get us in trouble. Something big and obvious and destructive.

But as she finished her spell, there was a tug in my chest, like an invisible string attached to my spine was tugged forward, and my eyes snapped to hers. The moment we connected there was a rush of heat along my core, a wave of energy that washed away in a moment.

"What is that?" The teacher had joined us at the window, and he leaned forward.

There was a cloud of... well, a cloud forming around Jenna, and distorting her appearance like a mirage on the horizon. Heated air, like the same that had just rushed through me, collected around her and then shot forward, straight towards me.

It struck the window and I braced myself, but that was it. The window fogged over with the sudden appearance of moisture, and a trail of warm air ghosted around all of us.

"That...was unexpected," I said, testing out my limbs. I *felt* fine. But without knowing what Jenna did, I couldn't say for certain that it was a dud.

That happened sometimes. Jenna liked to experiment with magic, since no one would teach her anything. She could cobble together a few tiny spells and create the most random result. But with all that experimentation came the duds. Spells that didn't go anywhere, didn't accomplish anything.

"Illana's not going to be too happy about this," the teacher muttered.

"Not going to be happy you stood around and didn't get involved either," Kevin pointed out, not too kindly.

Jenna and Justin split apart, with Jenna striding away in a fury. No, I couldn't imagine anyone was going to be happy about this. Especially not Jenna, and her fizzled spell. It was going to be a long ride home.

NINE

*Seven seniors were hospitalized before the
Invisible Congress ruled to investigate the
claims of the Moonset coven. No one is sure what
transpired during those three weeks in April—the
town of Carrow Mill was whited out from the rest
of the world. When it returned, a monster was
dead, and Robert Cooper was a hero.*

....

Moonset: A Dark Legacy

Jenna muttered obscenities on the way home, so whatever it was she'd been after hadn't played out. Maybe there was something to that whole "God is magic" thing. Maybe He was finally looking out for me.

Then I arrived at school the next morning. And realized that God didn't have my back after all. Unless he was just sizing it up for that knife.

"Hey, Mal." A girl I'd never seen before sauntered past my car, pointedly looking me over as she slinked past my open door.

"Oh my god, that's him," another girl whispered to her friend, not but seconds later. The two of them looked my way and giggled, and then grabbed one another for support.

I eyed them for a moment before turning away. "What the hell?" If Jenna started another rumor, or *worse*, talked Cole into resurrecting those pictures of me...

I caught up with Kevin and Maddy outside the front of the school.

Maddy scowled and Kevin was flush and neither one of them would look at me when I approached. I slowed, gripping the strap of my bag and looking around. Yup, people were still staring. "What the hell's going on?"

"Kevin was just talking about you." Maddy huffed out a breath and rolled her eyes.

"No I wasn't," he said quickly. Too quickly.

"Okay," I said, slower and with more emphasis. "*What's going on?*"

"Nothing!" Kevin still wouldn't meet my eyes. He shoved his hands into his pockets, the flush crawling down from his cheeks to the back of his neck. *Everything* about his behavior was off. The reason Kevin and I got along was because he was so chill. Literally nothing seemed to bother him.

This awkward, shy, *blushing* Kevin was someone else.

"Did you do something to him?" I asked, turning to Maddy.

"Did you?" she challenged, but just as quickly she deflated and shrugged. "Everyone's off this morning. I don't get it."

"Excuse me," another girl said as she barged past Maddy and knocked the purse from her shoulder. The girl stepped in front of the others, getting stalker-close to me. "Hi," she said, just as forward as could be. "You're Malcolm, right?"

"Nope," I shook my head. "Hate that guy. He thinks it's cool when people are rude."

She blinked rapidly, at least a dozen times in only a couple of seconds. My words curled right past her, leaving her amber eyes blank and blissful in their ignorance. "Whatever. Anyway, my friend didn't believe I'd actually come over here and talk to you—"

"—why are you?" I interrupted. Not that it mattered. She didn't stop talking.

"—because I mean, you're just a guy, right?"

"Right," I said faintly. Now I was starting to get more worried.

"And she never believes me that all you have to do is go up and talk to guys like they're normal people. I mean, I totally made out with the drummer from this band that we both like, and—" She was still talking when Maddy stormed past her, elbowed her out of the way, and then grabbed me and headed for the door.

"Idiots," Maddy huffed, her tone mocking as she repeated, "Talk to guys like they're normal people." Her head bobbed and everything.

Kevin trailed behind the two of us as Maddy led us into the auditorium. This early in the day, it was empty, but the curtains on the stage had been cleared, and chairs had been set up in a semicircle at the stage's edge.

Maddy glared over my shoulder at Kevin before turning back to me. His head was still ducked down so low his chin was nearly pressed up against his Adam's apple. "So since this has Jenna's fingerprints all over it, why don't you tell me what you did?"

Of course. That thing in the classroom yesterday. Her spell had worked after all. That was why everyone was acting like a freak. "She cursed me," I muttered. I knew Jenna had a habit of getting in her own way, but *really*? Cursing me was something we were doing now?

"Are you sure that she did something?" Kevin asked, voice soft with nervous pause. "Maybe it's more serious than that."

"It's not," Maddy said firmly. "This is a prank. Jenna's good at them; she's always bragging."

With good reason. Jenna was the mastermind of our inevitable upheaval. Every time she got bored and wished for a change of scenery, she created a reason for our schools to cut ties with us. Permanently and irrevocably. I think she'd been building up to blackmailing the principal in our last town, before the riot and, consequently, the wraith ripped control away from her.

If this was any indication, my guess was that Jenna was ready for a change of scenery.

So I just had one question.

"What the hell took her so long?" I growled.

———————

It didn't get better. It got worse.

Jenna was nowhere to be found during the day. It was

like she'd vanished after getting out of the car that morning. There were no adults to fix the problem—I tried calling Nick, but his phone went straight to voice mail. Same with Quinn. Aside from Kelly, who appeared to only show up to try to teach us about our "inner coven light," I didn't know any other adult witches in the school.

It only took first period before Justin and the others realized what was going on. I was almost surprised that Jenna wasn't bragging right out in the halls. Cole showed up at my locker after my pre-calculus class let out, though his attention was more on everyone *else* in the halls but me.

"Can you move out of my way?" I grunted, pushing at his shoulder where it blocked the lock on my locker. Cole shrugged and inched to the left, barely enough room for me to input my combination without him creeping into my space. I reached out, grabbed his shoulder, and *pushed* until he was a full locker away. He turned to give me a sour look and then lifted his head. "Hey, who thinks my brother's a hottie?" he shouted.

Oh my god, I was going to kill him.

There were catcalls and howls, guys who thought it was cool to jump on the "no homo" bandwagon, and girls. Lots of girls. Maybe all of the girls. Except no, Maddy was down the hall scowling. Bailey came down the stairs, looking like she had no idea what was going on. Which she probably didn't.

"I can't hear you!" he yelled, gesturing for the crowd to turn the volume up. Which they did. Enthusiastically.

I grabbed and dragged him towards me, clamping a hand over his mouth. "Are you freaking kidding me?" I hissed down at him. Cole squirmed, but even at his slipperiest, I was more than a match for him. I dragged him with me down the hall until he let his body go slack, forcing me to drag his weight. He thought that would be enough to make me drop him. Instead I shrugged, scooped him up, and dropped him over my shoulder in a fireman carry.

"Put me down, you jerk!" Cole punched at my back, getting one good shot in on my kidney before I reached the end of the hall. Teachers came out of their classroom at the disturbance, more than one looked like they wanted to intervene between Cole and me, but no one did.

Worse, a few of the teachers looked like they were only moments away from joining in all the noise themselves.

Maddy followed us into one of the back hallways, where the school had been expanded in the last twenty years. The tile was different, slapped down quickly sometime in between throwing up nondescript plasterboard walls and popcorn-spackled ceiling tiles. I dropped Cole once the crowd thinned out around us, and was surprised when Maddy appeared at my side. "Where is she?"

There are bad liars, and then there's Cole. He telegraphed every lie by doing the exact opposite of how he thought liars acted. Most people avoid eye contact, but Cole didn't look away, even tried not to blink. He never fidgeted or acted nervous, he actually became like a frozen mannequin, like if he stayed completely still everything he said, no matter how implausible, would pass inspection.

"I don't know what you're talking about," he said, followed up by a *too* sincere, "Jenna didn't do anything."

"How did you know I was talking about Jenna?"

"I mean—what? What are you talking about?" The more flustered he got, the more the facade started to crack. He started blinking rapidly, swallowing over and over again, even though his mouth was probably dry as dust. "Come on, Mal. It's just a joke."

"Jenna made the whole school fall in love with me," I said tightly. "That's not a joke. It's the precursor to justified homicide."

He squirmed back, holding up a finger. "They're not 'in love' with you. Love spells are against the law. But spells that help people realize their healthy attraction to the male form, well there aren't any rules about that."

That wasn't Cole talking, it was Jenna's words coming out of his mouth. Crap, she'd already started forming her defense. That meant Maddy and I were probably right, and this was all about getting us kicked out of school. "Why's she doing this, Cole? Didn't Quinn say that we weren't going anywhere no matter what?"

Cole didn't have an answer for that. He shrugged, looked away, avidly interested in what everyone else was doing. "Hey, how come you're not interested?" he said suddenly, focusing on Maddy.

"I—you—" Maddy's face went slack, the need to come up with a suitable response chasing literally every thought from her mind.

"It's doesn't work on anyone who's already in love with someone else." I smacked Cole on the head like he should have figured that out already. Maddy's mouth tightened, but the look she shot me a moment later was relieved. And yet suspicious.

That was a conversation for another time, though.

"It doesn't?" Cole frowned. He had the same look when he found out Santa wasn't real (Bailey had known for two years by that point). He was just too trusting sometimes.

"How'd she do it? How do I turn it off?"

"I—you can't?" Cole did his best to look helpless and innocent.

I grunted and turned away. "Can you call somebody?" I asked Maddy.

Her lips twitched. "You need me to call an adult before someone bad-touches you?"

A bad touch was the least of my worries right now. Now that we had a modicum of privacy, the extent of what just happened really started to sink in. The way everyone had stared. The crammed feeling of the hall when everyone stopped to see what was going on. All the eyes turned on me, watching, judging.

Everything grew hazy for a moment as the room started to spin. I reached out to steady myself, grabbed Cole's shoulder and held on. The dizziness passed, but the moment wasn't lost on him. "Are you okay?" He looked up at me with wide eyes. "Jenna said you wouldn't be hurt. She said it was just a joke, I swear."

My stomach gnawed on itself, as if to remind me what was really to blame. "I'll be fine once Jenna unravels whatever it was that she did," I said, not feeling entirely guilty about letting Cole think her spell was hurting me. It was better than the alternative.

TEN

Magic can do many things, but it cannot create something from nothing. Love spells are notorious, but impossible. The best you can hope for is an attraction, an obsession, a debilitating need that surpasses all other needs. It isn't love, though.

....

Magic and Subjugation:
Emotional Influence in the Modern Witch

My locker had been molested by an invasion of puff paint and glitter. Pink and red, mostly, heaped in oozing quantities as one poster had been pressed over top of another, the puff paint barely having a chance to dry and instead acted like a gluey substance, holding them all together like a serial killer's mosaic of victims.

"Malcolm," a voice called out from down the hall, "there

you are. Come with me, please?" Kelly appeared, face pinched in irritation.

"Thank god," I exhaled, feeling the tension already pooling out of me. "Where have you guys been all day? I've been calling Quinn since this morning. Do you have any idea what it's like—"

"I know exactly what it's like," she said crisply, leading me down the hall. The other students gave a wide berth, maybe it was something in her expression, or maybe she'd done some magic I wasn't aware of. Either way, we made it through the halls in record time.

She led us all the way back to classroom we used for Coven class. As we walked into the classroom, conversation stopped between a teacher and the two students who were still lingering by her desk.

"Get out," Kelly commanded, turning to look pointedly towards the door.

It was the chilling tone more than the demand that hustled them out of the room, I thought. Even the teacher didn't stop long enough to reclaim her purse, she went for the door with single-minded purpose. She didn't look back, didn't stop to wonder why a stranger was leading a student into the room only to clear it. She was even so thoughtful as to close the door behind her.

With that taken care of, Kelly spun around, pointing to one of the chairs. "Sit." But I was not a student, and I definitely wasn't going to be cowed by some grad school wannabe who thought she was going to put me in my place. I walked up to the teacher's desk, cleared a spot near the front and sat down at the front of it.

"I don't know who you think you are, but this isn't my fault. If you think I did this, clearly you're an idiot. I hate this kind of stuff. So go find Jenna, get her to undo whatever it was that she did, and leave me alone."

"Do you really think it's that simple?" Kelly asked, eyes dark. The lights in the room were off, the only light coming in from outside. "This school is nearly in a panic. One wrong move could set the whole thing ablaze. You remember what that's like, don't you, Malcolm?"

"I—" This wasn't my fault! Why was she freaking out like this?

"You think you're so special," she continued, "such a rebel. The witch who wants to be a real boy." She walked slowly towards me, each step a sharp snap of her heels against the tile floors. This wasn't where I thought the afternoon would take me, not by a long shot.

"I didn't ask for this. Any of it. You people dragged me here. If I could leave, I would." Frustration welled up in me, I could feel myself close to breaking. "They don't need me, and I'd be better off without them. I could actually stay in school long enough to make friends, maybe have a life. Maybe I could have been class president, who knows? I never have the chance because Jenna hates everything."

"It's so hard to be you," she agreed, her voice low now. Husky.

Oh. Oh no. Oh this was the opposite of what I'd wanted after all.

Kelly reached the end of the aisle, only inches from me. She placed her hands down on my knees, and as much as I wanted to, I resisted the urge to shove myself back-wards and away from her.

"I can help you." Her eyes were earnest, she really believed that she was doing the right thing, but then crazy people always did. She slipped out of her shoes, shedding any illusion of height. "I'm sure you've been very confused, Malcolm. It's okay. I'm here now. I can make you understand."

"This isn't you," I said, wondering how I could talk my way out of this. On a top-ten list of typical adolescent fantasies, getting hit on by the smoking-hot teacher didn't really work for me. At least not this smoking-hot teacher. Maybe if it was the football coach, but he was in his thirties, so maybe not. "You don't have to do this," I added desperately. "It's the spell. It's whatever Jenna did. This isn't you."

"And this isn't you." She traced her fingers in the air, and I felt a throbbing against my skin, like a second heartbeat trying to force its way into my body. It was foreign, uncomfortable, and made me want to run as far and as fast as I could. "But it will be soon. Don't worry," she cooed. "I can make it all go away. All the misery. All the confusion. Then we can be happy. You'll see. I'm doing this for us."

She continued tracing symbols in the air, and the pulsing around me grew thicker, stronger, like a blood pressure cuff squeezing my entire body. And then, for a glorious moment, it stopped. Everything halted. The universe took a moment to catch its breath.

"Oh I like this," a musical voice whispered, a symphony of pleasure and bubbling laughter before it ultimately soured, "but I don't like *her* very much." Fingers rubbed the back of my head again, pulling tight at the last moment, before the moment passed, the bubble popped, and the squeezing pressure returned.

"It'll all be over soon," Kelly promised.

"Miss Davenport, step away from the boy!"

I'd never been so happy to see Illana Bryer in my life.

———————

It took Illana less than fifteen minutes to not only save me from the substitute, but to also return the school to some semblance of chastised normalcy, track down Jenna and reverse whatever it was that she'd done. In the meantime, she made me wait in the English room. Quinn finally showed up with Nick a few minutes after Illana, both of them looking horribly unperturbed.

"So is this the part where you move us out in the middle of the night?" I asked, trying to figure out why I had not one but two Witchers guarding my back in the meantime. "Or is there another threat? Another wraith? A unicorn? A Cabbage Patch doll?"

"You're not going anywhere," Quinn said placidly. I would believe him more if the pair of them weren't lingering by the door like something was about to barge its way in.

There was something wrong with one of Quinn's forearms. It was distorted, the skin tone not matching the rest of his arm. The more I studied it, the less real it became until finally Quinn noticed my stare and snorted. "Shut up," he muttered at Nick, who was grinning furiously, before he scrubbed his hand over the space above the distortion. An illusion faded, revealing an arm brace of some kind. Black and strappy, there was a sheath laid into the interior, a knife blade lined perfectly to nestle against the crook of his arm. He pulled the athame out, holding it up as if this were show-and-tell.

"Never leave home without it?" he said halfheartedly.

"That's MasterCard," Nick replied immediately.

"Always?" Quinn tried next.

"That's Snape."

"Whatever, then. It's just a precaution," Quinn said, directing the words to me. "Not that there's anything to be really worried about, but Illana wants to make sure the situation doesn't grow any more out of control than it already has."

"I think it's pretty much as bad as it can get," I pointed out. "Or did you miss the part where one of your merry band of badasses tried out her cougar act a decade too early?"

"This was just a lust spell," Quinn said absently. "Though I don't know how Jenna managed it. She shouldn't have access to the kinds of spells that could put something like this together. But anyway, this is nothing. People just wanted to sleep with you. I'm sure that's not out of the realm of normalcy for you. It could have been a lot worse."

"There are worse things than hormones," Nick agreed. "Like that pitiful excuse of an illusion you've got going on," he said, nodding toward Quinn's arm brace.

"So, want to tell us what prompted this?" Quinn asked, flicking the lights on and off like a child who needed to find *something* to do to keep himself from dying of boredom.

Did he really need me to? Wasn't it obvious. "Jenna wants new magic. She thinks Eat, Pray, Coven class is her best shot. So she's buying everything you guys are selling. Because that worked out so well for us last time."

Neither one of them said anything. Most witches liked the idea of having a coven to belong to and were jealous of those who did. I'd even heard that there were summer programs for high school students specifically geared towards bringing as many kids together as possible for a few weeks just to see if any covens would form.

Illana's return a few minutes later was perfectly timed, as the awkward silence between the three of us only intensified.

"You'll be happy to know that your effect on the rest of the student body is at an end." Illana breezed back into the room, nodding sharply at Quinn as she passed him. Quinn and Nick disappeared out into the class, closing the door just as the bell rang, signaling the final break between classes before the end of the day.

"It's a bit premature, I'm sorry to say, but it looks like I will be taking over instruction of your lessons now. Kelly feels awful, of course, but we both thought it best if she took a few days to regain her footing. It's a shame. She's particularly well versed in aiding new covens control their bond. It's one of the reasons she was brought here to you."

"Yeah, you guys have been regular humanitarians, looking out for our best interests. Funny how none of that came up the first two months we were here." I rolled my eyes. "She's ... what? Twenty-three at the most. How much of an expert could she really be?"

"A double major in Psychology and Criminal Justice, as well as six years spent with the Witchers. The girl may be young, but I would think that you of all people wouldn't judge her so harshly based on her appearance."

I felt a flush of shame creep up my chest and into my face. "I didn't mean it like that," I muttered.

"Of course you did," Illana said blandly. "Some children grow up too fast because they have no other choice. Sometimes that pressure creates a diamond." Illana stared down my challenge, her look conveying regret and disappointment all at once. I never understood exactly what Justin feared from her—she had the ability to make him piss his pants on command. But being on the receiving end of her disappointment... I understood it a little better at least.

"She didn't teach us anything worthwhile," I said under my breath, like that was the problem all along. That I was absolved. And maybe I should be, especially after what happened that afternoon.

"You didn't want to learn," Illana countered. "And don't think I haven't noticed how you've yet to stop in at the hospital. I asked you to do something, did I not? Was I in any way unclear?"

And that was it. The breaking point. "Do you think I was just going to do it because you told me? *I hate this.* All of it. I don't *care* why Luca got involved in the black arts. I don't *care* that you did us a favor by not smothering us in our cribs. I. Don't. Care."

"Do you really think it's that easy?" Illana was controlled, calm. Surprisingly, she didn't seem angry at my outburst, or even offended. But her chiding disappointment was more than enough. "You may not see much value in your life, Malcolm, but that doesn't mean yours is the opinion that matters most." The strange words, and the strange touch against my head came back at once. I brushed my fingers against the nape of my neck, felt something slide against my skin. Ash on my fingers. There was ash in my hair. What the hell?

"I'm done with all this creepy monster shit," I snapped. "Do you understand me? Comprende?"

"Your uncle once thought he could speak to me this way." I swear Illana almost smiled. It was like watching a shark feel joy. "He never made that mistake again."

By that point I was yelling, but I still didn't care. "Get it through your head, lady. I'm not Justin. I don't jump just because you tell me to." An idea was slowly forming in my head. "You want my help? You find a way to break the Coven bond and get me the hell away from all of this. Get me the hell out of this town and away from all of you people, and I'll do everything you ask."

"Is that all?" Illana's voice was frost on glass. "Would you like the moon on a bauble, for an encore? You ask for the impossible, as you rightly know. The Coven bond survives even death. I can do nothing." There was something that flashed across her face, a look like remorse. "Even if we could, there is still Moonset's manipulations to contend with. Understandably, no one wishes to reignite whatever darkness they tied you up into."

There was a hiccupping sound from the door. I looked away from Illana to see Bailey standing in front of the others, different shades of the same hurt and disappointment on each of their faces.

ELEVEN

Charlie Denton took
Moonset harder than anyone.

....

Sara Bexington (S)
Personal Interview

I couldn't say why I ended up at the hospital. After seeing the looks on Justin and Bailey's faces, I left. Fled, really. I felt like a traitor, maybe because I *was* a traitor. All of us fought, but I think it was the first time any of us had really expressed how desperately we wanted the bond between us broken.

I think I was the only one who felt that way and that made it worse.

I had no intention of following Illana's orders, but when I left the school, the hospital was where I ended up. Their world wasn't mine, and I wanted nothing to do with it. So maybe one last job and then I could call it quits.

Maybe you just want to know how to walk away, my mind supplied.

The nurse directed me towards a waiting room on the third floor. Instead of the soothing colors of pale blue and yellow on the lower floors, these floors were a stark, unflattering white with mahogany-colored furniture. It looked less like a hospital waiting room and more like a warehouse break room.

There was only one person in the waiting room, surrounded by a half-dozen empty coffee cups. The television focused on an audience that didn't have anywhere better to be than a lackluster talk show, while a generic man in a suit interrogated a couple on a stage. The volume was off, so I couldn't hear whatever fake reality the fake couple was fighting about.

The man's head was turned towards the television, and I could see that his eyes were open, but they never moved to follow the action. Had he fallen asleep with his eyes open? Was he dreaming about these strange people with their silent problems and wondering how they'd invaded his mind?

The man himself looked grizzled—a face that hadn't shaved in a week, clothes that probably hadn't been changed in at least that long. At a glance, he reminded me of the crazy Moonset cultist that had popped up when we first moved to Carrow Mill. There was something about him that I couldn't put my finger on—something *off,* but the closer I got the more it slipped away.

"I know who you are," the man said, stirring from his slumped position. What was that saying, *he looked like forty miles of bad road?* He was more like forty years spent on those same forty miles, until they'd ground out every bit of hope and light in him, and left him a vagrant in his own skin.

"Everyone knows who I am," I replied.

"Yeah, but I know *what* you are," the man said with a slow, cruel smile.

At least it was exactly the kind of family reunion I'd been expecting. "Nice to meet you too, Uncle Charlie," I said, keeping my words to a bored monotone.

"You just going to stand their gawking?" he huffed, fumbling through his obstacle course of coffee cups, trying to find one with that last precious sip still intact.

"Not exactly how I expected this to go," I walked around his mess, finding a seat across from him.

"How'd you think it would go, tough guy?" he asked, squinting down at his cups.

I leaned back, crossed my leg on my knee, and stared at him. "Well, for one thing, I thought you'd be drunk."

I guess I could see the resemblance a little. But if I was going to look like that in twenty years, I might as well hunt the Prince down and get him to put an end to me now.

He chuffed out a breath that turned into a hacking cough. The tips of his fingers had a yellow, almost orangeish tint to them. Smoker. And from the sound of his cough, at least a couple packs a day.

"Probably would be drunk," he admitted, "if the coffee here wasn't so foul it would spoil good whiskey. You know how foul something's gotta be to make whiskey go bad?"

"Never had the pleasure," I said blandly. What was I even doing here?

A couple of nurses came off the elevator, chatting quietly as they came up on the nurses' station. I watched them for a few minutes, effortlessly going about their jobs. What would it be like to just drown yourself in normalcy. To wake up every day, head in to your job, and just … exist. Neither one of them had to worry about dead parents or being hunted for sport. They didn't know anything about wraiths, or the Abyss, or Maleficia.

"Guess the old bat finally convinced you to come gawk at your poor, broken blood, eh? Can't imagine there's a lot of sights that make a Moonset bastard look good by comparison."

The more the man talked, the more his foul odor crept towards me. I shoved my hands in my pockets after wiping them on my sweats. "Not really interested in what you have to say," I fired back. "Has Luca woken up yet? Said anything?"

"You think if he said anything that I'd still be here?" The man laughed until he choked. The coughing fit lasted longer this time, ending with him hacking up something that he spat into one of the empty coffee cups. I half-expected the cup to start sizzling.

I knew from the rumors going around that Luca didn't have a great home life. And it didn't surprise me that my uncle was a bastard. But I couldn't wrap my head around Charlie's presence here. "Why *are* you here?" I asked, half-demanding.

"Because that's what you *do,* boy. When you've known this day would come. When you knew it was a mistake to let her keep the baby, because she was still grieving and couldn't understand that bad blood is bad, no matter how hard you pray."

Bad blood. His. Mine.

"No wonder he turned out the way he did," I said thickly.

"What'd you say t'me?" Charlie leapt to his feet and threw

79

himself forward with a speed I didn't expect. He charged, thinking I'd fall back or run away. In that instant, I knew everything I needed to know about Luca's childhood. When I braced myself instead of running, he fumbled. The wash of confusion slapped the stupid right off his face. *This is what it was like for him. Submission. Fear. Like a dog that didn't know any better.*

"Maybe Luca never got the chance to tell you. Maybe he never will. But I'm happy to do it for him," I said, stepping forward. Charles Denton was used to being the intimidating bully. He didn't like it when someone stood up to him. Especially not someone who had probably thirty pounds of muscle on him. "You're pathetic."

I reached forward, and he flinched back, and I don't know what he saw in that moment, but something *terrified* him. "Do you know why you're so miserable? Because Cyrus has lived in your head every day of your pathetic life. You carved him out a little space and he made himself at home."

I would not let myself be dragged down into Moonset's fate. If the adults couldn't find a way to make it happen, I would find one myself.

Or die trying.

TWELVE

The Abyssal Princes are the worst of what hides in the Abyss. Born from the collision of chaos and cunning, they have become an abyss themselves, full of incessant hungers for destruction and degradation.

....

The Princes of Hell

Nick was at the table the next morning when I came downstairs. I bypassed the idea of breakfast and pulled my keys off the table where I'd left them. "Going to the gym before class," I said quickly on my way to the front door. "Quinn'll have to give them a ride."

"I'm sure he'll be thrilled," Nick said, all casual and unconcerned.

My mood was good on my way out of the driveway. The visit with Charlie had effectively countered the guilt

I'd had because of what I said in front of the others. Even the weather seemed in good spirits, as the sun burned away the lingering cloud cover and beamed down over the city. Snow was already melting a steady trickle down driveways and into puddles in the street. I felt it in the air. A fresh start.

My morning routine was a fast-paced version of a regular workout, my eyes continually on the clock. Stomach crunches, curls, and ten-minute forays on the elliptical. I couldn't spend more than an hour without being late for school, and the day was already going so well that I didn't want to jinx it, so I showered with plenty of time left before the first bell.

All of that changed once I stepped foot inside the building. Everything was back to normal; no one was staring or being especially creepy. But even still, I couldn't shake the feeling of being hounded.

There were dozens of connecting and crisscrossing smaller hallways between branches of the main couple of buildings. But every time I started heading towards my first-period class, which was a building away, traffic congestion sprung up out of nowhere. The more I tried to push my way through, the thicker the crowds seemed to get.

I headed down a side hall, cutting back the way I'd already come, only to have the same thing happen again.

Hallways started to blur together, and the more frustrated I got, the more I kept turning down random, open hallways.

It got to the point where I was so turned around and so focused on the bell that was going to ring *at any second* that I stopped recognizing any of the hallways at all. Like I'm pretty sure I took the stairs down at least three times, and the school only had two floors.

Then, finally, just before the first bell, everything around me grew quiet like oblivion. The sound around me stilled until there was nothing but me: the raised but steady pulse of my heart, the quickened breaths entering and then exiting my lungs.

I stepped across a threshold and the moment of quiet popped, a warm rushing in my ears like water that had finally worked its way free. When I looked around, I realized I was in the auditorium again.

I saw it again out of the corner of my eye. The curtain. Fluttering. Any other time I would have noticed and dismissed it, attributing it to a draft or a heating vent kicking on. But every time it moved, something crawled on the back of my neck, like a scorpion dancing before the sting.

I came down the steps and crossed the auditorium to the stage. Something was lit up underneath the curtain and flickering like a fire. *Moving.*

As I reached the stage's edge, I grabbed the material from the bottom and pulled them back. A symbol, lines all curving in towards the middle, spinning slowly and languidly like a whirlpool that had all the time in the world. One of my knuckles brushed against the edge, and that was all it took. My body reacted to it, trembling as I lost control of my hand. My fingers reached out and brushed against the tip of it, then centered over the middle as I pressed my palm against the glow.

The world rippled. Fell away. I fell *through* worlds, though it was more accurate to say that the worlds fell around me. I never moved. Reality broke apart in waves like it did in the movies when a character experienced a flashback. Or maybe it was like a pond after someone skipped a rock across the surface. One minute I was in the auditorium, trying to figure out why that symbol looked so damn familiar, and the next I was...in the auditorium.

Only it wasn't the auditorium. There was a stage, but it was a thousand times more extravagant than the one I'd just left. There were chairs everywhere. Dozens of them. But not exactly chairs. They were too...ornate. *Thrones.* I was surrounded by them. Some were gaudy, golden monstrosities. Others were carved out of bone, or emeralds, and one was leather, smooth and dark with brownish stains that turned my stomach.

My knuckles sizzled with the brief contact even as my palm burned the symbol into my skin. It kept moving, lazily spinning the same slow path across my lifeline. There was an awareness to it, a sense of *hunger,* or *need.* A vortex that wouldn't be satisfied until it drank the oceans dry. Even then its thirst would not slacken. That feeling was in me now, churning against the bones in my hand.

Whoever had been in charge of the redecorating had gotten into Lewis Carroll's private stash because it was...something dreamed up in the creepy side of Wonderland. The curtain had been pulled back and tied against the walls, revealing the blood and guts that would become the framework for the school's play. There were giant sheets of paper taped against the walls on either side of the room, brief sketches of scenery, or supplies still needed.

That was where the real ended, and the surreal began. The thrones, for starters. They'd replaced all the prison-block gray metal folding chairs. Someone had sketched out a tree in black on one of the walls, but now the drawing bulged out from the wall, the paper growing out as the tree took shape and became a three-dimensional monstrosity, erupting from the wall like a tumor. The tree shifted and swayed under a nonexistent wind. Papers hanging off the branches rustled with a breeze that didn't exist. And from a hollow near the base, a pair of yellow-and-gold eyes peered out. Whatever it was, I didn't want to know.

The worst of it was the fencing. Someone had started putting together a series of boards into a typical yard fence, probably for the Kansas scenes. But hanging off one of the boards was ... I wasn't even sure what to call it. It looked like a desiccated, road-kill version of the Scarecrow. Leather for skin that still had patches of hide to it, yet shrunken and damaged after a summer in the sun. The fingers tapered off into shards of something that looked like glass, and the eye sockets were deep, cavernous things lined with dark fur. But despite all the things that made it *not* human, it looked incredibly lifelike. I expected at any moment for the Scarecrow's liquid glass fingertips to slice through the marionette strings and for it to begin its career as the world's creepiest puppet. I was almost afraid to look away, because I was certain that even if I wasn't watching *it*, it was watching *me*.

"This is the part where someone drops a house on me, isn't it?" I muttered under my breath. Across the room, from the stage itself, there came a chortling sound that sounded like the stripped-down essence of laughter. Bubbling brooks and tinkling piano keys, summer breezes and applause.

The hair on the back of my neck stood up. But the creature sitting on the edge of the stage did not.

At first it was hard to say what I was looking at. At a distance, I couldn't tell if it was a boy or a girl, but it was immediately obvious that whatever it was, it wasn't human. White hair hung down past its waist and trailed to the floor beneath the stage—not just hair that was white, but hair that *glowed*— woven moonlight given form.

In a psych class a few schools ago, we'd done a section on how people perceive faces, and how important facial symmetry is to our subconscious opinion of attractiveness. The idea was that most people had an instinctive standard of beauty, recognizing immediately the symmetry of someone else's face. But it was also the flaws in someone's appearance that made them stand out, made them noticeable.

The creature in front of me didn't have any flaws, unless not being on Illana Bryer's Christmas card list was a flaw. A perfect nose, perfect eyes, perfect chin. It was like my eyes slid off whatever they saw, because they couldn't process what they were seeing. A face too handsome to be handsome, too beautiful to be beautiful, and yet too terrifying to be terrifying.

Time passed. It was impossible to look away, impossible not to want to *see*. I didn't even know what I was looking at. My eyes burned, and it was only after I forced myself to blink that I realized how dried out they'd gone. How long I'd been staring. And just like that, the spell—or whatever the creature was doing to me—thawed.

"What are you?" I finally managed to ask.

His voice was husky. Melodious. But definitely masculine. "Don't you know?"

Despite growing up as a terrorist cell's wet dream, I'd had

very few encounters with monsters. Bailey and I had already been evacuated by the time the wraith came after Justin and the others. But now her warning rang in my head again. "*One of them escaped. He's* here *now.*"

One of the creatures that Luca had been working so hard to free. One of them had managed to escape. "You're one of them. An Abyssal Prince."

A short nod.

"You tried to kill us," I said, already starting to inch my way back the way I'd come. Not that it would do much good. I had a feeling I wouldn't be allowed to leave until he let me.

"That's not quite how I remember it," the creature said. His words were strange, I could feel *wry amusement* dripping from the words themselves, as though his words were so heavily layered with meaning that they spilled out of the air waves that carried them. It was so overpowering for a moment that it completely shut me down. I pushed down the smile I'd drawn at his words. The warmth in my chest, and the embarrassment at his attention. My emotions were a violin, and he'd barely pulled the bow across the strings. He'd barely said anything at all.

"What's your name?" I asked, falling back on rote conversations that didn't require conscious thought. My brain was buzzing in the aftermath of his voice—I never wanted to hear his voice again, and for him to speak forever at the same time. I knew I was in danger, but knowing it and being able to *do something about it* were two vastly different things.

The creature opened his mouth, and there was a pointed pause, as if the words were on the tip of his tongue only to evaporate before they could be whispered into existence.

"Names...I remember names." His eyes turned towards me, violet and big. *Mourning and regret,* his words said. I whimpered. "Naming things. Deciding what they are; what they will be. Words to lock them into shapes that make sense. Names are glass cages, aren't they?"

Irrationally, I thought of Jenna. *"Of course her name is Meghan. I've never met a Meghan who wasn't a bitch."*

The creature nodded just as the memory faded, hands spread to reinforce his point. I shivered. He was in my head. He knew what I was thinking. But his voice was a lullaby, and kept my fear far enough away that it could not rule me. "Are names prisons where you came from?" This was one of the creatures that had nearly killed us—that Luca had almost died trying to summon. But back then they were creatures of green flame with voices that hissed and popped, not bodies that were a touch too human and yet not human enough.

"All names are prisons. Are you not defined by yours? Named for a man raised up in the wake of patricide."

I startled with a shock and turned away. "I don't know what you're talking about."

"Macbeth killed his father and was in turn killed by Malcolm. You are a prisoner to both name and history." He pulled one knee up and rested his cheek on it, looking to the side now instead of straight at me. "And yet, I miss it." The more he talked, the more his words buzzed in my ears and kept me from thinking too clearly. *I just wanted to talk to him, right? There was no reason not to talk. Just talk.*

"But you just said that names are cages."

"Not all cages are infinitesimal, you know. Some are as

large as worlds. But even still, one shouldn't forget that a cage is still a cage."

"Do you have a name?" I asked again, this time more delicate.

He shook his head, but still wouldn't look up at me. I almost missed it. His looks were a sharp knife that cut at me, kept me off my game, but when they were hidden from me it was an ache in my mind, a desire my eyes held independent of the rest of my body. They wanted to keep looking on him, feasting on the awkward, alien beauty of the Prince, even if I knew it was wrong.

You wouldn't be so calm if he looked like one of the wraiths that attacked Justin. It was true. I knew enough about looks—my own got thrown into the mix often enough—that I knew I was being stupid. I certainly couldn't trust this ... demon, just because he had a pretty face. And yet I still was. I couldn't help it.

"I don't blame you," he said. "I know you think of me as a monster. But I don't *feel* like one. Do you think that makes a difference?"

A strange thrill arced through my veins. My body was hot, all of the sudden. So hot, sweltering, smiling. "It matters what I think?" That he would think of me like that, the one who never mattered, the outcast even among the outcasts. That he would care what I think. How had I gotten so lucky?

The creature smiled, a tentative, shaky sort of smile. Like it would fall away at any moment and reveal the crushing emotion that was hiding behind it. Anger, contempt, despair. Whatever it was, it was certainly sharp and deep. "All the difference in the world. In all the worlds."

"Tell me your name," I promised, "and I'll tell you what I think of you."

The smile was brushed away by frustration. His eyes closed, his mouth clenched in on itself until it all but vanished, and there was a glistening sparkle that welled up underneath violet eyelashes. "I can't *remember*," he whispered harshly in reply. "There are no names in my home. No need to call out to your brothers, for they cannot hear you. We are bound at the bottom of a chasm that spans nearly the whole of creation. Even though the darkness has broken us and made us dark reflections, we will always be foreign. We are all strangers in the Abyss."

Justin had told us the story of the Abyssal Princes, creatures born of Faerie, lords and ladies of chaos. Further back than the written word, the Faerie lords had warred against the armies of the Abyss—of Hell—and lost. And for the rest of their existence, they would owe a tithe of a soul every seven years. When they failed to produce a human soul, one of their own was taken. The Abyssal Princes was what becomes of a Faerie trapped in the Abyss. Changed and twisted until it became a demon itself.

His eyes grew faraway. "I remember *pain*. I remember screaming. Even those are ageless memories of long-dead dreams. I am a shadow of a demon's nighttime sigh. My brothers gave up much for me." One single tear slid off his face and started to fall only to arrest itself in the air, inches from the Prince's face. "I fear they will never understand the failure I have become."

Tears pooled in my eyes, rolled down my cheeks as

sorrow and *regret* washed through me, a sieve to collect emotions too grand for one creature to hold on to by himself. "Who would ever call you a failure?"

A self-conscious twist of the lips. "I still *feel*, young one. Longing for things I shouldn't, desiring the fruits forbidden to me. My heart's song is a wish to be anything other than what I am." He reached out, touched the tip of his too-long fingers to the teardrop that hovered in front of him. "It must be a glorious thing, to be mortal. To love, and burn brightly, and let yourself be ravaged by passions and consumed by joys."

He finally looked up at me again, and I felt myself swallowing back my own feelings. "You know what I am, don't you?" he asked. I nodded, but couldn't trust myself to speak. "My people warred against Hell and lost. Only seven times have we failed to meet the tithe. I was the second they claimed. The second to break. Do you want to know why?"

He didn't wait for my nod this time, as though he already knew my interest was inevitable. He was right. "I sang a song during the war that was so painful, so devastating, that I brought the armies of Hell to their knees. Only once have the Hellborn ever shed tears, my human, and they have never, *ever* forgotten." Another sad smile. "My threnody, my *destruction*, was a discordant scream that rippled through the walls of the Pit like a soothing balm. My unraveling was particularly brutal. I'm told that the Abyss itself smiled that day."

"That ... is horrible," I said, because I had no better way of explaining myself.

"Horrible is just a word," the Prince returned quietly.

He reached for me then, and I leaned forward, eager

to feel his fingers upon my face, but something changed. Gravity fell away, the floor puddled at my feet, and I stumbled down into a chasm of darkness.

I woke up slumped against the side of the stage, one hand tucked up behind my head like a pillow. The skin in my hands was tight, reddened and swollen although there was no sign of the symbol burned into my skin. I stood up immediately, shoving back the curtain, but the symbol I'd seen there, the symbol I'd touched, was gone.

Holy shit, that was an Abyssal Prince. I survived an encounter with one of the Princes.

I slumped back down, waiting for that thought to make sense. My workout high was gone, vacated the premises, and the only thing remaining was a foggy memory of exhaustion. The auditorium looked the way it should be, the real-world version of itself. It was still empty, and I was alone again. But was it real? Or was it just a dream?

My head was swimming, wrung out and emptied in a way I had never felt before. When the Prince spoke, *feelings* washed through me. Now that they were gone, my body felt stretched out and pushed too far, like a particularly rough workout. If Justin was here, he would want to know everything. He'd see this as another opportunity to go off on his own and put the rest of us in danger. That it was our *responsibility.*

But still, if I didn't tell him, it was at least as bad as what they'd already done to me. Lies, betrayal. He may have gone about it the wrong way, but Justin's heart was always in the right place.

"Screw that," I muttered as I scrolled through the contacts in my phone log and clicked on Illana's name.

THIRTEEN

The magic of the witches is the only true magic amidst the darkness. Maleficia, Necromancy, Evanescence: monstrous birthrights for our monstrous counterparts. Our magic is the only thing that can stand against them.

....

The Book of Hours

There was a triumvirate waiting for me back at home. Illana had told me to leave school immediately, and of course, tell no one where I was going.

She was at the head of the table with Quinn and Nick flanked on either side. None of them said anything as I walked in. This time, instead of pretending like she wasn't there as I bustled around the house, I dropped off my bag and looked back towards the kitchen.

"I . . . coffee?" My brain was still a little foggy, but I was pretty sure I was asking permission in my own house. *There is definitely something wrong with me.*

Illana nodded her head graciously. I walked back into the kitchen, found a fresh pot of coffee already brewed and waiting for me like they'd already anticipated I would need something. But when I reached for a cup out of the cabinet, I saw my hands shaking for the first time. It slipped out of my grip, and would have probably shattered on the floor if not for the timely intervention of Quinn.

"I'll get it," he said, setting the cup down on the counter. "Black, right?" I nodded. "When's the last time you ate, Mal? Do you want something?"

My stomach chose that moment to rebel. I closed my eyes, feeling the shame rising up again. That was all I did anymore. Felt ashamed for the things I couldn't control. Just like I couldn't control this.

"Hey, it's okay," Quinn whispered, glancing over my shoulder. "You're safe now. Come on, go have a seat. I'll fix you a sandwich."

As much as I wanted to protest that I didn't want a sandwich (an extra two miles on tonight's run) my stomach wouldn't be denied. The blood rushed from my head to my gut, and I found myself walking back into the dining room and taking my seat at the table. Quinn followed behind me, deposited the coffee in front of me. Nick and Illana were pretending not to notice me, but when my head dropped I could feel their eyes on me. Judging me.

I didn't reach for the coffee cup again, terrified of what

would happen if I saw my hands shaking again. *Everything's spinning away. Spinning and rolling and off on its own.* My shirt clung to my skin, sticky with sweat and stinking of fear that hadn't reared its head until I came into this room. Until I was fully faced with what had happened this morning.

A Prince came to talk to me. To talk. Like we were friends. A wraith nearly killed Justin and Jenna, and I get the chatty, pretty boy demon. But thinking back, all I could remember of the Prince was a silvery blur in my mind. No impression had stuck, he was just a placeholder of feelings I couldn't explain and sensations that had hollowed me out. *I could have died, and instead I'm having a breakdown.* The thought made me laugh. And once I started, I couldn't stop.

"He'll be fine," Illana said crisply as I looked up, and saw Nick half out of his chair. "It's not exactly a trauma, but it is traumatic in its own way." She leaned forward, fixing her clasped hands over her knee. There was nothing of the harsh, knife-like woman I'd come to know. She smiled, her eyes sad but sincere. "It becomes easier, Malcolm. Take your time. Get yourself together as best you can. Then tell us what happened."

The plate being set down in front of me made me jump, the contrast in sound from Illana's soothing tone. Who even knew that Illana *had* a soothing tone? Justin would never believe it. Justin. I looked up at Quinn immediately, but the words tangled on my tongue. "They … it … what … "

"Everyone else is fine," Quinn confirmed. "We've got people keeping an eye on them. The creature didn't try to make contact with anyone else."

Just me then. I nodded gratefully and then looked down

at the sandwich. I devoured it with single-minded purpose, barely chewing before the entire thing was gone and there were only crumbs between my fingers.

I tested the coffee, taking only a small sip. Hot, but the burning sensation down my throat wasn't because of the temperature. I sniffed the cup, then shifted towards Quinn. Illana was the one who answered, though. "A bit of Irish whiskey to help calm the nerves. Drink up. There is still much to be decided today."

None of my siblings were big drinkers. Lowered inhibitions meant the possibility that someone slipped up, that spells were cast when they shouldn't. Now, though, I downed the rest of the cup gratefully, feeling the burn down my throat and settling into my stomach.

"That's a good boy," Illana hummed. "Now when you're ready, tell us everything that happened."

It was harder than it sounded. Once I started, I couldn't find a single thread to follow through to the end. My thoughts were scattered, broken things. Memories were disjointed and didn't fit properly together. I told them first what the thrones looked like, then followed it up with the Prince's talk about being human. Then jumped back to the beginning, and talked about the glowing symbol on the stage.

The more I talked, the more I couldn't hold it in, but I couldn't make my brain focus long enough to put the pieces in order. Finally, I stopped, mid-sentence, and looked up at the three of them. Their faces had gotten darker and more grim the longer I talked. "What's wrong with me."

Nick leaned back in his chair, thoughtful and relaxed.

None of this bothered him in the slightest, and I clung to that. To them, this was normal. They would make sense of it. They would take control and stop it from ever happening again. "An Abyssal is big, metaphorically speaking. It's a lot to take in. It's not unusual to have *troubles* after it's over. You know how some people go through a trauma, and they suffer PTSD after? It's like that. Sometimes it takes the mind awhile to condition itself. To put what happened into a context that makes sense."

"But this is normal," I pressed. "I'm not going crazy?"

"Of course you aren't crazy," Illana spat. "Don't be absurd. Do you know how many people have knowingly met an Abyssal Prince and lived to speak about it?" She held out a hand, took away two of the fingers. "Three that we know about, including yourself. It is rare for one of them to escape, despite their numbers. Rarer still for them to appear to humans."

Despite their numbers. "Seven," I mumbled.

Illana stared at me. "What was that, child?"

"Seven," I repeated. "There are only seven. That's what he said. That his people had only failed to pay the tithe seven times. He was the second taken. Second of seven."

A look passed between the three of them, one I didn't know how to interpret. Justin was better at that than I was. Somewhere along the way my hands had stilled—whether from the coffee, the alcohol, the sandwich, or the calm itself. The way they were all so quiet in between words, giving me moments and time to collect myself. My thoughts started to come together, organized and filed away in ways that made sense. Illana was right. It only took time.

I took a deep breath. The first time I'd felt like myself since walking away from the auditorium. "Can you stop him? Kill him?"

Illana inclined an eyebrow, her eyes careful as they regarded me. I wished I knew what she was thinking. "Perhaps," she said, making the word sound like a finality. "They are elusive creatures, the Abyssals. No doubt this one has found somewhere to hide, to disappear in plain sight."

There was a discomfort in the room that I didn't pick up on first. But Quinn scowled and Nick squirmed in his chair, and then I knew. "You still want me to be bait."

"What I *want*," she stressed, "is that you understand your place. For you to *want* to help."

If you help, a traitorous voice inside me whispered, *you'll get to see him again.* As bad as it had been, there was something about the Prince that confused me. They called him a monster, he called *himself* a monster, but he seemed so sad. Lost.

They all stared at me and waited for my response. Illana had a way of using her stillness as a weapon to club and batter until she got the answer she wanted. It was there, tucked between the clasp of her hands, there in the sharpshooter-narrowed focus of the eyes. In the way she was simultaneously leaning forward and yet completely at ease in her chair. It was like she wasn't waiting for my response at all. I was the one waiting on her reaction to whatever it was I would say next.

"I won't," I said finally, my heart thudding painfully in my chest. "I don't want any part of it." The lie burned a blistering score through me, but I grabbed hold of the goal, which was exactly the opposite of what she was asking. A normal life. Not a life filled with spells and Princes. "I did my part. I told you what's going on. Now I want you to leave me and the others out of it. Last time this happened, we almost died."

"The Abyssal came to you. We did not set any of this into motion." Illana lifted her hands, steepled the finger like a gun, and watched me closely. "But ask yourself, who will bear the responsibility this time if you walk away now? If someone dies, and you do nothing, how responsible are you?"

The woman was unbelievable. This was not my life. This was not my world. "Go to hell," I spat. I needed air. I needed to be anywhere but here.

———————

"You don't see it?" Jenna's voice carried through the front door. Guess they'd cut school too. I hesitated on Justin's porch—I thought maybe I could hide out in the living room, watch some television until Illana and the others left my house. But Jenna's serious tone caught me off guard. I pushed the door open quietly and heard her follow up with, "He's in trouble."

"Mal's not in trouble," Cole said, sounding so jaded and full of scorn that I almost didn't recognize his voice. "He's just being a baby about Luca."

"Maybe you shouldn't have antagonized him," Bailey added.

"It's more than that," Jenna said. I heard frustration, but that wasn't the part that was blowing my mind. I would have expected Justin to be the one with all the concerns. But I never would have expected something like that out of Jenna. "It was a bad joke, I get it. We joke about how he's always in a bad mood, but haven't you noticed him lately? Something's wrong with him. It's eating him alive."

"You're just trying to start something. Quinn told you to leave it alone," Justin commented.

I let the door slam shut behind me. The sudden silence coming from the kitchen was almost laughable. The four of them were spread out around the kitchen: Cole in front of the fridge, peering through its contents; Jenna, arms crossed in front of her, wary and pissed off; and Justin and Bailey, seated at the table, each of them swamped behind stacks of homework and textbooks.

"Am I dying?" I asked, feeling some sense of normalcy. The four of them against the one of me. This was good. It was usual. "Because I don't feel like I'm dying."

"Nobody's dying," Jenna said, a frown forming on her face. *She didn't like that I was here. She thought this was going to be private. I wasn't meant to overhear.* "Are you done being a five-year-old and ignoring the rest of us?"

"Are you done being a four-year-old who throws a tantrum when she doesn't get her way?"

It was a quick and easy change to the atmosphere in the room. However the conversation had started, whatever Jenna had said that initiated it, now things were different. Easier. Jenna was the spoiled, snotty sister, and I was the frustrated, irritated brother. My usual role settled around my shoulders like a mantle, and already I was breathing easier.

"Did you think they were going to move us again?" I continued. "Because we're still here, Jenna. And I can't walk the halls at school without people staring at me. Maybe they don't know that you infected the whole school with your weird prank, but they know it had something to do with me."

"I thought you liked the attention," she snarked back. "Aren't you Mister Popular?"

"Cut it out, Jenna," Bailey said, pen poised over her notebook. "Stop trying to pick a fight."

Cole peeked his head out from behind the refrigerator door. "Why aren't you yelling at Mal? He's the one interrupting a private conversation."

It was a slap to the face. *They didn't want me here.* Just because I'd walked in the front door didn't mean I should be privy to their conversation, that much was true. If they'd wanted me here, if this had really been some kind of intervention like the other day at school, they would have told me about it.

"Good point." I managed to hide my thoughts behind an even tone and a hesitant smile. Deflection was always a good response. "I'll leave you guys to it, then. Just put a list together of all my faults, huh? It'll save you lots of time in the future."

"No, wait." Jenna swore under her breath, and I could feel the heated look she shot at Cole, even though I'd turned my back to them. I didn't wait, though. It would be safer and easier outside. Away from here. Maybe I could get in my car and just drive, drive, drive until there was nothing but the memory of family in my rearview window. "Mal, wait!"

Jenna caught me at the door before I could make my exit. I should have moved faster. Then the conversation would be over and I could figure everything out by myself.

"I know it was a bitch move," Jenna said, her voice pitched lower than normal. If this was Jenna's attempt at an apology, it made sense. There were few things that Jenna hated more than anything, and admitting fault was at the top of the list. Jenna dealt with apologies in only one of two ways: she either wielded it like a weapon, loud and in someone's face, or it was a warm blanket, quiet and hidden away from the rest of the world. "I was just mad, and I wasn't thinking. It was stupid."

This was the latter, and I didn't know how to handle it. I was never on the receiving end of apologies like this.

"You know me, it got out of control," she added. Jenna kept her eyes low, hair falling into her face. That wasn't like her either. Jenna stood tall, always, but most especially when there was every reason for her to cower and bow her head. Her hand reached out like she wanted to touch me, and she looked down at it in surprise. Hesitated, and then let it drop with a shake of her head. "I thought if a couple of your new friends developed little crushes on you, it would be funny. Maybe torment you a little. It wasn't supposed to be the whole school. But it . . . spread. Like a virus. And then the whole school was infected."

I shoved my hands in my pockets, rocked on my heels. What was I supposed to do with that? Did Jenna really want forgiveness? Or was this an elaborate plan to win me over somehow? I could see her doing something like that, placing a moment of weakness down on the table as an opening bid only to collect my participation as her winnings.

"I know you're mad, and I know you don't want to talk to any of us, but if there's something you *have* to talk about, just . . . " She looked up through the fringe, studying my face, looking for something in my eyes, or tucked into my skin or streaked through my hair. "Just find someone who can listen. Please."

I grunted, which was about as well as I could do at the moment. My head kept saying that Jenna was playing me, that this was all a game to her. That she was just manipulating me the way she manipulated everyone else.

FOURTEEN

The Abyssals are captivated by humanity.
Their songs enslave us, but our humanity is
a fire that hypnotizes them too. In some ways
they are so very human. Dark gods of Olympus,
broken until they fit our molds.

The Princes of Hell

I had days to myself after that. I went to school, I had terse yet polite conversations with Justin and the others, and I started running after school. Maybe in the spring, I'd go out for track. There were no Witchers coming to me about any problems, no siblings pressuring me to take classes I didn't want to take. I worked on my homework in the library during last period, while they were learning all about Coven bonds and how awesome they were.

Everything went great. For exactly a week.

I dropped off my books at my locker—having finished the last little bit of my homework for the week, I didn't have anything to take home. People talked to me as I passed in the halls, some just saying my name and nodding their heads, others stopping me long enough to have a quick conversation.

I finally made my way to my first-period class when I saw it, in the instant *just* before my hand brushed the door-knob, which glowed with a golden, dangerous light. My hand connected, the symbol flared against my skin, and the world dropped away around me, like a curtain cut from the tethers holding it upright.

The hallways, which had been filled with the typical excited din of an afternoon free from the tyranny of school, dropped to a hushed murmur: a play on opening night. The longer I listened, the longer it faded until there was nothing but me.

The hall became grand, polished ivory and onyx tiles beneath my feet, columns of forest green and inlaid with gold and emeralds that held the ceiling back. They were impossibly wide, hundreds of feet across, a ballroom instead of a hallway. And when I walked into the classroom, I expected to find something like desks and knowledge. Instead, I found ... a toy shop. Santa's toy shop, if I was to be exact.

Everything was red and green, filigreed and overwrought. Explosions of color, even the doorknob was hideously intricate. The garbage can was molded out of fleur-de-lis, the light switch was a chain wrapped in ribbons, complete with a bell.

And the Prince, somehow understated, sitting on the bookshelf near the wall. Watching. Waiting.

It was like before, the way my eyes hungered to break him down into pieces and parts, to file them away as corrupted memories that would never be able to be played back. But I didn't care. I dropped my bag at the door and stared.

The silence gave me time for my mind to clear, to cast off the wonder like spiderwebs and remember where I was. Well, not exactly *where* I was, but who I was with. An Abyssal Prince, a denizen of Hell. A creature that lived a life of eternal torment and deconstruction, a demon whose very presence broke down the walls of reality around it.

"I resent that implication," his voice trilled.

"What?"

He looked disappointed, but not terribly so. The emotion was shrugged off his face easily enough, like water off a raincoat. Were the things he felt even real? Or were they just copies of real emotions, like a cell phone picture of a priceless piece of art. It wasn't the same thing by half. "Though I am cousin to the crawling chaos you call demons, I am nothing like them. Such an insinuation is offensive."

"You can read my mind?"

His neck popped in a series of clicks as it twisted to one side like a bird. He studied me in silence for a moment. "If you wanted to keep your thoughts private," he finally offered, "then perhaps you should hide them better. They dance behind your eyes like fireflies; how can I not be dazzled by their spark?"

I crossed the room, for a moment staving off the urge to shudder, and then finally giving into it. The idea that he was in my *head*. Inside my mind. Again.

After Bailey had been infected by one of them, she'd

spread the infection to us. It was slow at first, a pressure in the back of my head like a headache that was waiting for the sun before it was able to blossom. Each of us was abducted inside our own minds, tucked away behind locked doors and chains where we could see out, but we had no control.

The idea that there was something in my head—something that could control me—was something I tried very hard not to think about. I had enough trouble trying to control my own life. To have that wrested completely away from me, and there was nothing I could do to stop it—

"Send me back."

The Prince looked startled, *worry* radiating out from him like a spotlight. He reached out a hand in supplication, and for the first time I took in a detail I hadn't seen before. A ring, carved out of silver with a smoky gray stone across the top. "Have I done something to offend, my human?"

His words *claimed* me. I shook my head, anger surging inside of me that kept the rush of his emotions at a distance. I was my only master. No one else: not Illana Bryer, not Moonset and all their plans, and certainly not the demon standing in front me.

Stay out of my head. You have no right. You are not welcome, never welcome. My mind. Mine.

The Prince flinched and pulled his hand back. He didn't seem to move at all, and yet one moment he was seated and the next he was dancing. No, he was walking. Well, he was walking and he moved like dancing, like there was a pattern and steps he was following, and they just happened to bring him closer to me.

"Are you going to try to kill me?" I demanded, crossing my arms in front of my chest. "Because you should know that doesn't tend to work out for people."

His expression was hesitant, and I could tell he wanted to smile, but he refrained. Which was good because I don't know what I would have done. "I know all sorts of things about what your bond can do, little human. The question that hangs between us, though, is how much do *you* know?"

It was an open secret that Moonset had experimented upon us. That our Coven bond was...unique. But how would a creature straight out of Hell know about that?

"There's the Coven bond," I said, only a little uncertain, "and then something else. Another layer."

"Many layers," the Prince corrected, and now he *did* smile. "They were quite crafty, your parents. Never have I seen a darkbond crafted in such a way. You should be proud. There are those in the Abyss who would put you in beautiful bone cages and stroke your head when you sang, all for want of your vicissitudes."

"A *darkbond*." I kept my voice neutral, happy at least so my words didn't broadcast my feelings the way the Prince's seemed to.

The Prince hummed a few notes, and the walls lit up and became transparent crystal. He walked to one side of the room and stood at the edge, his feet brushing up against the glass. Colored lights moved beneath him, each a different shade and blinking with its own unique pulse. Fiery reds that were as slow as turtles, and brilliant viridians that were hummingbird fast. As many colors as there were colors, and as many speeds as there was speed.

His song continued, light and airy, spilling from his mouth with a presence that made it somehow *more*. It wasn't just a song, it was life and reality and nature all rolled up into one. There was a power to that voice, and though I could hear an encroaching finality laced between the notes, a song like that of universes collapsing, I didn't care. I would listen to that song forever if I could.

But soon it faded, and the lights below glowed just a bit darker. "Better to ask what it means to be one of the *darkbound*. To find yourself free from fate, to know that there is a place where you will always be cherished and safe. It is the greatest of honors and the sweetest of songs. Imagine your life, where all your cares and whims are cared for by another. Where you exist and serve in bliss. Where one controls many." A sour note escaped the Prince's mouth, then, that shattered the glass walls in an instant. The room around us shook and shattered, the walls splitting apart so that airy columns of green and gold became rust and steel, dripping red and hanging chains. Sulfur in the air and smoke in my eyes. From heaven to hell in an instant. "And all because your fathers stole something that did not belong to them."

"I—I don't understand what you're talking about." Moonset had done something, of course they had. This wasn't the first time something had come for us because of what our parents had done.

"You people call magic a language," the Prince sneered, and I crumbled to my feet at the *contempt* in his voice. My body shook with grief and despair, rocked beneath the wake of my own misery, summoned up by his ire. It was easy to hate myself, easy to hate what I was and where I'd come from. No one else would ever be able to hate me in all the ways I already hated me. "But you forget it's just *a* language. Just one. You think yours is the only one that's holy. Maleficia may be dark, but this world is a bottle of equal parts, containing just as much darkness as it does light."

With every word, with every ounce of spite, I curled up tighter and tighter, until I could not possibly make myself any smaller. And then, only then, did I start to cry, succumbing to my flaws. *I hate them because of what they did to me. I hate myself for not being strong enough to break free. I hate that I can only eat if someone's watching. I hate that I always have to pretend, always have to hide behind the calm. I have a fate I can't control, and I'm going to drown someday.*

"Zealots, the lot of you. So many languages: Necromancy, the songs of Evanescent, the shrieks of Maleficia. Your parents stole what they could not barter for, and killed for what they could not steal. I have waited for this time, Malcolm Denton. They ripped the secrets of the darkbond from my sister's mouth before they slit her throat. And then swaddled their children up in stolen magic. You will make reparation for what was taken from me."

There were books about Moonset, about what they'd been like before they'd formed a cult and turned into terrorists. Books that asked "where did they go wrong." Most people agreed it started with the Abyssal Prince when they were in high school. One had escaped, or been released. Sherrod, Justin's father, and my own were responsible for alerting the adults, but everyone agreed that it was Robert Cooper and his coven Eventide that ended the threat.

At least until Justin found out the truth. The Abyssals in the fireplace had claimed a different story. That it was Moonset, not Eventide, that saved the day. But letting people remember that story would only confuse the narrative that Moonset was destined for a dark end. They'd covered it up, and if it hadn't been for the five of us, that story might have stayed.

"Your ... sister," I said, trying to think. Trying to remember her name. "Kore?"

The Prince snarled, and I saw how beautiful could become a weapon. It hammered at me, each line on his face, the rage-contorted muscles and the unquenchable fire in its eyes. I could lose myself in that face, swallowed up in emotions that would shred me to pieces and leave me empty and dull while he could do anything he wanted to me.

The Prince looked away first, and the fascination lifted. I was breathing heavy, panting really, and it unnerved me. I was not myself around the Prince—the more I looked at him, the more I fell by the wayside. Determination coursed through me, though it was fickle and thin, like promises on paper.

A switched flipped, and the Prince was in control of himself once more. "That is why you are here. You will be my hand in this world. You will find the truth where it lies buried in a potter's grave, and bring it to me."

I stayed silent, and kept my gaze elsewhere. I refused to bow my head and look at the floor, though, so instead I focused on the grime-crusted ceiling.

"I have chosen you, Malcolm. There are few honors as great as this. Tell the tale of my sister's demise. Bring me the truth, bring me her bones, and I shall tie a bow around your heart that will make all ills well. If you would ask, I would give you worlds undreamt, but I don't need to." He leaned forward then, his hand sloped towards my face like he wished to caress my cheek, but he never touched me. I looked away, even though my body leaned to the side after his hand was gone, leaning into that phantom touch. "I already know what your heart desires most."

"What?"

"Freedom." A simple word that rang with *hope* and *promise*. Feelings of possibility and closure flooded through me, and he didn't have to explain. I knew. He could free me from the Coven bond. He could free me from the darkbond. And whatever other bonds our parents had laid over us, tying us tighter than fate should ever allow.

"How—how do I know that you can really do this? How do I know you're not lying to me?"

"I may wear a different face and speak a different tongue, but I am still bound by ancient laws. If I say it thrice, it cannot be construed as false. Bring my sister's killer to me, and I will unravel the bonds laid upon you. Bring her body to me, and I will free you from the chains that trap you. Bring me my vengeance, and I will make it so that no man may claim your soul again."

Before, his words had made me drown in emotions that were as vast as an ocean, but this was like a shiver and a promise up my spine, reaching out and tugging on every bit of hair on my skin until they all stood straight as soldiers. These words had a weight I could almost touch, and hold and lay down against.

To be free of Moonset's curse upon us—what the Prince called the darkbond. Freedom from it, and from the Coven bond. He was right; he knew what I wanted more than anything.

Would I really help him?

FIFTEEN

During the day, they ran with different crowds.
Emily was a cheerleader, Diana the brilliant rebel,
Cyrus the most popular, and Sherrod the all-star.
But once the day let out, they always came together.

Moonset: A Dark Legacy

What if the Prince is telling the truth, and there's an escape clause?

The thought haunted me so completely I was a zombie in the halls. I think people tried to talk to me once or twice, but I couldn't concentrate enough to distinguish one voice from another. Somehow, I made my way to the office and managed to alarm someone enough that they showed me to a conference room and shut the door behind them.

No one escaped the Coven bond. It didn't happen. They were immutable, sturdy, and built to last. A coven didn't sever if a member died, the bond just became smaller. Tighter. Until finally there was only one or two. There were stories that said the last members of a coven always died within hours of each other.

"I saw him again," I said without preamble when Illana, Quinn, and Nick came into the room. "I know what he wants."

Illana let out an aggravated huff when I let that one hang in the air. "We're not concerned with what *it* wants, Malcolm." The subtle reminder that what I'd seen was a monster, not a person. "We don't negotiate. There is only one outcome to this situation."

They would kill him. The same way my parents killed his sister. I was sure that if the Prince was in the room, that thought would have bothered me, but outside in the real world, I knew it was the only right answer.

"How did they manage to kill Kore? What happened back then?"

Illana was shrewd, not stupid. "That is not something you need to know. Besides, weren't you the one shirking away from any sort of responsibility in this manner?"

"I just don't like lies," I said, raising my chin and staring her down. "For all I know, the fact that you covered up what Moonset did here had a direct hand in how they ended up where they ended."

Her lips thinned. "At the time, the only ones who knew about the Abyssal Prince in Carrow Mill were those who needed to know. The *revised* version only became public knowledge after Moonset's crimes were exposed, no thanks to that confounded book of Adele's." Adele Roman had been the chief historian who'd cobbled together the rise and fall of Moonset. Nearly as famous as Illana Bryer, she'd made a career out of our parents.

"So it wasn't a conspiracy at all. Robert Cooper just found a way to bolster his reputation by claiming the takedown of an Abyssal Prince, and the rest of you backed him up. Because it would be too *confusing* for people to think that even monsters are capable of a moment or two of heroism."

Quinn's face flared into an expression I hadn't ever seen before, a kind of lumpy eyebrow shock. Or maybe his eyebrows were like air-traffic controllers, trying to wave out a signal of danger. Either way, it only lasted a moment before his face smoothed into the mask I was used to. A mask that said I was on my own.

"Outside of this room," Illana spoke slowly and distinctly, each word selected and released with infinite patience, "a comment like that would be considered treasonous. Especially from Cyrus Denton's son. I understand you are under pressure, Malcolm, but you should remember where you are. Your parents did good things, once. Do not fall down the same path that led them astray."

"You're right," I said evenly, trying desperately for some of the calm that Illana had in buckets. "But I need to know what happened before."

"Grandmother, we'll be alright," Quinn said suddenly, pushing himself off of the wall. Nick didn't say anything, although he shot his friend a quick look that Quinn ignored. "I'll find out what Mal knows while Nick helps you set the wards around the school." Off my look, Quinn added, "It's come after you twice at the school. Safe to say that this is where it feels most comfortable right now."

Illana gave the pair of us a sharp-eyed look as she headed for the door. Whatever it was that Quinn was planning, I had the feeling that Illana knew exactly what he was up to. He waited until they were gone before he moved, but even then all he did was to pull down the window blinds, to wedge a doorstop underneath the closed door, and to dim the lights.

"What did it offer you?"

I flinched even though I knew better, turned away like it would somehow protect me. I exhaled. "I'm tired, Quinn." Part of me wanted to confess everything, but another part of me was jealous, hoarding the information for as long as I could. "If you can't stop him—"

"We *will* stop it," Quinn said grimly. "Trust me on that."

But I don't. I don't trust any of you. I don't even know if I trust myself. That was the crux of the problem. One tiny little promise and everything I thought I was came up in question. I was seriously considering helping a monster. I could *go*. Justin and the others, they could keep living the dangerous life they wanted. They could be chased, pursued, hunted. And I could have a career. A life. Maybe even a dog.

This was what I wanted.

I kept him behind me, walked to one of the windows and leaned against the counter. Peeked out from the corners. But I didn't answer his question. "They said my dad was the one who set the bombs. That he'd figured out some way to trap Maleficia inside little vials, and he'd build an entire bomb up around them. That way, when the bombs exploded, the Maleficia was released to spread the violence as far as it could. It was the only reason they managed to kill everyone they did in that first strike. Normal bombs wouldn't have caused half the damage it did, not once someone was aware there was an explosion."

The London bombing had been Moonset's first "official" strike, their coming out as a terrorist organization. The witch Congress, then known more predominantly as the Invisible Congress, had met in the building the Covens had owned for two hundred years. There were committees and branches to the government then, each Coven dividing themselves up by interest. A centralized location where the strongest, most powerful, and most importantly, the battle-tested Covens were all located at once.

A week, maybe a month's worth of planning and Moonset crippled the opposition in just a handful of minutes. Human rescue crews worked to put out the fires and look for survivors, while in the magical circles, no one knew what to do because everyone who made the decisions was buried beneath the concrete and ash.

"They also say that your dad was one of the first ones to realize there was an Abyssal in Carrow Mill, feeding on his classmates," Quinn pointed out. "Just because he went down the wrong path doesn't mean it should negate everything he's ever done."

I snorted out a laugh. "You are *literally* the only person I've ever heard who has that opinion. He's the Bogeyman, he's Jeffrey Dahmer with a spellbook. I've heard all the stories, Quinn. Cyrus was the playground bully, the monster in the halls, the scourge of seventh grade."

"You've read Adele's book, haven't you?" Quinn asked, unusually gentle. I shrugged. Adele Roman might have written everything there possibly was to write about Moonset, but that didn't mean that anyone took it as gospel truth. People skimmed the early chapters, only gaining interest with the London bombing. No, that wasn't actually correct. People gained interest during Moonset's missing years: after high school, the six of them had vanished into obscurity, only returning after whatever it was that inspired their descent into a Maleficia-fueled cult. They took jobs with the Congress, ingratiating themselves amidst the very people they planned to murder.

"We've all read it," I said tonelessly. At one point or another, we couldn't help ourselves. Sometimes, it was a teacher who wanted to rub our noses in where we'd come from. Other times it was personal curiosity. To see exactly where our blood had come from. When we were younger, I'd tried to keep it from the others, but that only lasted so long. There were only so many times you could be called Moonset like it was the foulest insult before you had to *know.*

"People loved your dad growing up." Quinn leaned against the wall. He was looking away from me as much as I looked away from him. "I've talked to some of them. The humans who don't know about *Moonset,* at least. They never understood his bond with Sherrod Daggett, but he couldn't go anywhere, or do anything, without a crowd of people following in his wake."

"I don't want to hear this." Because it was safer not knowing. Safer to blanket my thoughts of him in the crimes and monstrosities. It made him less human. It kept him a monster. Monsters were safe because they lurked in closets and in the shadows under the bed. They weren't people with blood in their veins and full of mistakes made and insecurities and bonds that they couldn't break no matter how much they could have wanted—

"The only person responsible for his actions was him. And the only person responsible for your choices is you." I heard the door twist, the lock give way as Quinn made for an exit. "Let us handle the Abyssal, Mal. Whatever it offers you, remember that Moonset got an offer once too. All it takes is one slip, and suddenly you're someone you don't recognize."

———————

Charlie Denton was in the same waiting room I'd left him at a week ago, surrounded by the same litter of Styrofoam cups and self-loathing. The cups themselves might have been different, but the contempt curling the air was identical. "So are you just waiting here hoping you can get one last beating in?" I asked.

Livid red eyes squinted up at me. "You think you're so smart. You've got it all figured out. Mean old Uncle Charlie ruined poor little Luca's life. Well, you listen to me, you little bastard. That kid was *wrong* from the first time he screamed. You can't beat the Devil out of someone if that's what's under the surface."

"You beat your kid and you think *he's* the Devil? Looks like the drunk didn't fall far from the family psychopath tree."

The glare he shot was weak and unstable, an offense that

toppled out of his eyes like a dimmed light. "You'd know all about that. Rotten fruit, rotten tree."

I sat across from him, leaned forward and invaded his space. It smelled like stale cigarettes and gasoline, which thankfully drowned out the smell of Charlie himself, who still hadn't showered. "Spoken like a withered branch. Hey, you remember Kore, don't you?" I watched his eyes, waited for a flicker of the old Charlie, back when he was probably Charles, or Chuck, or maybe he was even a Chaz. "Did you try to stop her? Cyrus was a monster, but he fought her. What did you do?"

A complicated series of muscles flexed and atrophied in Charlie's face, and I couldn't tell if he'd suddenly aged a few decades, or if the last few decades had been wiped from his face completely. Eyebrows stopped and started like remote-controlled cars with spotty batteries, lines appeared and disappeared. I saw more of his eyelids than I'd ever seen before with the way they fluttered.

"I don't have to take this." The man they all said was my uncle stumbled to his feet and spilled out of the room, his feet wavering under a floor that seemed to rock beneath him. He couldn't get away fast enough. The elevator chimed a moment later, and by the time I walked out of the waiting room, a pair of nurses split their shocked stares between me and the blinking elevator light down to the lobby.

———————

They let me see him, because they didn't know any better and because they were just nurses. No witches in sight, which was strange. Suspected of acts of Maleficia, unconscious in a hospital, and Luca wasn't under guard?

I understood why once I was led through gated doors one at a time, each round of security for my protection, the nurses claimed. Despite the fact that Luca was catatonic, the hospital was worried about his mental state. Thus, they'd sent him for monitoring on the long-term psychiatric floor, with the patients who would live out their days in the same tepid hallways.

The nurse waited outside, giving me a five-minute window to see my cousin. The boy who'd been responsible for bringing us here in the first place.

There were more tubes than I expected. Tubes leading into his mouth, tubes running along his hands, tubes leading into machines that did more than just monitored his vital signs. They'd said Luca was just in a coma, but this was more than a coma. This was keeping something alive that would be dead on its own.

Underneath the equipment covering his mouth, his skin was pale, almost translucent. Freckles stood out stark against his skin as if they were drops of ink across snow. And there were lines like scars, raised bumps that ran along both cheeks, above both eyebrows, and I even saw a peak of them cutting up from his chin. A half-dozen lines. One line too many to link up to fingers, and yet it was so perfect a comparison that it had to be.

Maybe it was the result of whatever the Abyssals had done after he'd summoned them. Maybe when they marked him, it had been physical. I don't know what I was looking for in his room. Maybe a sign that Luca wasn't as bad as they seemed to think. But I wasn't getting any answers out of him tonight.

Justin said he looked half-finished, like someone had dulled and smoothed all the edges, created smoothness and youth where edges and age were meant to go. There was an undeniable list of things that Luca and I shared. Cut our hair and set it side by side, and no one would be able to tell the difference. Underneath papery eyelids were eyes the exact same shade as mine, a spattering of green surrounding a brownish-orange interior. He was probably due another growth spurt, if he ever woke up again, which would put him close to my height.

"I don't know what he did to you exactly," I said, lingering in the doorway, "but that doesn't make what you did okay. You should wake up, just so you can pay for what you've done. You don't deserve the easy way out."

But wasn't that always the way?

I didn't stay much longer than that. There was nothing to do—Luca was out of it, and no amount of talking would change that. Whatever happened to him, it wasn't like a normal coma. The Abyssal Princes had done that to him. So maybe he would only wake up when they were ready.

It wasn't until I was on my way out the front doors of the hospital that things really went to hell, full stop. Flashing red and blue lights, shouting, a dozen more people than I expected to be crowded around a trio of headlights. A constant spin of red and blue lights. And the sound of Justin, shouting, "Get your hands off me, you stupid motherfu—!"

SIXTEEN

*Let everyone in love come and see. I want to break
Venus's ribs with clubs and cripple the goddess'
loins. If she can strike through my soft chest, then
why can't I smash her head with a club?*

....

Graffito left on the walls of Pompeii

It was some sort of standoff. A small crowd of people frozen
around an angry center. There was a cop car off to one side,
their lights spinning. Through the crowd I saw a sharp motion,
and then one of the police officers went hurtling into the air.
Like *way* into the air. The kind of lift that only magic can
accomplish. "I'll kill you, you piece of shit," Justin snarled. I
finally pushed through the crowd—easier now that he was getting violent and people were trying to get *away*—and found
something I wasn't sure how to handle.

It was definitely Justin, but it was Kevin standing across from him that caught me by surprise. Justin wasn't a slouch in the size department, but Kevin was a varsity athlete. There was no contest. Justin looked...wrecked. His hair stuck up at all angles, he somehow managed to look like he hadn't gotten any sleep since last July, and he was panting like a madman.

He snarled out another spell, a pitch that Kevin almost casually connected with. He brushed his hand casually to one side and muttered something, and the spell bounced away from Kevin. *That was what sent the cop flying* I realized. This time, he avoided the innocent bystanders, but Justin was still advancing.

I ran between them and grabbed my brother by the shirt. "Justin, what happened? What's wrong?"

"Get out of my way, Mal." The growl was barely recognizable as my brother's.

"He just went nuts," Kevin, on the other hand, was totally calm behind me. "He rammed into my car when I got here. Started threatening me." His eyes trailed away for a moment. "And now there's an unconscious cop to deal with."

"Not to mention a crowd of witnesses," I muttered. "Call someone," I ordered Kevin over my shoulder.

"You're *helping* him?" Justin couldn't believe it. The betrayal in his voice was so thick he choked on it. "How could—why are you—" And then he snarled another word, one I didn't know and hadn't heard before. His shirt fell out of my hands at the same time the ground fell out from underneath me.

I landed some distance away, the concrete slamming and scraping against my back. The breath whooshed out of my lungs and I struggled on *how* to breathe for a moment. And then, with a rush, the air came back to me, my lungs inflated, and my body processed the rush of pain.

Someone came to my side, helped me up. The crowd had grown sparse now, backing away slowly from the two boys at the center of it all. But now, Justin's attention was on *me.*

"Justin, what are you doing? Did something happen?" I gasped out, struggling to my feet. Justin always tried to be the levelheaded one.

"He was talking to *her,*" Justin spat. Literally spat. Like, it flew from his mouth and he didn't even realize it. "I saw him."

"This is because I was talking to your girlfriend?" Kevin stepped back into the frame. "Are you kidding right now? Dude, you wrecked my car!"

"There's got to be more to it than that," I assured him. "Right, Justin? There's something else?"

My brother's expression was completely blank. His words carried his rage, his posture and his hands and everything about him expressed *fury* and *frustration.* But there was nothing written across his face, no explanation for what had set him off.

"You're helping him." The words themselves were empty. But the condemnation they carried was clear as day.

"No, Justin, I'm not—" But again, Justin reacted before I could finish defending myself. But this time, when his spell ripped me up and threw me back, I was more prepared. Instead of slamming down into the ground, I rolled with it, and managed to avoid a repeat of the last time. I was back on my feet in a moment, although my back was probably going to be a mess of bruises in the morning.

"Ash doesn't belong to you, she's mine!"

Okay, this was clearly more than just some sort of lovers' quarrel. Justin pulled a knife out of his jacket pocket—where the hell did he get a *knife*—and it wasn't just a knife but one of the black-hilted athames Quinn kept locked up in his room. All the guardians had a ritual knife—it was the reason they could stand up against creatures stronger than they were.

So what was Justin going to do with his?

"You need to calm down," I said, holding up my hands, palms facing him. I tried to relax my body, to project every *I am not a threat* vibe I could. This wasn't like Jenna's first spell at all. This was worse.

And it had to be Jenna. She'd already used magic against me, maybe Justin had said the wrong thing and now she'd targeted *him*. I *knew* random attack of conscience was a front. She was just playing me, buying time until she could finish cobbling together her new spell. Only this time it had turned out worse than expected. If Justin killed someone or hurt them seriously, he'd never forgive himself.

I'd never forgive Jenna either.

"This isn't you, Jus. Take a deep breath. No one's trying to take Ash from you." And where was Girl Friday when all this was going down? If she'd been there when all of this started, why wasn't she here now?

"I'm not after your girlfriend, Daggett. I promise, I'm not into her." Kevin had adopted the same pose as me: nonthreatening. Calming.

"No, you're just trying to get between us," he said, voice shaky and yet sure of his words. "I won't let you take me away from her. She doesn't belong to you."

"She belongs to you," I agreed. "And she doesn't want you to do this. Kevin's her friend. Just her friend." I swallowed, and prayed that Kevin could keep a straight face. "Kevin's with me. Remember the other day, how weird he was acting? Jenna made that happen, but afterwards we talked."

"You—you talked?"

"Yeah, we talked. So he's with me. He's not after Ash." I held out my hand, prayed to something I didn't believe in, and almost smiled when Kevin slipped his hand into mine. He was going to owe me so big for this later. Seriously, it was too bad I wasn't into him at all. Or that he wasn't into me.

"So you don't have to do this," I said calmly. "Okay?"

A war raged on Justin's face, the power shifting with every flicker of his eyes. They would latch onto our linked hands and waver, but as soon as he looked away the rage took hold again. And then he'd look back, and struggle. He was still in there, and whatever was controlling him hadn't totally won him over.

"If I don't do this," he finally said, "then she won't know how I feel. She won't *understand.*"

Just as Quinn and Nick appeared at the corner of my eye, just as Kevin pulled his hand free of mine and shouted out a spell, or a warning, or a plea; just as my body froze up and my mind refused to process what was happening, just as someone lingering in the parking lot screamed…

…Justin turned the knife on himself, and plunged it deep into his own stomach.

SEVENTEEN

*It took twelve covens summoned from the seven
corners of the world to free the town of Hamelin
from the Abyssal's grip. But it was too late for
their children, swept into a hidden world never
to be seen again. That is the price Hamelin
pays for making bargains with monsters.*

....

The Princes of Hell

Justin dropped, just like that. I caught him just before his
head smacked against the concrete, cradled his head even as I
panicked at the sight of the knife. Correction: the hilt. It was
the only part I could see.

I screamed, I yelled, but I couldn't remember if you were
supposed to take a knife out or leave it in. It didn't matter.
Someone called security, or begged for help, or lit a rescue fire

or something. Either way, once someone realized what had happened, nurses and trauma personnel streamed out of the hospital and collected Justin like ants on the hunt for food. It happened fast, like the world was moving twice as fast as I was.

They dragged him back inside, and disappeared down into the ER. It wasn't until after he was gone that I realized I might have just seen my brother for the last time.

Hours passed.

No one told me a thing. There was a lot of movement around me, a lot of serious tones and sharp actions. But I didn't care about any of it. I knew Quinn and the others had a job to do, but I didn't care. It took me over an hour to realize that the two visitors waiting by the doors weren't visitors at all. They were guards.

The waiting rooms were exactly the same as the ones where Luca was being kept, the same walls painted the same shade of Depression Off-White, and the same untouched coffee cups on the end table. Quinn stayed at my side, probably afraid I was going to do something drastic (if it was Jenna's fault I was going to kill her) while Nick coordinated everything else.

Every time something happened to one of us, something happened to *all* of us. Wherever they were right now, Witchers were locking down the other three, making sure they were safe and stayed under guard. It was a toss-up how much they were being told—a lot of the time we didn't find out there had been an attack until much later. But I doubted any of them knew Justin was even in the hospital. Or why.

It was past midnight, and even though the rational part of

my brain kept wanting me to slow down, to take a rest, I was too keyed up to even consider it. I leapt up out of my chair, determined that this time I was just going to walk through the double doors that separated me from answers, and demand that *someone* tell me what the fuck was going on. The hospital was full of witches, so why was I still *waiting*?

Quinn blocked my path. I grunted, pushing him out of my way, but as I did, he grabbed my arm and held on.

"Let go! They have to know *something* by now."

"We'll know something when they want us to know something." I tried again to shake his hand off, but he grabbed harder, refusing to budge. "You need to stay calm." And then when I didn't seem to be reacting fast enough, he added a sharp, "Malcolm!"

"Justin could be dying," I pointed out. There were a lot of things I hated about my life, but there were far fewer things that I feared. Few things that made me want to grab my things and find a dark, quiet space where I could trap myself where no one would ever find me.

Justin couldn't die. That just...that wasn't possible. The curse wouldn't let him die, right? Attempts to separate us, attempts to harm us, and most especially attempts to kill us always fell back on the attacker. In a manner of speaking, it was like we were invincible. But I'd never once stopped to wonder about what would happen if one of us tried to kill ourselves. Was there a loophole in our parents' design?

"You can use magic to heal him," I pointed out as Quinn led me back to my seat. Witchers could do that: use magic to heal. Cole barely had a scar from the last attack. Quinn had done that himself.

"They can," Quinn admitted, "but that's only part of it. Justin perforated organs—did damage to his body's systems. Magic can close up the wound and speed the healing, but it can't un-pierce a kidney or a liver. The doctors have to do their part first."

Magic was useless.

Justin could be dying, *dead*, in there and I didn't know. I *should* know. We were all supposed to be connected. The connection had defined our lives from the beginning. So why was I still *waiting*.

Imagine what you could have done, if you'd learned to access the Coven bond. Maybe you could have stopped him. Saved him. Or maybe you'd know exactly how he was right now. All that knowledge was right there at your fingertips, and you turned it away. It was Jenna's voice in my head, Jenna's and my own. I couldn't tell which voice loathed me more.

I'd already thrown up once, but I wasn't ruling out a repeat performance. Seeing him . . . with the knife. It slid into him so easily it looked fake, but the force that must have gone into it. There wasn't any hesitation at all.

"They should be here," I muttered.

"You know why we can't do that," Quinn said, just as patiently as ever. "*You* shouldn't even be here right now. I'm supposed to evacuate you until we know more."

It was a long night. I dropped off somewhere around two, only to startle awake every time a pair of shoes squeaked on the tile. When I looked down at the coffee on the table next to me—a coffee that had been there for six hours at this point— the cup was still freshly steaming. *I'm hallucinating, that's all. No big deal.* But when I reached out to touch the side of the cup, it was warm against my skin.

Quinn nudged me in the side. I looked up, followed the turn of his head and saw Illana walking out of the double doors with a white-coated doctor. I was so busy studying his face for signs of Justin that I barely even noticed the woman at his side. There was another woman in her wake, doddering behind with a strange gait, though she worked valiantly to keep up. She listened intently as Illana spoke quietly with the doctor, a conversation that dwindled and drifted away as they approached.

"Justin will make a full recovery." Those were the only six words I needed to hear, and the moment I did, I slumped back down into my chair. I hadn't even realized I'd come to my feet in the first place, the trip back down unsteady enough that my vision blurred. An exhaustion I hadn't paid enough attention to was suddenly roaring in my ears, but how was I supposed to sleep?

Justin was going to be okay. I swallowed because there were things that needed to go back down, thoughts and feelings that needed to be chained up and dropped back into the ocean where they could sink to the bottom.

"I think that will be all for now, doctor," Illana continued, making a shooing motion with one hand. She moved in front of me, although all I could see of her at the moment was her black and purple skirt that hung down to her ankles. I put her out of my mind, though, and focused on pulling myself together. My head throbbed and I couldn't tell if I'd been ignoring a headache for the last few hours, or if Illana's news gave it permission to finally come out of hiding.

Okay, I needed to go home. Figure out what to tell the others and what to do about Jenna. "I have to go. The others need to know he's going to be okay."

"The children are all probably asleep," Illana said dismissively. "First we need to—"

"No, they're not."

She didn't seem to mind the interruption. "And how can you be so sure?" she asked smoothly, like she'd asked for my perspective in the first place.

"You've met them, right? Bailey always knows when something's wrong. And even if she doesn't, I'm sure Jenna's climbing the walls already." Though they weren't actually twins, Justin and Jenna acted like it often enough.

"Yes, I'm aware of that, but I still don't understand..." she trailed off and looked to Quinn.

There was a silent conversation between Illana and her grandson, before he finally shrugged out a *do whatever you want* look. She sat across from me, taking care to arrange her skirt just so. "Malcolm, I want you to meet a very old friend of mine," Illana started.

The other woman scoffed and interrupted her. "*Very old.* Bite your tongue, Illana Bryer. That boy doesn't need any reminders of how many years I've spent trying to keep your behind out of the fire."

Something very nearly like a smile flickered across Illana's face. It only lasted for a moment, so I could have been mistaken, but she almost looked *normal* for a moment. It was eerie, like seeing a shark smile. "Malcolm," she said firmly, "this is Adele Roman. She's one of the foremost historians of—"

"—Moonset," I finished. "Yeah, I know." I eyed the woman again, this time paying more attention to the sharp awareness in her eyes. Illana was definitely a shark, but this woman was something else. Something that didn't mind lying in wait for her prey. A crocodile, maybe.

"It's been a long time, Malcolm," Adele said. She remained standing, just barely taller than the seated Illana. "We met once after you were rescued. Of course, you wouldn't remember."

Rescued. It was funny how things were remembered. Like we'd been prisoners, the subjects of horrible war crimes, and the Congress had stepped in and saved us. The truth was that it was a capture. When Moonset left their hidden compound in order to surrender, we'd been left behind in cribs and playpens, just waiting for someone to find us.

"I was barely three," I pointed out, "so no, it's all a bit hazy."

"Illana asked me to come after your encounter the other day," Adele said. Her demeanor shifted quickly, becoming more energetic and focused. I almost didn't notice the limp. She moved, and her arms gestured as she spoke, and her words became crisper and more careful. "I know a great deal about Moonset, but I'm also something of an expert on the subject of the Abyssal Princes."

Ahh. So that was it. I felt my guard go up, some lingering reaction to the sound of the Prince's voice in my head. There was nothing she could tell me that I needed to know. Now wasn't the time.

"She's also informed me of a few discrepancies in my own account," and with this, Adele shot Illana a dark look that the Coven leader pretended not to notice. "It seems that history was indeed written by the victors, wasn't it? Maybe if your parents had been recognized for their efforts to halt the Abyssal's curse, we might have met under different circumstances."

"What curse? What are you talking about?"

Adele waved a hand. "The Abyssals used to be Fae: chaos-wielding miscreants if there ever were any. But when the Abyss remade them in its image, it placed a hunger in their bellies that can never be sated. To be in this world, an Abyssal must feed. What your father and the twins' father noticed was a listlessness in their fellow students. Children who once loved art, or sports, or even each other, suffered from melancholy and depression. Nothing could pierce their malaise.

"We believe that each of the Abyssals fosters something in their victims, that a connection forms between them as they come more and more under its sway. And when the connection becomes strong enough, he can collect all of them at once, and feast for years to come."

"You already know this story," Illana added quietly. "From the history books. The Pied Piper of Hamelin wasn't a gifted musician at all, it was an Abyssal. It stole the children away after making itself the center of their worlds."

"I don't know what that has to do with anything," I said, looking between all of them. "How can you be sure this wasn't Jenna? She just attacked me the other day, and made everyone fall in love with me. She must have done the same to Justin." But in my head, I knew that no matter how angry she was, Jenna would *never* have attacked Justin like that.

"Justin tried to *kill* himself to prove his love," Quinn said gently. "That's something stronger than spells. Jenna's spell made people *want* to like you. Some were uncomfortable, some were happy to go along with it. But none of them were consumed by their feelings the way Justin was. His rational mind was completely suppressed."

"So you're telling me a Prince did this?"

"That is what we're telling you," Illana agreed.

"What the Abyssals do is an infection. It will spread. It probably already has. But the good news is that we have time to stop this," Adele added. "In the meantime, Justin will be kept safe."

"Kept safe where? *Here*?"

"Your brother has been passing this plague on to God knows how many people." Illana pursed her lips together. "We've established a quarantine around the town. Wards and fascinations to keep the humans from asking too many questions. Everyone will be on the lookout for new infections, and we'll bring them here until this matter is settled." Her voice had an iron finality to it. There was only one way things would be settled here, and they'd end with something in a grave, one way or another.

"I don't understand. How the hell do you *quarantine* an entire town? Are you kidding? You're not the CDC."

"We're the next best thing," Illana replied with a haughty sniff. "Magic can make any number of problems disappear, if you know how to approach it best."

"Can it bring Justin back?"

At this, all three of them turned away, looked down, looked anywhere else. "What?" I asked, aggrieved. Now wasn't the time for them to bite their tongues.

"As far as we can tell, the spell is only broken with the death of the Abyssal."

I thought back to the monster who lamented his inhumanity. The moment of understanding I'd felt—like I was the only person in the world who could understand him. Who *got* it. "Oh. Okay then." And with only a moment to process, I made my decision. "So we kill him. Tell me how to do it, and I'll do it myself."

"It's just," Adele started, flummoxed for words. "That is to say... there aren't any records of *how* Moonset killed the last Abyssal Prince. All we know is that there were once seven, and now there are six."

"This is why the Abyssals are considered so dangerous," Illana added. "They escape so rarely they are almost myths, but when they do, they are nearly unstoppable."

"Okay," I said, thinking about the blossoming trail of red as it had spilled out of Justin. The look on his face, sincere and fevered in his quest. "Okay." I took a deep breath. It was one thing to wish for another life, but it was another to do so at the expense of the old life. "Okay." Third time was the charm. I closed my eyes, feeling a lifetime's worth of buried feelings struggling to reach the light. There were many good reasons why I was the way I was. And not a single one of them mattered a damn.

All I could see in my head was Justin and the knife, and how casually he'd almost thrown his life away.

I looked up at Illana then. Saw her slow nod. She already knew.

"I'll do whatever you want. I'll help."

EIGHTEEN

*Denton was the lieutenant, Sherrod's right-
hand man. He understood strategy and war.
Sherrod may have called the shots,
but Denton lined up the targets.*

....

Moonset: A Dark Legacy

They were all in the living room, waiting for me. I could see
it in Cole's unnatural stillness, in the way that Bailey picked at
the same threadbare spot at the back of her pants, and in the
way that Jenna wouldn't sit down, wouldn't stop pacing because
at least pacing was *doing* something. The waiting was driving
them crazy. Anything was better than waiting. Even bad news.

"Oh, Christ," Jenna said, despite the fact that none of
us had ever been religious in our lives. She ran a hand over
her forehead and into her hair, and looked up and away.

"She thought you were going to be Justin," Cole said quietly.

"Is he okay?" Bailey asked, almost running over Cole's words in her haste. Jenna stilled at the question, her hand still caught in the tangle of her hair.

All three of them had gotten dressed, or they'd never gone to bed, it was hard to say. A pair of Witchers stood in the kitchen, leaning against the counters and pretending like they weren't blatantly eavesdropping on every word. I tried to blank them out, like the giant, black construction paper backdrops they were.

"Justin's fine," I lied. We were always lying to each other. Even when we promised no more lies, not this time. It was a lie.

"They wouldn't tell us anything," Bailey added, before anyone else could take the lead. "But we knew that something was wrong."

"Of course we did. They pulled us all out of bed," Cole snapped, a night without sleep taking its toll on his mood.

Bailey pulled herself up to every inch of her diminutive height. "Some of us knew even before that. You said so yourself. You had a bad feeling."

"I always have a bad feeling," Cole muttered, shoving his hands in his pockets.

But Jenna was the quiet one. She was also, ironically, the one I worried most about. An hour ago, I'd been ready to rip her head from her body. But now things were different. She thought Justin would be the one coming home. The one that was happy and healthy and whole.

I would say that for most of us, Jenna's love was a theory.

Sure, we all loved each other, but it was a strange thing. Family but not family. Friends but not friends. A coven but not a coven. Our bond might have been unbreakable, but it was always up for debate.

On the surface, I knew Jenna cared for us, but I had to wonder if Justin was the only one she *loved*. We called each other brother and sister, but it was make-believe. Justin and Jenna, though, they had the same blood coursing through their veins.

The rest of us were just outliers. Pretenders. Jenna might have been sad if I'd been the one in the hospital instead of Justin, but no more so than if it was Quinn, or Maddy, or anyone else that casually made her acquaintance over the years. Justin was a different story. Justin was *real* to her in a way that the rest of us weren't. He belonged to her.

"He's going to be fine," I said to her and her alone. This time I meant it as much as I'd ever meant anything in my life. Justin *would* be fine. And I would do everything I could to help Illana make sure it was so.

"When can I see him?" Jenna asked. Demanded, really. I'd expected their first questions to be about what happened. Who had done this to Justin, and how bad was he hurt? I should have known better. Jenna wouldn't trust any of that until she saw him for herself. Jenna wouldn't trust anything she couldn't touch, or see, or experience for herself.

I checked my watch, did the math. "We can go back after they're done with rounds. But he hasn't woken up yet," I warned, "and they don't know how long he'll be out. So we can only go a couple at a time. Jenna and I'll go first, and then you guys can come this afternoon."

"We're not going to school," Cole warned, crossing his arms in front of him.

"So don't," I replied easily. "But you're going to sit here, in the house, until they let you go to the hospital. You're not hanging out there all day, getting underfoot. School might be a good distraction until you can see him."

"Whatever," he said. I knew that was as close to an agreement as I was going to get, so I decided to take the victory where I could get it.

Getting the kids settled in wasn't nearly as difficult as I expected. Both of them refused to go home, instead choosing Justin and Jenna's as their home for the night. They also refused to be separated, which was interesting. Bailey slept in Jenna's room, and Cole slept on the floor. It was always a little weird to remember how divided we were. There were barely three years separating me (the oldest) from Bailey (the youngest), but we were split in two groups.

Justin, Jenna, and I always had to be older than our years, and responsible for each other. Somewhere along the way, it became an unspoken agreement that Bailey and Cole should get to enjoy the childhoods we missed out on. Most of what we did was to shield them from the worst parts of our lives, even now. That's how it always had been. That's how it probably always would be.

When I came back downstairs, it was no surprise that Jenna had decided to forego sleep. She sat on the couch, facing the window behind it, completely oblivious to the world. It was clear she didn't want to talk. I wasn't about to push her.

I'd never had to be in the role of "oldest sibling" before.

Justin was always the one that took charge, played the mediator. I was surprised at how easily I slipped into the position, and then felt ashamed for even thinking about it like that. It wasn't like I was replacing him. But someone had to step up, and seeing Justin hurt himself, how could I not? It put things into a perspective I'd never had before.

"I'm going to take a shower," I announced. I knew she heard me, but she didn't react. The two Witchers were in the kitchen still, both bent over a cup of coffee. I didn't like the idea of leaving Jenna on her own, regardless of who else was in the house. She was unpredictable on a good day. I didn't want to chance it.

I was gone barely a minute when it happened. The Prince's sigil flared into the door the moment I pushed my way into the bathroom, and I tumbled through the ether into another world.

———

The bathroom was an eastern European bathhouse straight out of a torture porn horror movie. Huge, vaulting arches separated one bathing pool from the next. The walls were a dirty rust color, filigreed with something that might have once been brass but was now so tarnished it simply looked black in the dim light. At the bottom of the pool was an entire scene painted over tiles, a woman surrounded by many tiny creatures swaddled in white cloths.

There was no water in the pool, nor in any of the others that I could see. The pools themselves weren't that creepy. The chains, though, were a different matter altogether. Thick, rope-like links of metal hung from the ceiling in a variety of configurations, some of them thick with viscera and dripping rust and carmine onto the floors.

"I know you're here," I called, when after several minutes I was still standing there, waiting for him to show his face. "Are you a coward now? Ashamed after what you did?"

Steam rose in the air, a hanging cloud of mist despite the fact that the air was dry as dust. It grew thick and left a slick sheen on the surface of everything around me, but didn't so much as brush against my skin. Nothing more than illusions. There was nothing in this world that was real.

One moment I was alone, and the next he was seated at the edge of the bath, long and muscular legs stretched down where the water would be if there was water here. By this point, I recognized the effect he had on my senses, the way my eyes couldn't help but try to pick every piece apart and keep it for always, but every time made him a little more human. A little easier to process. The face wasn't a blank glow of eyes and mouth anymore, but made up of a strong, chiseled jaw and long eyelashes.

Waves of discontent and nerves filled the room with a careless energy. The air grew heavy with something incendiary, like it would only take the smallest spark for everything to be blown to kingdom come. Which meant that the Prince, whatever else he might be, wasn't an idiot.

"Do you know what lip service is?" I asked, crossing my arms in front of me.

He didn't speak. But then again, if I was an ageless, demonic orphan I probably wouldn't advertise my ignorance either.

"It means when someone tells you that they wish they weren't a monster, and then they turn around and do monstrous things, they're just paying you lip service. They don't really *want* to be different. They're happy being monsters, and coloring outside the lines. They *like* it."

There was a very long moment where the Prince didn't say anything, didn't *share* anything, and then he surprised me. He smiled. A beaming, bright smile that was as captivating as it was hideous. "You should be happy," he exclaimed, a cavalier joy spreading from his words to my limbs, electrifying my body with his excitement. "It weighed heavily on your mind. Our bargain: my sister for your freedom. To give in to your own selfish, human desires or remain true to the principles of your masters. I took away the heaviness on your heart. You no longer have to help me because you want to. You will help me because you have no other choice."

Justin was recovering in the hospital and the Prince was making it out to be my fault. "You're sick."

Confusion puffed out into the air between us, a cloud of *trying* and *failing* in equal measure. Thoughts that would not process, connections that could not find the proper sockets to fit into. "But I've given you what you wanted," he said slowly, each word more hesitant than the last. "I do not understand. How have I disappointed you? I removed all obstacles to your salvation."

"You infected my brother! And now it's going to spread, isn't it? You're going to do the same thing to the rest of us."

"The rest of *them*," he said gently. "I told you once. You are my champion. I've *chosen* you, Malcolm. The best and the brightest the world over, and you surpass each and every one."

He meant it as a compliment, but all I could think of was Justin's madness spreading and all the people who would get hurt in the aftermath. Thoughts that curdled around in my head, thick and viscous.

"Make it stop," I demanded. "I told you I'd help you. There was no reason to bring Justin into it."

"Ahh, but the human heart is fickle. You've already turned away from me, haven't you? They try to turn you away from me, even as they teach you to bow your head and beg for favors. You've become their pet. All this, for want of punishing me." He made a tutting sound as I opened my mouth to protest. "Their time will come soon, my champion. Never fear, I will free you from their chains, just as I promised."

"You started this, not me. You shouldn't have gone after my brother."

"I don't plan to *take* the Daggett scion, nor any of the others. For now they are a loan. I have merely borrowed your brother's vessel and will return it more or less intact at the conclusion of our arrangement. "

"It's the 'less' part I have a problem with. We aren't defenseless." The Coven bond would have to kick in eventually, wouldn't it?

"I am not so ignorant of the darkbond, my sweet. The travesties they wreak will be theirs and theirs alone, but I made an oath to you. I have not come for your bondmates. A melody of witches brings nothing to my table, the harmony never quite achieves its true reach."

"I don't want *this*. And if you're going to hurt the people I care about, I don't want any part of you either!"

"Again, I don't understand. *You hurt them every day.* You keep them from their destinies, you tie their hands and legs and throw them into the water to sink. You hide behind a mask of indifference and tell lies with every look. I could not possibly hurt them any more than you already have. So why do you cast me as the villain? All of this, I do for you, my Malcolm."

"I am not *yours!*" I snapped. There was a single moment where I saw eyes that glistened blue and shimmered with hurt before the bubble we were in collapsed around me. Just like that, my vision cracked in half, and the pieces of the Abyssal's world fell before me, a shattered mirror into another reality.

———

I didn't tell anyone about the Prince's appearance in my bathroom. If I had, they would have woken up Bailey and Cole, moved them to another location, swept the houses so thoroughly that none of us would be able to go home for days, and generally be pains in the ass. I had something much different in mind.

The Prince was watching me, stealing me away only once I was alone. I felt it when the connection to his world broke—something inside of me cracked a little at the same time. There was a bond between us. Maybe not the dark-bond he always talked about, but whatever the connection was between a Prince and his champion. Twice now my anger had displaced me out of his world, only this time I saw the hurt first. My anger was a knife, and when tempered with my frustration and disappointment at the Prince, it was enough to cut me free.

I never ended up taking the shower, just stripped down and changed my everything, scrubbed my face with the morning scrub that Bailey had promised would make a morning person out of me. The bags under my eyes weren't nearly as bad as I was expecting, but I studied my reflection for a long time anyway, tilting and turning at different angles. Was my face thinner? Was all my baggage starting to show? It was hard to tell, and the more I studied the Malcolm in the mirror, the more the knots in my gut tightened.

I had to wipe my hands onto my jeans three times before they felt dry enough to make the trek back over to Jenna's. She was in almost the exact same position she'd been in when I left, only she'd gotten up and changed at some point while I was gone.

"Ready?"

Jenna didn't reply. She didn't even look at me. It was almost eerie.

When we left the Witchers in the kitchen were caught up in quiet, but furious conversation. One of them had their phone out, texting faster than even Bailey could. They looked up exactly once as we left the house, and though neither of them said anything, I could feel their eyes on us up until the door closed.

Did they know? No, there wasn't any way. Unless there was some residue left from when the Prince collected me, but I didn't know the first thing about it. Didn't even know how the symbol made the world warp around me. It could have triggered any number of warnings, but then they hadn't stopped us at all, which made me think I was overreacting.

If they knew anything at all, then they would have stopped us from leaving the house, right?

We sat in the car for a few minutes before we left, waiting for the heat to kick on. At any moment, I expected Jenna to launch into a tirade, demanding answers about what happened to Justin, or explanations. Or *something*. But the longer the silence stretched out, the more awkward I felt. Every time I shifted, the noise was unbelievably loud, the shift of my jeans against the leather an audible nightmare. And what was worse, I couldn't shake the feeling that something was watching me. That no matter how fast or slow I drove, there were eyes on me no matter what.

I could count on one hand the number of times Jenna was shocked into silence. For her, silence was like everything else that came out of her mouth. The sharpest kind of weapon that she could wield with deadly accuracy. But this was different. This wasn't Jenna cloaking herself in quiet and ready for war. This was a Jenna I'd never seen before.

"Do you … want to talk about it?" I knew it was awkward, and I did it anyway. Justin would want me to.

Nothing. She didn't even look away from her window.

Was I supposed to push? What would Justin do in this situation? No, Justin would never *be* in this situation, because he would have diffused Jenna already. He would have her making jokes and snide comments, tossing her hair back and relaxing instead of stressing.

"Illana said he should be fine in a few weeks," I continued, now desperate for anything other than the silence. I would have taken raging Jenna on a power trip any day.

Quiet Jenna was scary as fuck. "Healing magic is pretty difficult. And they don't trust just anyone." There was a coven somewhere in New York that was supposed to have specialized in healing magic, but I had the feeling the quarantine would make it impossible to bring them here now. Besides, the rumors said that the coven only performed healings for those who could pay.

Still, Jenna said nothing. I thought for sure that between the topics of magic and danger, *something* would have stoked a fire. Even a roll of her eyes would be welcome at this point.

"I ... really don't know what to do here. So if you're about to have some sort of breakdown can you at least try to warn me? Because Justin knows what to do in these situations. I don't. And this doesn't have to mean anything. We can go back to hating each other tomorrow, I'll even promise to call you a bitch if you want."

"Bailey thinks it's your fault."

Five words that stopped my heart. *Bailey is almost right,* I almost confess immediately. It was there on the tip of my tongue. Confession was supposed to be good for the soul, but I just ... the Prince took Justin because of me. It *was* my fault. No almost about it. And it occurred to me now that Jenna was the person who could help me with that.

"The thing from the fireplace. It's still here. It ... infected Justin. But it's not going to stop there. It wants all of us, maybe everyone in Carrow Mill. The one that Moonset stopped, it tried to take the whole senior class before they stopped it." Maybe a selective truth was the way to go.

"How do you know all this?" she asked, her hair still a shield hiding her face from me.

"Illana and Quinn for some of it, and the Prince for the rest. He … likes me. Said he *chose* me, whatever that means."

A short bark of a laugh tore through the car and made me flinch. I looked across the aisle cautiously, and saw so much of the old Jenna in that moment that my body relaxed instantly. "You've got a demon boyfriend," she exclaimed, laughing and then just as quickly covering her mouth as she realized where we were headed. It wouldn't be right to laugh when Justin was in a hospital bed, trying to recover from what had happened.

"It's not funny," I said seriously. "He went after Justin because he wants to make sure I help him."

"With?"

I sighed. "Something that seems like it wouldn't be a huge deal, which probably means it's going to be catastrophically bad."

She got so quiet then that I thought the moment was over, and I'd look up and she'd be facing the window again, lost inside her own head. But she was looking at me, open curiosity painted across her face, and it was stupid, but I felt so exposed that I had to look away.

"If your gut's telling you it's the wrong choice, then you know what you have to do."

"Since when did you become a therapist?" I demanded, but there was no real heat to my question. I thought she might flinch back, or turn away or something, but Jenna smiled like she'd expected nothing less from me, and then lifted her shoulder once in a lackadaisical shrug.

"Part of me did it just to see how they'd react," she said, and it took me a minute to realize we were talking about something else, and not the fact that Jenna had become a therapist overnight.

I squirmed. "Do we really have to talk about this right now?"

"I just … we're supposed to be a team. And I guess I never thought about what it must be like for you on the outside."

"And suddenly you're enlightened?"

"No," she said, shaking her head. "Not suddenly. Just because I play a raging bitch in real life doesn't mean … I don't know." Jenna huffed out a laugh as we pulled into the hospital parking lot. "I'm glad you were with him," she said finally. "If it couldn't be me, I'm glad it was you."

What was going on with Jenna? Had the Christmas spirit finally infected her, two months after the fact? Or was I still being small-minded and refusing to see that she'd changed in the meantime, that she'd *allowed* herself to change. To grow up, to become less selfish. Justin's accident could have done that, or anything that had happened to us since coming to this damn town.

"Moonset beat the Prince because they worked together," Jenna continued, and it was like she'd laid down the path for me to follow perfectly. I'd bought into it, hook, line, and sinker, and now I knew where she was going with this. And I was almost powerless to resist. "That's what we need to do now. Work together and hope that we can stop this one too."

"Coven class," I said flatly.

"*Class,*" she stressed. "Knowledge. Information. Maybe Illana and the others can stop this thing, or maybe it'll fall to us again. But maybe if we start trying to actually stick together and learn what we're capable of, we can stop this from ever happening again. That's part of what you want, isn't it? For us to be out of danger? For Cole and Bailey to be able to have normal lives someday? Or as close to it as we can get?"

I didn't say anything, which was the same thing as telling Jenna that she'd won.

Damnit.

NINETEEN

No one knows quite how strong the Abyssal Princes are. At least as strong as the Fae they once were, but now their songs are dark and destructive. They create armies out of innocents, and hide themselves amidst the rank and file.

....

The Princes of Hell

The parking lot was a graveyard. When I left in the middle of the night, there were still dozens of cars in the front lot, a line of reserved parking for hospital staff that was filled with cars, and people were still coming and going. There were hints of dawn in the skyline to the east, a dash of color against an otherwise black sky. The stars fading into existential black. It was too quiet.

Something was wrong.

Nick was in the lobby, elbows on his knees and head balanced between his hands when we walked in. "No change," he said, like it was somehow good news. He was the only one in the lobby, but the room didn't feel still and quiet. I looked around, unsure why the hair on the back of my neck was standing up.

Jenna seemed to notice it too. "What's happening? What's wrong?"

Nick's eyes were lazy and hooded, focused on me, despite the fact that beneath the show of despondency, his body was taut, fingers digging into his thighs and shoulders squared. He seemed to be waiting for something, but I honestly had no idea what it was.

Until I did.

The elevator doors flared golden, reflecting the Prince's symbol in the stainless steel surface.

"What?" Jenna said from my side.

"No, no, no," I whispered, breaking into a run. He was here. *Why* was he here? He'd already infected Justin, what more could he do? There was a bad feeling in the pit of my stomach, and for once it wasn't something the Prince had put there first.

I reached the symbol at the same time as Jenna, only realizing she was still at my side the moment her fingers mimicked my own and pressed against the golden flare vibrating softly against the door.

The elevator button spun away as the threads of the world unspooled. The ground fell up, the ceiling dropped, and the world dissolved into the strange reality of the Prince.

This time, it was red velvet and opera, the hospital lobby transformed into an acoustic marvel where every sound reverberated off the walls. The walls were covered in thick crimson fabric, gold rope threaded with streaks of green, each looped off into a giant gold tassel that looked thicker than the curtain it was holding back. Where in a normal opera house there would have been chairs, there were only empty gaps. The size and shape of the rows seemed to change from one moment to the next, growing less stable the more I looked at them.

In fact, that was how everything looked at second glance. The curtains warped and waned, scattered by winds that couldn't be felt or heard. The ceiling was both a thousand feet high and a wondrous stained-glass masterpiece, and at the same time low enough that I could have nearly brushed my fingers against the tips.

My eyes couldn't focus. Every time my vision shifted, the world around me writhed and deviated. Everything cycled between two versions, two different and yet completely stable worlds inhabiting the same space. Both wondrous in their own way, but they crowded in upon each other, and it was making my head spasm.

"Is this what you see all the time?" Jenna asked, one hand cupped over her eyes to shield them against the light. "How do you stand it? Everything hurts."

"You can fight it," Nick said. I turned to him, and he made my eyes burn. He'd risen from his chair, but around him, the world was real. Or not; no, it wasn't real. This was real, and he was surrounded by drab hospital carpeting, navy-blue hospital chairs, even the sign on the wall behind him pointing to Radiology. He was like a gravity well, drawing reality in all around him in a concentrated pocket. But it hurt to look at him, because the only thing worse than the Prince's fantasyland was the real world. I had to look away.

"What's going on, Nick?" Jenna was not playing around anymore. The Arctic winds could learn a thing or two from Jenna when she was in a mood, and right about now her fury was palatable.

"It's going to be okay," Nick said, only he'd adopted the "soothing adult" tone that never seemed to work on any of us. We weren't children to be placated. Especially not now, when the Prince was somewhere in the shadows, probably just holding off so he could make a proper entrance.

"*What* is going to be okay?" I piggybacked on Jenna's frustration and rage with some of my own. Justin was here, and they were putting him in danger by ... whatever it was that this was. The Witchers had set something in motion. Of course they had. How could I have been so stupid?

"Time to go, guys," Quinn said, stepping forward into the half light. The last time I saw him, he'd been wearing jeans and *flannel*, for Christ's sake, and now he was like ... Goth pro wrestler or maybe ninja infantry. A balaclava covered everything on his face except for eyes, nose, and mouth. Everything else, even his fingers, was swaddled in black military garb. He pulled a blade from a sheath wrapped around his forearm, a matching one on the other arm. The world warped around him, the same way it did to Nick, as though they were both too heavy to carry, and it had given up. Around me the air spun faster and faster, the mirage warping and waning.

The walls bulged and stretched and contracted, and my center of gravity kept shifting. If this was what it felt like to be on LSD, I could see why people went crazy.

"Quinn?" Even Jenna's brain couldn't quite match him to the guy who made us pancakes with the paramilitary uniform he wore now.

"You know he's here," I said, half in wonder. "You planned this." After everything that had happened, we were still bait. Did they let Justin get hurt? Had they been *waiting* for this?

"Now's not the time," Quinn said firmly.

I looked to Jenna, who had the same frown lines marring her face. She grabbed for my shoulder, and I steadied her arm with mine.

But before either of us could respond to Quinn, a peal of bells signified the opening of what had previously been the elevator doors. Now they were a pair of giant doors that swept up towards the ceiling that hung impossibly high in the distance, so far from us that the moon was even visible underneath it.

The doors swung open, rolling on wheels that were tiny clockwork creations, gears and springs that rattled as they rolled. Behind them was the Prince, long haired and dressed in an embroidered gold imitation of Quinn's outfit. There was an empty pommel at his side, but it wasn't like he needed the weapons. He *was* one, the deadliest thing in the room by far.

"You invited friends," the Prince whistled, making a beckoning motion with two of his fingers. He bared his teeth, bright like moonlight and just as bewitching. "Hello, friends."

"Go," Quinn commanded again, barely sparing us a glance. A pair of Witchers emerged from the stairwells on either side of the hall, falling into line behind him.

"Stay," the Prince countered with a wink and a smile.

Even if we wanted to leave—and I was certainly content with letting Quinn and the others handle this—the room still swayed between worlds, each dragging against us in a heavy, metaphysical version of tug of war, one in which we were the rope, destined to split apart under the equal forces at play.

Two more Witchers came in from between a pair of cherubic busts, glossy gold monstrosities that looked rather like the Prince himself. The new duo came to stand behind Nick, who wasn't dressed in the same battle gear as the others, but he had an athame of his own and looked just as ready for a fight.

Six against one, and I could see the Prince do the calculations as his eyes drifted over each of them in turn, a wealth of information processed in only a single moment. With some, the corner of his mouth twinged as if hearing the funniest kind of joke, while others caused an eyebrow down into sharp edges, the entire shape of the brow changing in that moment.

Quinn was a threat, of course, but surprisingly so was Nick. None of the others, though. Until after another hurdle of time passed, and two *more* Witchers appeared from somewhere behind each of the men, bringing their numbers to ten.

This wasn't a raid, this was a full-court press. "Tell us your name," Quinn said, surprising me. I didn't picture him as the negotiating type. "This doesn't have to get ugly."

"Obviously," the Prince said, throwing a smirk in Quinn's direction.

"You didn't answer the question." If Quinn was daunted, he didn't show it. But then, he looked almost alive in a way I'd never seen before. There was a light in his eyes that screamed for reckless abandon—a thrill-seeker gene where I hadn't expected to find one. *Quinn was having fun.* Not exactly what I expected.

"You don't interest me enough," the Prince said, words weighed down under the prickling thorns of spite, growing and spiraling out of control. His lie curdled in my stomach, and snarls of emotions that were thick with contrast rolled up underneath my skin. I shivered, and tightened my grip on Jenna's arm. It was easier, with her at my side.

The Witchers didn't let it affect them, though. Each of them was empty and blank, a canvas that the Prince couldn't affect, and once he realized that simple fact, his entire demeanor changed. The joking, the jovial outlook, all of that was cast aside like the mask that it was. For the first time, I got a glimpse of the creature underneath the costume.

The Prince cocked his head to one side, the expression going thoughtful and reserved on his face. For once, the emotions at hand were muted, dulled down until I could barely tell what *I* was feeling, let alone anyone else. "You're stalling," he said in wonder. "Oh, tricksy boy. You like to play games." And now, broad, beaming approval radiated outwards like its own personal sun. "*Devious* I can deal with."

The Prince opened his mouth and whistled a few notes, the opening strands to something haunting and slow. It quickly gained in tempo as the whistling continued and was yet joined by a deeper hum. Only the Prince's mouth moved, and the only sounds were coming from him, but somehow he could split his voice into complementary parts. And those parts were weaving something together that made my skin itch with longing.

"Stop!" Quinn commanded, but the Prince ignored him.

"Quinn!" But Nick's warning was ignored. Because the Prince's voice split again, and this time it was a dark sonata that he sang in piercing tones. Each of the notes carried its own heft, one hammer strike after another. All three of the pieces of his song sailed above us, around us.

At first I was relieved, because despite the fact that I looked all around us, there was no sign of danger. No change to the status quo. I'd expected a plague, or an attack of some kind, but the Prince's song started to fade out and nothing had changed.

"What was that?" Nick demanded, when a moment of silence had passed. "What did you do?"

The Prince used his smile as a shield, hiding all his secrets behind it. Quinn had the kind of patience that could have kept him peaceful for forty years of wandering, but Nick was not cut from the same cloth. Nick wore his deficiencies on his sleeve for all to see. "What'd you do?" he demanded again, as if by repeating the question it would somehow compel the Prince to tell the truth.

The Prince screamed and every window on the hospital floor shattered from the sound.

TWENTY

We know Moonset believed all power had merit.
That Necromancy could save lives, and Maleficia
could be weaponized. We believe they learned as
many as they could get their hands on.
They even sought out myths of a primordial
magic, stronger than any other.

....

Council Report
Eyes Only

Witchers poured from the building, far more than the half-dozen that had originally appeared. The Prince was right, there were more still waiting in the wings. *The one you see has a dozen siblings lurking in the walls.* Someone had told me that once, but I was pretty sure they'd been talking about rats at the time.

Jenna and I were caught up in the evacuation, as some

of the black-garbed men and women stayed behind to put out fires and check for injuries. The largest part of the force, though, streamed outside after the Prince, who had walked casually through the wall where windows had once been. Fire alarms ran through the building, though there were no fires that I could see.

He seemed heedless of the danger he was in. I doubted he feared the Witchers even a little. The sun peeked out at the center of the sky, a sliver of light that set the building behind us alight with faint oranges and yellows.

At first it seemed like no one had noticed us, but Quinn was on top of one of the black metal benches near the door, eyes scanning the crowd. When he found us, he hopped back down and started moving through the crowd, but the Prince intercepted him first.

"No hospital staff," Jenna said out of the corner of her mouth, her eyes trained back on the building behind us.

I turned, realizing quickly that she was right. There were Witchers filling the parking lot, but not a single ordinary human. Not a doctor, a nurse, even a patient. They'd evacuated the hospital already. They were *waiting* for this. "We are so out of our league," I whispered, half to myself. Quinn knew the Prince was going to show up here. Maybe to finish what he'd started with Justin, maybe for some other reason. But he *knew*. Enough to empty the hospital during the handful of hours I was gone.

"I believe you have something of mine," the Prince said, circling around Quinn with a dark smile.

"You're not taking Malcolm," Quinn replied tightly, chin

up and keeping his reactions to a minimum. He didn't show any fear, which was good, but he still looked like he was enjoying this too much.

"Malcolm already *belongs* to me."

Quinn snarled, and like a well-oiled machine the three dozen Witchers fell into order. Jenna tried to step in front of me, blocking me with her much smaller body until I snorted and reversed our positions. She gave me a pointed look as we jockeyed for position, and instead ended up side by side.

All of the Witchers had broken up into rings of five. Quinn was the only one who stood alone. Nick looked up at a wordless nod from Quinn. Just as the first real burst of sunlight flew over the horizon, he shouted, "Now!"

Shouts of magic punctured reality, as ice and stone and flame were summoned, each attack streaking forward just a second later than the one before. It was genius, really. No one could have dodged *all* of those attacks. To dodge one was to put yourself directly in harm's way for the next, and the next, and so on.

Only... that was exactly what the Prince managed to do. He spun and dipped and pranced like this all was a dance, and he was the only one who was enjoying himself. The Witchers knew exactly what they were doing and had their timing down perfectly. He *shouldn't* have been able to dodge everything they threw at him. But he did all the same.

Quinn called out directions I didn't understand, things about gnomes and numbers that made no sense to anyone who wasn't a Witcher. But with every command, the tactics the army displayed changed. Magical strike attacks—fire and force—were abandoned and area attacks taken up. The ground around us trembled as multiple shouts severed the land, created chasms and gashes as the blacktop concrete split apart.

The Prince continued his dance, running and sliding and evading everything that came his way. The Witchers' attacks were controlled and careful: despite the fact that everything they threw at him missed, the collateral damage was minimal. Spells faltered and vanished before they could strike one of the hospital buildings, the light posts, even the landscaping. Only the parking lot itself was damaged, torn up and split apart like the gates to the Abyss were going to open right here.

Twice, just when it seemed that two or three attacks were going to meet with the Prince in the middle, he shimmered and vanished, only to reappear five feet to the right and completely unmarked.

Once, an attack veered wide, arcing towards both the Prince...and us. By the time we saw the spell (which was like storm clouds and purple lightning), it was too late for Jenna and me to even move. But the Prince surprised me again, darting behind and scooping us up, one in each arm. He leaped backwards, five or maybe ten feet off the ground. And despite the fact that I was the better part of six feet two inches, in his hands I was an infant who could be easily moved and carried.

"Watch yourselves," the Prince said, the harsh current washing my features out in red and a sudden snap of anger. Shame welled up in me only long enough for me to realize that he wasn't chastising *us* but Quinn's soldiers. "What if you'd hit one of them?" the Prince called, sounding outraged. "You could have hurt him."

Quinn held up a hand, and immediately the incipient magic in the air faltered and vanished, recalled back into the ether it had come from. There was an impasse, and it had everything to do with Jenna and me. The Prince's arm was still around me, hot and disturbingly comfortable against my skin. He smelled like my favorite body wash, but on his skin the scent was somehow *more*, the most perfect version of itself. He released us, then turned to look at me, as if he'd forgotten that he was one against dozens. As if it didn't matter.

A discordant note in the symphony flowing from the Prince's mouth lasted only as long as his eyes on mine. The first two fingers of his right hand sliced through the air to point somewhere over his shoulder and a piercing note hit my eardrums like Charybdis itself swallowed me whole.

I had been ripped between points and from one version of the world to another so often by now that the transition hit me no harder than a bit of turbulence, but Jenna grabbed my arm in surprise.

One moment we were in the shadow of the main building hiding amidst some of the wreckage, and the next, we were on the roof of the hospital overlooking the battlefield.

There was a moment when it looked like Jenna was about to lose her dinner all over the side of the hospital, but the queasy look soon passed and she straightened.

Quinn spun around once he realized we were gone, but he and the Witchers were like ants to us, all the way up here. "Hey!" I shouted, waving my hands, but the sound didn't carry that far. Up here, the wind was more ferocious, angry and sulking like Cole on a summer school morning.

"He wants us out of the way?" Jenna tucked some of her hair behind her ear, but the wind just whipped it out again like a wild serpent refusing to be tamed.

"I don't think we really know anything about what he wants," I replied. We tried the only door to be found on the roof, but it was locked from the inside, and when Jenna tried the only unlocking spell she knew, it didn't work. Because there were so many different kinds of locks, there were an equal number of spells that each catered to a different type. And Jenna's spell could barely jiggle the handle.

There was nothing to do but stare at the battle below us.

Someone would call out a command, and then as a unit the Witchers would lob a series of attacks, their magic rocking through the air as loud as any jet engine. So many attacks, fire and ice, lightning and force, shadows and light. Dozens of attacks, all spread out on different levels, different heights, different wavelengths. No one could escape all of it.

But that was exactly what the Prince did. He leapt through the fray with a triumphant trill, feet catching on to empty air and propelling him off the ground. Some attacks he hopped over, a few he rolled underneath, and then there were the ones where he stretched himself out until he was no more than an inch wide and slid between them.

To their credit, the Witchers never broke ranks. Each wave of attacks was just as calm and focused as the ones before.

But with each round, and the way the Prince darted around them, the Witchers shifted position. Sometimes they stepped back. Sometimes they moved for cover, as wayward magical strikes hurtled their way. It took several minutes for me to see the pattern. For me to understand why the Prince wasn't returning any of the attacks himself. The Witchers, all thirty of them, kept inching closer to one another and none of them had realized it yet. The Prince wasn't just dodging their attacks. He was *herding* them. And that could only mean one thing.

"Oh no," I whispered, once I realized what was going on.

Jenna leaned over the ledge, seeing almost instantly what had taken me minutes. "He's playing with them." And then. "He's going to kill them." She grabbed for my hand, threading her fingers through mine. "Come on. We have to do something. We have to *help*."

"What can we do?" I tried to pull my hand free, but she wouldn't let go. "We need to stay out of it." The image of the spell hurtling towards us, and the way the Prince had leaped into its path, rather than letting us be hurt. I wasn't a coward by any sense of the imagination, but this wasn't our fight. It wasn't something we *could* fight. If it was something that wanted to kill us, then maybe we would have stood a chance. We could have used the curse for some good.

But if that spell had come any closer, it might not have been a demon of the Abyss that was destroyed by its activation, but one of the Witchers. Maybe even one of the ones we knew.

She grabbed me by the face, and I expected fury or something like it, but Jenna was calm, controlled. "Listen to me. He's going to kill them. Quinn's down there. Nick too. People we *know*. I know you *hate* me, and I know you hate *this*, but it's the only thing we can do right now. We have to help them. Somehow."

"What do you even think I'm going to be able to do?" I

asked, flustered and frustrated. I didn't know spells. I didn't have nearly the same kind of drive that Justin and Jenna did, the hunger to unravel every spell they could find, to teach themselves everything that they could. I knew about as little as I could help, and Jenna knew that.

"We're stronger together," Jenna said firmly. "We're part of the same coven, Mal. Together we're more capable than either one of us on our own."

I didn't know what she expected me to do but listen. It turned out that was all she wanted.

"Close your eyes," she said, and I did. "Feel your heartbeat. Feel the part of you that's alive and kicking, the adrenaline that's in your veins right now." She took my hand in hers, pressed it against her neck. "Now feel my heartbeat. You and I, we may not share any blood, but we're family. I'm the only one who gets to make fun of you for your demon boyfriend."

The laughter escaped me suddenly, and it should have broken the moment between us, but it had the opposite effect. The more Jenna talked, the deeper I fell inside myself.

"There's a cord that connects us, light like angel feathers that will stretch to the ends of the earth if it needs to." Her voice was low and serious, the perfect voice to be hypnotized to. "And with our hands on this cord, we can access the Coven bond.

"It's just there, it's under the surface. The five of us are connected in a way that no one but us will ever understand. For me, the four of you are like fires burning in the distance. When I close my eyes and concentrate, I can feel you somewhere just beyond my eyelids."

I concentrated, trying to use the sounds and feel of our heartbeats to tap into the hidden world she was referring to. But in the dark of my mind, there was nothing. No fire, no feeling. No connection to any of the others, least of all Jenna.

Her words grew hesitant, slow to regain their fire and passion. They stumbled, the truth hard against her lips. "I hate you sometimes, but Justin never will. And I hate that because someday he might decide I'm not worth fighting for anymore, and you'll win. And some days it feels like he's all I have, that he's the only thing that keeps me here. I don't know what I'll be without him, and what's worse is that someday I know I'll have to find out. We can't be together forever."

The confession did what Jenna's soothing tone could not. My mouth opened, and words spilled out. "None of you know me. I play the part and give you the only mask I can, even though it's not enough. And there's so much fear. Sometimes I can't push it down fast enough, it grows like weeds and the only thing I can do is drown it out with more anger. And I'm always angry, and always frustrated, and none of you will ever know why."

And there was no time for guilt or blame, because even as I confessed to the person I trusted least in the circle, my mind expanded, like another world opening up inside my brain, a world of more than three dimensions, where light and air were the same thing. I couldn't just feel the connection with Jenna, I could *see* it. It stretched far beyond the two of us. I could feel Justin inside the hospital, sleeping and dormant, his presence a gray node inside my head. Cole and Bailey, each slow to sleep and dreaming fitfully, bright spots even in a world that already seemed composed entirely of light.

There was more to it, though. The Coven bond between us was *right* and *fitting*, but there were other ties. A chain made from tar and melted black licorice, that bound us hand to hand. Another that was a strange sort of gravity, as if our bones were all pieces of a greater whole, just waiting to be dragged together. Even now, I could feel my forearm being pulled towards Jenna's leg. The femur, maybe, or her ankle bone. And one I couldn't see at all, could only feel in the way it made my soul shiver and stand on end, a thunderstorm of potential all around me.

It wasn't the bonds themselves that fascinated me. It was the layer of something between them. A spinning stream of energy that slowed when I focused on it. Green and gold and silver, lights or threads that separated when I focused on them, when the spinning slowed and I realized they were *symbols,* or something like them, spinning so fast they'd blurred together.

I'd always had a knack for reading sigils and symbols of magic. It was just something I never tried to hone, because... magic. Sometimes I could look at a symbol and discern something about it without even knowing what it was for. When we first came to Carrow Mill and the Moonset symbol started appearing everywhere, I could feel it there under the surface. Electricity and something living, the meaning behind the word.

There were thousands of them... not quite in my head, and not in the heads of the others, but somewhere in between. A streaming circle of something greater than all of us, trapped just outside my head like a halo.

Something told me Jenna couldn't see it. If she had, if

Jenna knew it was there, she would have reached for it already. Abused it. Taken it apart and figured out how all the pieces fit together. As it was now, it was beautiful. A pretty display of lights and colors that watched over us like guardian angels. *This could be the curse,* I found myself thinking. *If I can figure out a way to take it apart, I could still find my freedom.*

"You feel it, don't you?" Jenna's voice intruded on my headspace, but for the first time in my life, I didn't mind. I opened my eyes, and viewed the chaos below. The battle continued to rage, only now the violence was extreme. I vaguely remembered the building rocking once or twice while I'd been focused internally, the feel of the building taking a hit.

The thirty Witchers had been spread across the parking lot, taking strategic placements to cover all angles of escape. But now they were all on one side, and the attacks came more infrequently now, because everything they sent forward was repelled towards one of their colleagues.

It was easy to pick Quinn out of the crowd. He still stood at the front of his little army, putting himself in harm's way before any of the others.

With the Coven bond racing between us, it wasn't anything like what I thought. Jenna was there, in my head, but she wasn't in my thoughts or intruding somewhere she didn't belong. Instead, it was like the two of us had expanded until we were greater than the sums of our bodies, equally sharing all the space between us. She was part of me, and I was part of her. We were separate, and yet together.

He doesn't just want to kill them. He wants me to watch. My thoughts took the place of my voice, but I knew she could hear only what I wanted her to hear.

The Prince looked up to us, and even though it was too far to say for sure, I was almost positive he was looking me in the eyes. Making sure I watched. Held off his victory until the audience was primed and ready.

Is there something you can do? He likes *you.* Jenna was uncomfortable with the idea. Hell, I wasn't exactly a fan of it myself. But she was right.

I grimaced, the momentary lull was over, and now the fight had regained its fervor. The Prince stopped obeying gravity altogether, and when attacks came from too many directions he jumped into the air and ran on the air itself, raising and dipping, despite the fact that there was nothing holding up his feet. One time, he jumped and ran parallel to the side of the hospital for almost a dozen floors before he pushed off and swan-dived back towards the ground.

Now that he knew I was watching, the Prince's tactics changed. No longer was he so worried about dodging attacks and staying on the move. He allowed things to hit him, though they never slowed him down. He walked through spells meant to contain him, and wardings meant to hold him off. With Jenna's knowledge at my beck and call, I could see and understand things about the battle that I would never have known about by myself.

The only sound we could hear all the way up here, despite the rushing wind all around us, were moments of the Prince's serenade, now a sharp thing of cymbal clangs and percussive slaps.

He doesn't like. He thinks he loves me. Because it was true. The Prince loved the idea of being in love. The idea of ownership, and how one was the same as the other. He thought

I belonged to him, because he thought he knew the person I really was.

Maybe for a minute I had believed him. Maybe I, too, had wondered. But attacking Justin had changed everything. That wasn't love. That was psychosis.

The Prince advanced on Quinn suddenly, the pair of them dancing like tiny toy soldiers.

"Mal," Jenna warned, her voice rising.

Quinn didn't back down the way the Prince had. When the demon invaded his personal space, Quinn held his ground. He would not be moved. But the Prince wasn't after intimidation. I saw movement, but couldn't see what at this distance. But when I saw the flash of metal in the demon's hand, I knew what had happened. He'd taken Quinn's knife from him. And yet still Quinn stood there, still like a statue. Frozen, or unafraid. Either way, he was in trouble.

The knife raised, glowing holy white as the sun struck it, and just before the Prince brought it back down, knowledge poured into me from Jenna's mind. We both screamed at the same time, her the spell that would amplify my voice, and mine a commanding "STOP!" that reverberated across the parking lot, the woods on the far side, and all around us into Carrow Mill itself. My voice was a thunder crack and a sonic boom, and the ground shook after its passing.

The Prince stayed his hand, eyes again turning towards me. Quinn was also looking, but if he said anything, his words didn't carry.

"They raised arms against me," the Prince pouted, his words carried softly on small gusts of air, traveling whole and unbroken up the entire length of the hospital. It was like we were only inches apart instead of a dozen stories. "A lesson needs to be taught, my human."

"I won't let you kill them," I said, and though the words barely left the roof before the wind ripped them away and apart, I saw something change on the Prince's face down below. A frown, maybe, or a darkening of the eyes. Something unpleasant.

"You cannot stop me from this, my Malcolm."

But the spinning wheel of knowledge above the crown of my head begged to differ. One moment it was a wheel with a thousand different spokes and the next it was a book with thousands of pages, the pages flying right to left until they stopped and there was a symbol in my head, crowding out my thoughts and tearing memories loose from where they'd always been stored.

It was something too big for my head, a symbol that was more than me and more than ... everything. It wasn't magic the way I thought of magic. It was *more.* It was real in a way that nothing else was, more fluid and eternal than anything else I'd ever known. It was what I thought power must have felt like to the Abyssal Prince, and how callous a god felt next to a Toyota.

"Mal?" Jenna said. Then again, worry in her voice. "Malcolm?"

My vision sharpened to an impossible level, and I could see every detail of the battlefield all at once. Quinn's face showed no fear, but the droplet of sweat on his forehead suggested otherwise.

I opened my mouth and the symbol crawled out, and all

I could think of and see was the knife poised above Quinn's head, and the absolute lack of fear in his expression. And even as my mouth struggled to shape the words that would bring the symbol to life and activate its power, I felt the page in my mind ripped out and turning to ash, the knowledge used up and burned away.

Quinn's eyes locked on mine, and my tongue pressed the magic from my body, the symbol tearing through me with the kind of pain that only came after a really good workout. I spoke the word and the ground quaked beneath us, shaking the hospital from the basement all the way up to the roof. The clouds hammered against each other in the sky. The raging wind quelled. All around the Prince the air darkened, black and fragmented. Shards of onyx covered him over like a coffin, all sharp angles and solid shadows that compressed upon themselves, breaking down and shrinking piece by piece until there was nothing but a crystal the size of a golf ball where the Prince had once stood.

And then even that vanished down into nothing.

TWENTY-ONE

I've never seen someone so cold as the day that Cy broke up with Savannah. They'd been together for years. It ended the spring that Moonset formed.

....

Sara Bexington (S)
Personal Interview

"Tell me again what you did."

Quinn looked exhausted, as did all the other Witchers. Hell, even Jenna looked exhausted, but I felt like I could run a marathon. Despite whatever it was that I'd done, my body had recovered quickly. Insanely quick. I knew this wasn't the way magic normally worked, but what I'd done on the roof—that hadn't been magic. At least not the kind of magic we were used to.

The Prince had pointed out that we considered magic

a language, but that humans also thought it was the *only* language. That any other language was evil. So when Quinn asked me to tell him what had happened, I lied.

"I don't think it was me. I told him he couldn't kill you all, and I guess he must have listened." It irritated me that I had to put the onus on the Prince, that I had to give him credit for a mercy he didn't feel. He would have killed them all and then walked me along what remained of the parking lot, bragging about each kill. Showing them off like their bodies were trophies he'd collected just for me.

Quinn didn't believe me. That's because he wasn't an idiot.

"The Prince did that," he said flatly. "Folded himself up in a crystal cage and disappeared. For no reason. He was *winning!*" I'd never seen him so close to actual anger before. Quinn never lost his temper, but it looked like he was about to.

Jenna didn't know what happened either, but for once she had my back. "That's what he said." She crossed her arms in front of her and stared down Quinn. "Is there anything else?"

He looked between us, and of course there was something else. There were lots of things else. But Quinn didn't ask any more questions, he didn't push things any further than necessary. "You should have run when you had the chance," he said gruffly. He looked weirdly uncomfortable and kept looking at Jenna and ducking his head down. Never at me.

Quinn stood up and headed for the door, pausing just before he crossed the threshold. "You can see Justin in a few minutes, once we get the wards down from the upper floors."

"If you warded the hospital, then how did he walk right

in?" Jenna asked, because she might have had a change of heart where I was concerned, but she was still *Jenna*. "What was the point, then?"

Quinn shook his head, but he still wouldn't look at me. "The point was to keep all the patients safe. Justin and Luca were inside; we needed to be sure they wouldn't be harmed."

Luca. That's right, he was here too. "You go see Justin," I told Jenna. "I'll be by in a few minutes."

Luca's floor was now entirely empty except for the pair of guards on either end of the hallway. None of them batted an eye as I walked past—all the locked and secured doors had been propped open with doorstops, shoes, really anything that could be found to make them stay open.

There was no change in Luca's condition. I didn't stay long, as the sound of breathing machines was enough to unsettle any good mood I'd managed to maintain after the day and night I'd had. But I had to wonder—the Prince was up and moving around, and Luca slept. When the Abyssals had come for us the first time, they said we were supposed to be the restitution for what Moonset had done—that through possessing us, Moonset's debt for killing Kore would be paid.

Each of the spirits needed a host. So who was hosting the Prince? Was it literal, like was he walking around inside someone's body. Or could it be something more complicated, and as long as Luca slept, the Prince had free rein over the rest of the world?

The easiest thing to do would be to find a way to wake Luca up, and see if it made a difference. He'd been the one to summon the creatures in the first place, so he probably knew as much about them as anyone.

"Has your dad been back lately?" I asked, my voice so quiet the machines drowned it out. Even if he was awake, he probably couldn't hear me. I liked it that way, though, to be honest. There might have been a few words I could have eked out while Luca lay on the bed with his eyes closed, but an actual conversation ... I wasn't ready for all that.

There were more guards outside of Justin's room. It was hard to say if it was because they were more worried about protecting him or more concerned about what a crazy Moonset kid could get himself into. I recognized a few of them from the battle outside. Most had washed up in the meantime, changed into clothes that weren't singed and ripped and bloody. A few, though, were new. Reinforcements who hadn't spent the early morning hours fighting for their lives.

I didn't say anything to them either. The idea of acknowledging them annoyed me, in some way. Like they would suddenly become captors instead of guards. It was stupid, and I couldn't figure out why I was suddenly so bothered, but the hospital was crawling with Witchers and the Prince had nearly killed them all.

Jenna stood in the doorway when I approached. One of the Witchers told us to hang back and let Justin sleep. That the doctors said only one visitor at a time, and only for a few minutes. We compromised and looked in on him, neither of us saying anything for the longest time.

Justin was all pale skin and limp hair, even blacker than usual against the ivory hospital sheets. Deep lavender circles had swept over his sunken eyes and his hands were a mess of bruises even I could see from here. Each hand was also wrapped in a thick cuff that swallowed up his wrist as well as part of his forearms.

"They're afraid he's still going to hurt himself," Jenna said, her voice atypically flat and empty. "I thought he was better. I thought all they were worried about was the surgery. And now that he was done, everything was going to be okay."

I knew she wanted to be Bailey in that moment, naive and willing to believe in any story. "I think he's going to be like that until we find a way to stop the Prince."

"Didn't you? Stop him? I know what you told Quinn," she dropped her voice down to a murmur, "but I saw what you did. I don't even know what that *was*." But it was clear that she wanted to find out, exactly as I knew she would.

But even if I could figure out what it was that I'd tapped into, or even what it was that I'd done, there was no way I'd share it with Jenna. The spell, or whatever, that I'd used had saved everyone, at least for right now. Just before I'd lost the connection to whatever power that was, I'd felt the page burn away, the knowledge vanish.

I think whatever I'd tapped into was a limited resource. The things there could only be used once, and I certainly wasn't equipped to decide if it was okay. But I also wouldn't trust Jenna with it, especially after seeing what it could do. There was every chance she would squander any real power she was given, and while my stomach still clenched at the idea of doing magic, I'd seen just how much it had done today.

Besides, once I had some real sleep, I had something more important to focus on. The Prince was gone, not defeated. And he'd attacked Justin for one reason and one reason only:

for my cooperation. The first step towards that was to start finding out what really happened in Carrow Mill twenty years ago—and to discover exactly what kind of legacy our parents had left here.

This was a town with a higher-than-average concentration of witches per capita. *Someone* had to know something.

––––––––––

Jenna and I slept outside Justin's room, waiting for him to wake up. Neither of us was quite ready to leave, and we'd both clung to the hope that he'd wake up any minute, and we'd be there, and that would help us come to terms with it all somehow.

But Justin didn't wake up, and someone needed to check on the kids. I volunteered, since even the idea of separating Jenna from her hospital chair seemed designed to send her into a panic attack. Her hands made claw marks in the wooden arms when I talked about Cole and Bailey, how they were sitting at home and waiting for updates. Her breathing had increased, and I even saw a sheen of sweat on her forehead.

"I'll go," I said, deftly plucking the decision from her hands. There was no moment of grateful appreciation, and it was better that way. I liked Jenna better when we kept each other at arm's length. "Call me if anything changes."

Someone had to drive me home, because I'd actually *parked* in the parking lot. The whole area had been cordoned off, with someone having whipped up a construction crew in the handful of hours since the fight. I don't know what story they spun to make the town forget that a hospital had been evacuated and a monster had used some of their loved ones as a meat-puppet army, but it was a good one, because when we drove through town it was business as usual everywhere we went.

Illana was there when I walked in, as I'd expected. But the startling thing was that she had Cole and Bailey spellbound, seated at her feet like grandchildren on Christmas morning.

"Shh," Cole said immediately, annoyed at what little interruption my arrival had caused. Both of them were almost a decade too old for bedtime stories, and to that point, it was still daylight out. Regardless, they hung on her every word.

Illana raised a heavily penciled eyebrow in my direction, but never stopped weaving her story.

"And they called him the 'heart stealer' because he was beloved in a way that only the Princes can be. Now the town of Hamelin never quite forgot what happened, even if the truth was ground away like a pebble in the ocean, worn down to sand after hundreds of years. But they still remember the salient points of the story. There was a man who came to the town of Hamelin, whose music was ribald, though it was more his personality that was pied than his clothing."

Almost in stereo, Bailey and I both turned to Cole, and he didn't disappoint. "How could he wear pie, though? They didn't have pie in the Dark Ages. Everyone knows that." He was confident at first, certain in this one truth, but after a moment that certainty wavered, and he added, "Don't they?"

"Pied meant that he wore a coat of many colors," Illana murmured with a soft smile, which put Cole at ease even as I swallowed down a momentary flush of relief and Bailey hid her smile behind her hand. Cole would always be Cole, and for that I was incredibly thankful. "But what our own records suggest is that the man was foreign in a way no one else is ever really foreign. He grasped the language with ease, yet he lacked social cues. He could play a complicated melody on any instrument you handed him, yet he did not understand the human way of life.

"And so he became close to the people of Hamelin, and they fell under his spell. He did them favors at first, even protected them from threats that they could have fought off themselves. With every favor, he deferred all talk of payment until one day, he spoke to the town elders, and he revealed what he was truly after. He wanted the children. *All* of the children."

"Wanted them for what?" Bailey, always the pragmatist. "They were his friends, weren't they?"

"The Princes feed on souls, but only certain types of souls. There was a Prince named Kore, and she fed on passions, on souls who had something they loved more than anything else in the world, and she could only take them when that passion had died in them, and they were broken, vacant creatures. The Prince in Hamelin, though, he was particularly seditious. For it was love that he sought. Love above all other things. And sometimes, when love is forced or artificial, it becomes a dark thing. A snarling tangle between bestial urges: to hurt, to control, and even sometimes to kill."

The pair of them were quiet for a very long time, and then Bailey said, with complete clarity, "That's what happened to Justin. He was crazy for Ash before, and now he's just ... *crazy* for her."

She has to know how I feel! Justin's shout echoed through my head.

"So what happened to the Prince when the town told him no?" Cole asked. "They did tell him no, right?"

Illana smiled the same humoring smile she had every time Cole spoke. Illana wasn't a people person, so where the hell did the story-time lady come from? She wasn't their actual grand-mother, and this wasn't a bedtime story.

"They told him no," she confirmed. "And he went away in a terrible rage. But by then it was already too late, because the children were already infected. Word spread to the nearest coven, who contacted the Congress, which at that point was headquartered in Italy. And within the month, a dozen of the strongest covens rode for Hamelin. But it was all for naught. The Prince faced off against the strongest witches available, and held his own long enough for the power of his song to steal away the last child. And once they were all infected, he col-lected them all and spirited them away to an unknown place."

"And now he's here?" Cole asked.

"And now he's here," Illana repeated, in a far more con-fident voice. "Magic isn't the way to defeat a creature of the Abyss. Not one that thinks and moves and breathes. Maleficia can be overwhelmed and destroyed. Creatures, though, are something else entirely."

"So how did Moonset kill one?" Bailey asked, and I flinched, realizing even Bailey saw there was more to the story.

Illana spread her hands wide, the blank curiosity that was painted across her face exaggerated to the point where I had to roll my eyes. "I suppose that's what your brother intends to find out."

"I want to help," Cole said, flinging himself around to

stare at me. Bailey chimed in a moment later, offering up her own desire to help. I glared daggers into Illana, because the last thing I needed was the pair of them getting underfoot.

"I think this is something Malcolm must do on his own," the woman confided, as if it was a very great secret. I don't know what kind of spell she'd cast on the two of them to make them revert to the childish personas who sat on the floor and listened to stories, but all of this was too far. "But there is something that is integral that you must do. A part of the story I haven't shared yet."

They turned back to her eagerly, their pleas to Malcolm forgotten for the moment.

"As I told you, love in the wrong hands can become a most terrible weapon. Your dear brother is proof enough of that. And if the Prince plans to replicate his old plans, Justin is only the first. There will be others. Many others. And we must contain them as quickly as possible, before they hurt themselves, or anyone else. Imagine the kind of harm we could cause, if we let ourselves be slack in our vigilance."

"Why don't you just lock them all up before they get bad?" Bailey asked. "I can help." Off the sharp look I turned towards her, she wilted, and shook her head. "I just meant, I could talk to them. Get them to a pep rally at school or something, and then you lock them up until it's safe for them again."

"Because we don't use coercion on children," Illana said. The two of them believed her and I snorted. The Congress did nothing *but* use coercion. We were living proof. "It would be easier, certainly, but if we break the laws for this, then the next time the justification becomes easier and easier, until the laws hold no meaning. We will protect the children as much as we can, but we will not strip their freedoms from them. Not until we have no other choice."

Being given a task, even one as serious as the one Illana had thrown them, set the two of them into a frenzy. Bailey and Cole started arguing one moment, trading ideas back and forth the next, electrified by their chance to be useful. To be part of something.

I watched them with shock and an itch on the back of my neck that wouldn't quit. "What did you do to them?" I demanded the moment the pair left the room. Because the whole thing had been surreal in a bad way, and I had no doubt that for all Illana's protests against coercion, that was exactly what she'd just done.

"What needed doing. They would get underfoot, and at least now they will worry for their own safety. They are children, not warriors." Illana's face twisted unhappily. "Not yet."

"Not *ever*," I snapped. "Not if I can help it."

"But you can't," she said, wrapping calm around her as a shroud. "I know you think of them as having something that was stripped from you, the innocence you were never allowed to have. But they are still your greatest weakness. I would have thought your recent trials would have proved that. You can't shield them forever."

This was not a conversation for me. It was a conversation for Justin, or maybe Jenna in his stead. "I'm not the one in charge," I said, loathing in my tone. I wasn't sure which one of us it was for, but I let it ride. "You want them to trust you? Stop manipulating the people they care about."

Illana got up carefully, her spine stiff the entire way, and glided into the kitchen. A moment later, I heard a methodical sound, the thwack of a knife against wood. I followed her to the edge of the kitchen tile, but stayed on the outside like a vampire.

"Where were you, when that was all going down this morning? If it was all hands on deck, shouldn't you have been there?"

"Dear boy, who do you think played sentinel over your wayward siblings? As if I would trust their safety to anyone else." Illana moved in broad, sweeping strokes. Everything she did was precise and expended just as much energy as she needed, not a bit more or less. She tossed a kaleidoscope of colors into a pan: reds, yellows, whites, and greens. Others she set off to one side before she turned back and grabbed a whisk from the counter.

You trust their safety to anyone else all the time. You only turn up when you need something from one of us. "Is your friend still here? The one that wrote the book about Moonset. What's-her-name. The nosy one." I knew exactly what her name was. I'd known who she was since I was nine years old.

"Much to my chagrin," Illana said, "Adele will remain until this business with the Abyssal is taken care of. I think this news of your parent's secret victory has undone her good sense. She longs for a chance to get the story right. I think she believes you all will follow in your parents footsteps."

"And what do you think?"

There was a hideously long pause, where the only sounds were the hissing vegetables in the frying pan and the occasional tick of the coffee maker reminding itself it was still on active duty. "You're going to dig up the old bones, aren't you?" she asked flatly. "You're going to help that thing."

Her back hid what was happening on the stove, the origin of the sudden pouring, bubbling liquid that I could hear but not see. Illana made it all sound so simple. Monster, evil. People, good. But there weren't any other options, if there were, I would have been all over them already.

"Do you have a better idea?" I asked, and finally I'd found an outlet for everything that had been bottling up inside of me. "Can *you* stop him? Because your grandson carved a spellform into the Prince's chest cavity and he walked away without a scratch."

"Until you made him go away," Illana said and she turned fully around, still hiding the stove behind her. Her hooded eyes shined with renewed curiosity. Everyone wanted to know what had happened on the roof. I may not have liked Illana much, but at least I trusted her. More than I trusted the others.

"The curse…" I said instead. "How much do you know about it?"

I watched her eyes work as she tried to connect the dots, only to realize there weren't nearly enough of them on the page. Her hand stilled; she'd been about to bring it up to tap against her lips. The move was so typical, so natural, that I was almost surprised that she resisted. "Something happened. Something new."

I nodded. "I think you should start being more careful. The Coven bond isn't the innocuous power you think it is. Not for us."

"Tell me." So intent was she on the conversation that she

hadn't turned back to the stove in several minutes; the realization caught her a moment later, and she spun back around with the kind of foul-mouthed curse I would have expected from the boy's locker room.

I found out what she was doing a few seconds later when she shoved a plate down onto the table in front of me and stabbed a finger towards the chair. "Sit. Eat."

My stomach revolted. The concept of food was so glorious that by the time I realized how hungry I was, the plate was nearly licked clean.

"Malcolm," Illana said, as gentle as she could be, which was about the same thing as saying gentle like concrete.

"The curse … the Coven bond. The Prince told me that Moonset stole the secrets of the darkbond from Kore before they killed her."

"So they managed a darkbond between the five of you? Interesting. Although I'm afraid I don't see how they would have found that useful." A momentary pause, and then Illana continued, "But then, they could sometimes see things in a way the rest of us couldn't. I'm sure if they incorporated the darkbond, they had a reason."

I exhaled. "There's more. It's … actually, I have no idea what it is," I said, scratching the back of my neck. "There's a lot of layers in our Coven bond, and I think one of them is a grimoire."

She was quiet for so long I grew nervous, afraid of her reaction. She waved a hand for me to continue, but the severe look on her face didn't change.

"He was going to kill them: Quinn and the others. Jenna

talked me into trying to help, and we managed to tap into the bond somehow, but when I saw him about to stab Quinn...I panicked. And then there was this book of symbols in my head, flying through my head so fast I could barely pick one of them out. And then it stopped, on this one particular symbol." *And then it crawled out of my mouth,* I didn't say, *because I don't think it was magic at all. I think it was alive somehow. I think I got lucky.*

"And then you banished the Prince." Illana's voice was hoarse like she'd been the one talking for so long. I nodded, a rapid jerk of the head. Awkward and uncomfortable.

"It burned away, after," I added. "The spell...or whatever. I think it all burns away after." Illana started to relax visibly, but that was because she didn't understand. "What I did today, that was weak, compared to some of the others."

"And you're worried about what Jenna or the others will do if they can access that part of the bond." At first I thought she was asking a question, so I nodded. It took a few minutes to realize that wasn't what happened at all. That she already knew how I felt and about what worried me. It hadn't been a question at all to her.

"None of the others have reported anything like this," Illana said after several minutes of quiet thought. I'd sat there the whole time suffering through it with the queasiness in my stomach. It was supposed to feel good to confide in someone, to rely on an adult to make things better.

"That doesn't mean they won't," I said, quiet with certainty.

"It might be that the Prince's influence has somehow allowed you to tap into this hidden layer," she said finally. "I've worked with your siblings, run them through many different exercises. If there were anything amiss, I would think something would have come up before now. Especially if it was something so easy you could stumble into it on your first real attempt."

I didn't know what to think. Didn't know if I believed her or not. "So what am I supposed to do with that?" None of that was a real answer, just a dismissive theory about why Jenna hadn't broken into the secret magic factory.

"Nothing for now. Be cautious, and listen to them. If they discover it, let me know immediately. And Malcolm? I don't think this needs saying, but we never had this conversation. We maintain your lies from this morning. The Prince vanished himself. No other explanation is nearly plausible."

"And me? I think I could still tap into that magic, you know."

Illana smiled, and it wasn't the first time I'd ever taken a moment to admire her, but it was the first time I realized that I was right to do so. "I know how much you fear the power inside of you, Malcolm. I think there would be no better caretaker for this power."

But if Moonset put this power there, then doesn't that automatically make it evil and bad, and the kind of thing we should never, ever touch?

She saw it in my face, and this time her smile turned sad. "Even monsters have moments of clarity, Malcolm. Monsters can have children just like everything else, and want to protect their children, and still be monsters. I admit I've always wondered if the curse was all they'd done for you. I suppose now we know the truth."

"And what is that?"

But Illana wouldn't answer me.

TWENTY-TWO

We knew Moonset was destined to go places.
Even then, Sherrod was charismatic. They could
have ruled the Congress within a dozen years.
They chose to burn it down instead.

....

Robert Cooper
Transcript from the Moonset trial

It took two days to track down Adele Roman, the person who knew the most about what Moonset had been like in high school. She was the first person I wanted to talk to— the one who'd know exactly where to start trying to track down what had happened to the Abyssal Prince during Moonset's senior year.

Two days where I dealt with my siblings bouncing all over the place, shuttling people back and forth to the hospital to visit Justin who, by all appearances, was the picture of health (minus the stab wound in his gut). The adults were taking things slow, and he was still in restraints when I visited on the second day. Justin was the most wary of his freedom.

"It's fine, leave them on," he said, resisting any suggestion to the contrary.

There'd been no sight nor sign of the Prince. Maybe it meant he trusted me to get to the bottom of what happened, or he was busy with something else. I wondered if he was really doing all of this for his sister, or if there was more to the story. But then, if Justin hadn't survived the attack, I wouldn't have let up until I tracked down *his* killer. So I could understand it.

I tried to use my time wisely to track down Adele Roman, but the woman didn't lay down tracks easily. I asked Quinn and Nick, but they couldn't find her. I even called the motels and hotels in the town to see if she was at any of them, but no one was registered under that name. I even tried to get word to Illana through the Witchers, but of course she wouldn't return my calls. Why make anything easy on me.

Maybe it should have been obvious, but when I finally found Adele on Tuesday morning, she was in the public library, seated behind the librarian's desk in the far corner, a happy but absent smile on her face.

If Illana had taken to acting like our new grandmother, Adele Roman was the one who looked the part. She wore comfy-looking sweaters, her hair was just a bit frazzled, and she smiled so much she almost looked deranged. In a good way.

"I expected you days ago, Mr. Denton," she said, like it was completely understandable that I'd tracked her down to the local library when she was neither local nor a librarian.

"No one knew where to find you," I said, thrown off a bit by the kind tone and the smile. Adults weren't nice without a reason, not in my experience. They were easier to deal with, easier to handle, when they were up front with their hostilities or their limitations. Illana was easy to get along with, for example.

"Oh," she said slowly, "oh, dear. Yes, I guess I can see where you're coming from. I suppose I should have told someone where I was staying."

Was the woman for real? I studied her and then shook my head. No, this was some sort of game. She knew who I was. She knew all of us probably better than we knew ourselves. Maybe she wanted a follow-up to the Moonset book, the story of the sequel.

"Have a seat, Malcolm. Why don't we talk?"

I expected an interrogation, the cost of doing business with a historian who'd made her life's work a retrospective on my dad's crimes.

"Illana asked me to aid you, but I don't know how much help I can be. I repeated the story that was told to me, only to find out it was fiction. Robert controlled the narrative, but I can't help but wonder *why*. This was years before Moonset's decline, so why did he feel the need to wrest a victory from them?" She spread her hands and sighed. "Moot, I suppose. Without him here to answer for his lies, I can't even begin to unravel what really happened. That's exactly why I argued against immediate executions, of course. There was so much we could have learned from them..."

She trailed off, and I was struck dumb by how casually she talked about my parents like that. Not that I was offended, but it didn't even occur to her that the subject was touchy.

"I suppose there's nothing to do about it now. Robert is conveniently in the field somewhere, unable to be reached by phone or spell." She snorted. "'Unreachable.' More like hiding out overseas, as if that's far enough to escape his wife's wrath."

"Well, her *wrath* should bring him here. His lies are the reason this thing is here now."

"Oh, I'm aware. And the Congress will someday soon be made aware as well."

I snorted. The idea that Illana would turn against her husband after helping him cover up his lies for twenty years made me laugh.

Adele gave me a curious eye and a sympathetic smile. "You seem to know a thing or two about complicated relationships. Don't think that theirs is any simpler. Their marriage was symbolic. The Congress has always been her real husband, though one that doesn't seem to mind if another man shares her bed."

Since I hadn't sat down at her invitation, Adele climbed to her feet, sliding a small wooden cane out from under the desk. She used it as she walked, gesturing me along with her free hand, though I hadn't thought her limp all that bad in the hospital. Now it seemed a bit more pronounced.

She tapped the edge of a metal cart that was tucked against the end of a bookshelf. "Push this for me, if you'd be a dear."

I pushed, and Adele shelved, one book at a time. She barely looked down at what was on the cart, simply grabbing volumes one at a time with her good hand and slotting them onto a shelf, sometimes having to step on the tips of her foot to lunge up far enough to slide the book back.

"I don't think any truth Robert has would even be worth the paper he printed it on. I've looked into some of the records again, and I suppose if you squint at them in the right light, you can see how Moonset's involvement was greater than written. But it's far more likely that they themselves stayed out of the spotlight for their own reasons."

"But why? They managed to kill something no one else could. They saved their whole class. So why wouldn't they want anyone to know?" My mind stuttered to a halt and I realized. "Was it … were they already dark by then? Maybe saving the other kids was a side effect of whatever they were really after." *The darkbond. They got the secret of it out of Kore, and they built one into our heads.* Was that why they did it?

"I think there are a lot of things about Moonset we still don't know," Adele said carefully, "though I wouldn't put it past them to have done something good for their own selfish motives. There aren't any heroes to find in this story, Malcolm."

"So where should I start?"

She pretended to think, but it was obvious she'd already figured out the answers I needed. "Start with your uncle. Charles was a good boy once, misguided, but what boys aren't at that age? I've heard he's gone a bad way since then."

"You could say that again," I muttered.

"You could speak with your father's old friends," she mused, "but I doubt any of them are still around. At least not the ones worth talking to. You can try the Dugard boy. He was friends with your father up until senior year. They had a falling out a few months before graduation."

"Do you have a first name? Or should I go up and down the streets asking if anyone knows the 'Dugard boy'?"

Adele smirked and waggled a finger at me for a moment, a little bit of grandmotherly judgment in her eyes. "No need for that kind of tone, young man. His father taught at the high school for years and years. Never was a fan of your dad's, though."

A slow ripple ran through my chest. I remembered an old man who hadn't been a big fan of Justin's father, who'd been a teacher at the high school. A man whose son now ran a curio shop of random knick-knacks right down on Main Street.

He'd known my father?

We crossed into another row of shelves, and by this point Adele's limp had become more severe, and her other hand came down on the front end of the cart, which she used as a second support. "Are you okay?" I asked, looking back the way we'd come. We could have this conversation just as easily at the desk. There was no reason for her to hurt herself more than she already had.

"Nothing you can do for me," she said with a smile. "Besides, just because you have a weakness doesn't mean you have to let it be used against you. You don't grow up in Fallingbrook without learning to bite down on the pain."

Fallingbrook was Illana's coven. "You... You're part of Illana's coven?"

Her smile was bright and proud despite the pain. "Surprised? I've never been half the witch that Illana is, but I have my own uses."

My scowl came sudden and quick. "Then she knew where you were the whole time. I know covens can track each other down like that."

Her smile never failed, serene and a little pleased. "And if you're especially talented, you know exactly how to hide from it too. Ana's dear, but I like my independence, and I don't like knowing she can peek over my shoulder any time she wants."

"You sound like you don't trust her."

A sharp laugh at that. "Sometimes the people you trust are the ones you have to keep at arm's length, Malcolm."

TWENTY-THREE

The war changed no one as much as it changed
Cyrus Denton. Just a few years before, he'd been
the popular, charismatic leader. But by the
end he was a grim, emotionless assassin.
I can't even say which one he really was.

....

Elizabeth Holden-Carmichael
Carrow Mill, New York—
From a written account
about Moonset's development

"Explain to me again what we're doing?" Kevin asked. With
Luca on lockdown, and no sign of his dad after I'd scared him
off, I needed someone who knew where Luca lived. Uncle
Charlie might know something about the Abyssal Prince, and
he wouldn't talk to the other witches. But I had a much better

scenario in mind: I'd gotten a reaction out of him at the hospital. Maybe he'd let something slip if I could get under his skin.

Like what really happened when Kore came to town, or *how* she arrived in the first place. That was the part of the story that bothered me most. *Someone* invoked Maleficia and summoned her. When Luca had done the same, everyone knew immediately what was happening. There was evidence of damage all over town. But in all the stories about Robert Cooper's victory, there wasn't a single explanation about where the Prince had come from, who had summoned it, and what had ultimately happened to them.

"He knows something about what's happening here. He has to," I said, slowing when Kevin pointed to a lone driveway on the west side of town. I couldn't see any sign of a house, but there was definitely a mailbox on the side of the road.

We followed the gravel path back and around, slipping behind several thick oak trees, and a weeping willow that blanketed a large portion of the driveway in swaying tendrils. The house was tucked away in the back corner of the property, as far from the road as it could possibly be. It was a decent-looking log home, not the trailer trash gutterslum I would have expected from Charlie.

It was the house of a family man, and even now the yard looked well maintained. Garden beds and plants in hibernation lined the house, a flag hung from the porch, amd there were curtains in the windows.

"This ... is not what I thought it would be," I said, slightly in awe. Luca might have grown up with a drunk bastard for a father, but he lived in a Martha Stewart house.

"Mr. D never seemed like a decent guy, but Luca never complained, and this is where he grew up," Kevin said with a quiet resignation from the passenger seat. "I always figured that he was just awkward because of who his family was." He glanced quickly across the car, shame on his face. "Sorry, man."

I waved it off, cut the engine, and climbed out of the car. Kevin got out and followed me, throwing his jacket back on. For whatever reason, he claimed that Luca's dad had always liked him, and he was pretty sure it had something to do with being on the football team. So when I'd asked him to come along as backup, the first thing he did was grab his letter jacket, which mostly just hung in his locker. Kevin normally wasn't one for showing off.

"You think he's here?" he asked, looking around the house and yard like he should have already been visible.

I nodded to the bag full of empty beer cans tossed with neglect towards the corner of the porch. Someone must not have felt like dragging them all the way to the garbage can, and that someone probably still had a hangover.

I hoped so. Hungover Charlie seemed like he'd be easier to deal with.

I pounded on the front door, taking a small bit of pleasure at the way the door shuddered underneath my fist. How many times had someone come to this door and wailed on it until Charlie stumbled out because of something his family had done.

He lumped his loathing for his son in with his feelings for his brother, that much was obvious, but the real person Charlie hated was himself. Why else would he stay in Carrow

Mill—where people would have no choice but to remember him? If he hated it all so much, he would have left, whether it was his home or not. On some level, Charlie *liked* being reminded of his brother's crimes, and as someone who went as far as he could to *not* know about his father, I was pretty sure that wasn't something healthy people did.

"Uh, dude?" Kevin stood by the front picture window, peering inside. "I don't know if he's home or not, but I kinda hope not."

I peered inside. It looked like it had been a normal living room or sitting area... once. Furniture was overturned, the contents of a bookshelf spilled out across the floor as loose pages were sprinkled like a garnish on the chaos.

"Call someone. Illana, or one of the Witchers."

Kevin already had his phone in hand, but he hesitated. "Not the police? Dude's not a witch anymore, not really."

"Yeah, but Luca is. And he may not use magic anymore, but he's still a witch." I went back to the front door, only this time I went straight to the knob. It turned without resistance. The door wasn't locked. "Stay out here and keep watch," I whispered. Kevin started to argue, but I silenced him by walking inside and shutting the door behind me.

He didn't follow.

I had to step over a coatrack in the foyer—who the hell had a coatrack anymore? But from the amount of dust coating each of the arms, it didn't look like the thing got much use, anyway. The living room was to my right, and there was barely any room to walk amidst all of the chaos. Both couches were overturned, end tables, even the television had been knocked over. In fact, someone had taken great pains to trash every single piece of furniture in the room. Even the wall hangings had been torn down, pictures broken and mirrors shattered.

I walked through the kitchen next, which was better in some ways, worse in others. Someone had taken all the sharp knives and dumped them into the sink, and then emptied everything else out onto the floor. I turned and tried to find another route through the house, rather than walk across the broken ceramic shards.

There was a lot of destruction, but no signs of a struggle. No blood spatter, no droplets around the dishes. It was like the house had been trashed by someone with a clinical grace, managing to break down everything room by room without giving up anything of themselves.

Did Charlie do this? There were kids running around with the Prince's infection inside them, maybe one of them had stopped by. Retaliation against Luca, maybe? But there were only a handful that knew who Luca really was, or what he'd done, and almost all of us were being watched.

Charlie, then.

I walked past a closed door in the hallway, opened it to see the eye of the storm. Luca's room. There was a team poster of the Patriots, featuring Tom Brady and Chad Ochocinco. I wouldn't have picked Luca for a sports fan, but his room suggested otherwise. The bed was made, a somber blue that belonged in the room of someone older and more mature. In fact, the room was untouched, the only bit of normalcy in the whole house.

That left two more doors at the end of the hallway. I backed out of Luca's room, and headed for the first, the door to the master, which was trashed just as much as everything else in the house. The word was *overkill.* The bed wasn't just ripped apart, it was literally *ripped apart*—pillows hacked and stabbed through-and-through, the mattress shredded, the sheets ripped into strips of fabric.

The other door, though, squeaked when I pushed it open. Charlie was sprawled along the tile floor of the bathroom, half asleep in a puddle of a creamy blue shampoo that had pooled off the side of the tub. There was destruction here too, but it looked like Charlie had passed out in the middle of it.

An empty bottle of whiskey sat to his left, not the knock-off swill I expected, but the kind of bottle that screamed expensive. None of it matched up. The house, the landscaping, the way everything must have looked before Charlie had demolished it all: it didn't match up with the man in the hospital. There, he'd been the bitter, angry drunk.

Someone had told me that Luca's mom had left, but now I wondered when. If she'd left only recently, maybe that would explain the schism. Or maybe her influence had stayed in the air like old perfume, keeping the family together on the surface.

"Whazzat?" Charlie didn't even lift his head or open his eyes, but with the stirring of his neck and the smacking of lips, he came back to life.

There was a gold coin on the bathroom counter, I leaned over and brushed my finger against it. Charlie had missed something when he'd trashed the room. The coin was faded and tarnished, more brass than gold now, with the image of a heart on one side. I flipped it over, a spade on the reverse. Some sort of playing card theme?

In the back of my head, I remembered the conversation with Kevin and Maddy, about the amusement park that had been abandoned outside of town. It must have been some sort of token, then. Maybe a keepsake from when Luca was younger.

"It's your loving nephew," I said loudly, hoping his hangover was hellacious and I, in some small way, would be able to make it worse. "What happened here, Charlie?"

"Ain't gotta neph…" he trailed off again, whether unconscious or just because he couldn't stand to vocalize the word, I couldn't say.

I waited almost five minutes before I remembered Kevin, and the phone calls. I left Charlie in the puddle of his disgrace (which smelled remarkably like Head and Shoulders) and returned to the front of the house. Illana and Adele were just pulling up in a town car.

Neither one of them looked surprised to be called out in the middle of the afternoon. "Is he alive?" Illana called out, her presence somehow managing to drop the temperature around her, so brisk that it was now actually a bit chilly.

"Drunk," I said, which was as much an explanation as it was a description of being. "The house was self-inflicted."

Adele chirped something low at Illana's side, but her words didn't carry across the driveway. Now that backup was here, and I knew there wasn't any danger, I went back inside to track down the uncle I didn't want. Charlie had managed a sitting-up position by the time I came back, a soapy blue residue staining half of his head. He was propped between the toilet and the tub, with a hand thrown over each for support.

"Remember when I said you couldn't be more pathetic?" I told him, leaning against the only spot on the sink counter that wasn't a mess of product and water. "I stand corrected."

"G'outta my house." He smacked his lips a couple of times, and I could only imagine what foul taste lurked there inside his mouth, sticking to the words like molasses.

"Not much of a house anymore, is it? You do that all by yourself, or did you have someone helping you?"

Charlie didn't answer, and I didn't exactly care, so I moved on to the reason I was really here. "You were close to his age, right? You guys went to high school together."

"Go t'hell."

"So you must have been there when the Prince came to town, right? Why didn't you ever say anything? How come no one knows what really happened?"

My questions were met with a snort and a slump.

"You're an epic kind of dick, aren't you? Cyrus saved your worthless life and killed that thing, and you let someone else take the credit."

The silence from the other half of the room was only interrupted by the occasional sniffle, throat clearing, and coughing fit.

"You never said anything. Is that how you afforded the house? Did someone pay you off after Cyrus went to the dark side? Bury the real story, pretend your brother was nothing but a monster every day of your life when you know that was a damn lie."

If it was possible for him to slump down any more, he did, and his eyes wouldn't meet mine, but I recognized the self-loathing when I saw it. I'd struck a nerve. Maybe all of them.

"Tell me what really happened, and I won't walk out of here and tell everyone what a liar you are. Tell me what Cyrus did, and we can go back to pretending he was the monster he became."

Charlie's lip curled up, and the self dropped out of his loathing. "You think you're so much smarter than the rest of us. You've got it all figured out. Your daddy was dark as sin, but ain't none of that keeping you up at night." A sudden smile, a light flaring behind something that had rotted away long before I came to town. "You know what I know, you little shit-stain? I know what your daddy was. I know all about him, and that means I know *you*. All the parts you think you carved out for yourself, but you just put the pieces together. Your daddy designed the blueprints."

He was trying to strike back, trying to get under my skin the way I'd gotten under his. I wasn't Jenna, who took every slight personally, or Justin, who felt the need to defy his heritage. My father was a monster. My cousin was a monster. And I didn't *care*. It could only affect me if I let it, and I refused.

"He let it all slide off too," Charlie said with wicked relish. "He could know horrible things, do even worse things, and it never affected him. He was a cold, little boy. Calculating. You think you know him because you read about him in a book? Daggett's boy may be the spitting image of his daddy, but you've got the soul of yours."

My leg moved on autopilot, slamming into Charlie's

stomach with every ounce of force I could muster. He collapsed around his stomach with a groan, his voice leaping an octave in a whining cry while I tried to suppress a smile.

I wasn't just like my father, and I certainly wasn't anything like any of the other Dentons. Just because we shared blood and a name didn't mean they had power over me. I wasn't anything like them.

I wasn't.

Charlie, though, he *howled* with laughter. It shook him, made his body jerk and tremble as the laughter spilled out of him like a bag full of worms, oozing out all over the place. I backed up, rather than let that laughter anywhere near me.

"The … the Prince," I said, licking my lips and struggling against the faintness in my voice. *I kicked him and he thought it was funny. The funniest joke I never told.* "Tell me what happened."

"Don't you already know?" His was a sly look, marked with all the knowledge I found myself wanting no matter what. My fist clenched at my side, and it was a surprise.

"He never told," Charlie confided. "He liked it better that way. All those dark secrets, locked up inside to keep him company."

"You're lying," I said, my eyes narrowed. "You were close. Everyone knows that. If he told anyone, he would have told you."

"But why would I tell *you*? He'd hate the sight of you. Last thing my brother and I had in common. We both hate the sight of the things we spawned."

"You're a psychotic little fuck."

Charlie coughed again, a hack into a loose fist that left it dripping with a lifetime of bad decisions. "It's got something you want, doesn't it?" He smiled around grimy teeth. "That's how they do it. You'll do anything for it, just like he would. Monsters make you crave something so bad you'd sell out your own brother. He didn't care what he had to do—he was getting what he wanted. You'll do the same. Ain't that right, boy? You don't care about anything except what that little Prince has been whispering in your ear."

This time, when I kicked him, I knew exactly what I was doing.

TWENTY-FOUR

Missing: Savannah Rowe, 17. Last seen by her sister Alice at Carrow Mill High on April 14th. She was wearing blue jeans and a black leather jacket. Please call the CM police department if sighted.

Police blotter
April 16–April 23

"You're supposed to be the levelheaded one," Illana said half an hour later in Charlie's living room. Some measure of order had been restored to the room. The furniture was righted, though the collective destruction had been shifted into corners and out of the way. The front yard was occupied by a half-dozen Witchers, most of them barely out of their beer pong days.

I ignored the disapproval in her voice. No one had been particularly pleased to find Charlie hunched over, clutching his stomach and groaning about assault charges. Then again, they weren't surprised either.

"He's not going to tell you anything." I took up a seat on the arm of the couch, resting my feet on the coffee table. Adele clucked at me in disappointment, but the look faded when I offered her a simple smile. Like it or not, she was a girl, and girls liked it when I smiled. It was a weapon I didn't use often enough.

"That's not the same thing as 'he doesn't know anything.'" Illana turned her own version of a smile on me: tight, shrewd lips and a hint of calculating steel in her eyes. "I've been told I'm a bit more influential than a teenage boy with a tendency to roughhouse."

"But only slightly," Adele offered helpfully from the love seat she'd claimed. The chair was so big that it swallowed her up, giving her a certain Alice in Wonderland vibe where the furniture was too big for the person using it.

"So they say." But the moment for levity faded quickly, and Illana clasped her hands in front of her, rocking them back and forth briefly as she eyed the broken shell of a man sitting across from her. I hadn't realized at first that each of us had taken a different side: Illana across from Charlie, and Adele and I on either side of them. Adele's eyes twinkled at me from across the coffee table, as if realizing the same thing I had.

"I told the shit-st—" Charlie swallowed down the profanity, and then swallowed again for good measure. "I told the *boy* that I don't know anything. Cyrus never told me nothing."

"Now that's not true," Illana said, unleashing the rarest weapon in her arsenal. Kindness. "You and he were close. Isn't that right, Adele?"

"That's right," the woman agreed, her feet dangling off the floor.

"Almost like brothers." It took me a moment to understand the strange note in Illana's voice. She was *teasing*. There were all sorts of weird things happening today.

"We hated each other," Charlie spat. "Never hated no one more."

"Double negative." Adele grinned at Illana. I almost expected her to conjure up a box of cookies, spilling a fistful of crumbs into her lap. "He *could* hate someone more."

"Tell me when you decided to hate him." Illana leaned forward, and her blue eyes were suddenly strong and bright. I could feel something like magic in the air, making the air hum, though no one spoke a spell. "Was it when you slept with his girlfriend? When you stole her away?" The woman canted her head. "When she *died*? When you married her sister? I know Cyrus is tangled up in there somewhere. Just tell me which thread to pull."

I ... what? In just a handful of words, Illana had created a dozen different things about Cyrus Denton, images about how he fit into Carrow Mill, how he fit into his family. And just like that ... I could feel him becoming more real.

That was exactly what I didn't want. I didn't care what they were like when they were teenagers. I certainly didn't care that Charlie might have stolen my father's girlfriend, or that she died. That he'd married her *sister*. The woman who must have been Luca's mother.

Jesus, what was wrong with these people? Was this the effect of Moonset, or was their family drama to blame? Did

Cyrus fall in line with Sherrod Daggett because of what his brother did to him? Betrayed and hurt by blood, he reached out for a family that had been created for him, allowed them to close ranks around him, and give him a new purpose.

Had Sherrod used that information to manipulate my father? Did my father even ever need manipulating?

The thoughts kept racing through my head like trains set for collision. Each one narrowly missed striking the next, but eventually they would collide and the fireworks would be intense.

"You use an awful lot of words just to say you're a bitch," Charlie said sourly.

I was up off the couch in an instant, though it was hard to say whether I was defending the honor of a woman I didn't particularly like or just taking the chance to hit Charlie for a third time and make it really count.

Illana made a tut-tut-tutting sound and waggled a finger. "It's a compliment, Malcolm. Small men call a woman a bitch because they're afraid to say that she scares them."

Then you're definitely that. But at least I was smart enough not to say it out loud. She smirked, probably reading the thought right off my face.

"Tell me what really happened, Charles. Tell me, and we all go away. Otherwise, I will drown every part of your world. I will have people in your home, at your job, waiting in your bar every night. Even that restaurant you go to on Thursdays. We will be everywhere, and we won't stop. Because this stopped being your town, and your home, the minute your son took up his uncle's mantle."

For a second, Charlie wavered, and I blinked in surprise. It was going to happen. Illana would break through his walls. He would split apart at the seams and admit that he'd treated his son badly but it wasn't deserved. That he was scared, but the good man underneath wanted to help. That he knew something crucial.

But it was only a moment. And there was still too much liquid courage in his veins, giving Charlie a backbone of Scotch and stubbornness. Whatever he'd been once upon a time, years trapped in his skin had rotted Charlie Denton through.

"It keep *you* up at night? Knowing that you and Robert pulled the trigger and Moonset was the cost? *You* caused this, lady. All of you, smug little Covens. Whoring yourselves out to each other, protecting your legacies."

Illana gracefully rose to her feet. "Cyrus turned to the blackest of magicks to escape his family. You did that. Not us."

Charlie surged up, but that was exactly what Illana wanted. Something small was in her hand, but at his first movement she flung her wrist, and a telescopic baton sprung to life. With three swift, economical strikes she clubbed the back of one knee, deflected an arm, and then slapped it across his windpipe and held it there, bracing it between both hands.

"Now you're going to tell me everything I want to know," she said calmly, somehow managing to overpower the drunk despite her age, "or I'm going to give your nephew his first lesson in how to beat a confession out of someone. I'm confident we'll all learn a thing or two. I can be quite creative."

She didn't have to make good on the threat. Charlie talked. A lot.

Charlie told us all about how the senior class came under the Prince's spell, and how Sherrod and Cyrus were the first to notice. But when they went to the authorities, looking for help, they were written off and ignored. Moonset was newly formed, and they didn't have the clout to make anyone take them seriously.

Moonset became Cyrus's world. And it wasn't Charlie's fault, he claimed, that he was there to pick up the pieces. Then there was a three-day blackout, and Cyrus didn't come home. Two days into it, when he finally showed up battered and bloody, it was to announce that an Abyssal Prince had come to town, and now it was dead.

But in all the chaos, Charlie lost the love of his life when she ran from the darkness in Carrow Mill. Savannah took off on the first bus out of town and never looked back. Heartbroken, Charlie married her younger sister a few years later, but it was never the same.

Charlie never knew anything more than that. He'd always believed the stories that Robert Cooper had saved the day.

Or so he claimed.

"He spins an interesting story," Adele said when we met outside after. Two Witchers stayed behind to keep an eye on Charlie, while the rest prepared to leave.

"You think he's lying?" Illana asked, slipping on a pair of sunglasses. The afternoon sun wasn't too bad, but she looked a bit more pale than she had earlier.

"I've always found that life is hardly an orderly pursuit. People are the ones who trim threads, who make tangles into knots and shave away all the things that don't fit. They want things to make sense, and I think Charlie makes quite a bit of sense."

"He's lying," I said with conviction.

"Oh?" Now Illana was amused. "Please, share your expertise with the rest of the class."

I knew she was mocking me, but I didn't give a crap. "Notice how helpful he was? What are the odds he had a change of heart? He's a dick, he'd happily tell you a story peppered full of lies just to mess with you. He doesn't care if anyone gets hurt. He just likes misery."

"I agree with the boy," Adele said happily. "I think I'll stick around, see what else I can jog loose from the man. I think there's more to the girl's disappearance than he's saying. I think we might have found the Abyssal's host after all."

Illana tapped on her lower lip. "Get in the car, Malcolm. I've been meaning to pay a visit to an old friend of your father's. I think having you around might prove useful in this instance."

———

Illana drove the same way she did everything else: with a cool demeanor, incredible poise, and a soft undercurrent of terror that she was going to kill everyone in her path. She drove into the center of town and parked near the curio shop.

"Why'd you want to bring me along?" I asked, once the car was stopped. Illana didn't seem in any rush to get out, and I followed her lead.

She held up a hand, displaying all five fingers towards me, wagging one with each point. "He's a witch I've never heard of. Born and raised in Carrow Mill. He stays under the radar and I dislike that. He was a friend of your father's. You might shake something loose without knowing it."

"But I've already met him," I said absently. "Never even looked at me like I was familiar."

"That doesn't mean anything," she said, though there was a faraway look in her eyes. "You look more like your cousin than your father. He might not have realized."

I followed her inside, ducking my head down as we passed through the front door. The curio shop was about what I remembered. Ten acres worth of garbage packed into a half acre's worth of space. Dogs played poker next to cats in togas, and there was a buffalo head hanging on the wall with a trio of silver necklaces hanging from its snout. A ceremonial-looking knife was stabbed into a small end table etched with elephants so that the knife passed right through one of the elephant's eyes. Chessboards were filled with something on every square: crystals, keys, and even a Hershey's Kiss.

"Hi there, can I help you?" A red-haired man popped up from behind the counter like a jack-in-the-box. The only way the effect could have been stronger was if the welcoming chime had actually played "Pop Goes the Weasel."

"Matthew Dugard?" Everything Illana was screamed "Police." Tasteful pantsuit, hair pulled from her face, serious tone, and severe expression.

"Yes," the man said slowly, letting the word stretch out for a span of seconds. "Can I help you?"

"You knew my friend's father," she said, indicating a hand towards me. Like I would really be friends with a woman like

Illana Bryer. A woman old enough to be my mother's mother. Or maybe my mother's grandmother.

Mr. Dugard looked towards me, but there was no recognition in his eye when he shrugged. "Could have."

"You went to school with him," Illana prompted. Normally she wasn't one for dragging things out. She liked to cut right to the heart of the matter.

"I went to school with a lot of people. School's big enough for more than one at a time." His tone was pleasant, easy. Whoever he was, he wasn't intimidated by her. That alone was enough to make me think that Charlie was wrong, and this man had barely even known my father. Unless he wasn't a witch at all: that might still be a possibility.

Illana didn't seem to agree. "Town full of Witchers and you don't know who he is? That seems odd."

At the word, the man stilled, like she'd said something foul. Satanist instead of Witcher, maybe. More than the fake smile, the phony cheer, this was a real reaction. Something he couldn't mask behind a shopkeeper's veneer.

"The Denton boy," the man said, studying me closer. "Right, yes. You were in here a couple months ago."

So he *did* know who we were. "Your dad went a little nuts last time."

The man shrugged. "My dad spent four years tormenting and being tormented by Sherrod Daggett. His doppelganger walks in the door, what's he supposed to think? Senility's a bitch, but sometimes remembering is worse."

"I'm afraid you're a new one to me," Illana said, her voice as soft as pillows. I didn't trust it for a minute. Neither did Matthew. He stiffened up behind the counter, and then made a show of relaxing his body, spreading his arms. Communicating without words that he had nothing to hide. "Exactly how is it you live in this city and I don't know you. I know *all* of the witches."

The man sighed, ran a hand through his frizzled red hair, and turned his head to the side. He pointed to the plastic device curled up inside his ear—a hearing aid. I hadn't noticed the last time I was here. "Not a lot of call for partially deaf witches," he said. I expected him to sound bitter about it, but he wasn't. To him it wasn't anything traumatic, just a fact of life.

"Your father taught you?"

He shook his head. "My mother. Elizabeth. They divorced when I was young. Elizabeth Raines."

Illana inclined her head, though I couldn't tell if that meant she believed him, or she was still skeptical. She didn't press the issue any further, though. "How long since you started losing your hearing?"

"Little bit all my life. It keeps falling away like bread-crumbs, gets a little worse after time. The hearing aids make it impossible to cast. I can't hear the words right, so I can't repeat them with the same inflections."

Magic was all about the mouth and the ears. Words spoken and heard. Inflections memorized and tasted on the tongue. If one of those senses was damaged, then it would make the whole process harder. I'd heard of witches who were born with problems: ones that couldn't speak, others that couldn't hear. It had to be incredibly difficult, being able to touch something they couldn't fully master.

At least, I assumed it would have to be difficult. For me, not much would have changed.

"How is it that no one knows about you," Illana pressed. "You are still a witch. Still a part of our society regardless of what challenges you face."

The man looked at her and laughed, and then hesitated like he'd heard the joke wrong. He sobered quickly when her expression only sharpened. "I'm not a witch. Not really. I'm not in a coven, but I'm not a Solitaire either. I don't use magic, so I don't participate in the government. If I fell through the cracks somewhere, I'm sorry, but that's not my fault. As far as the Congress is concerned, I'm useless, therefore I don't exist."

The speech only managed to intensify the cold front warring across Illana's face. "No witch is useless to the Congress. Or do you not realize to whom you are speaking?"

"You didn't even know my name yesterday," the man said sadly. "I'm not one of you. And claiming me now doesn't do either one of us any measure of good. I accepted that I was an outcast a long time ago. I keep my head down, stay away from trouble, and live a normal life. That's fine enough for me. Nothing shameful in it at all."

I noticed he hadn't admitted whether or not he knew who she was. Illana's expression changed—softened, really—as I think she came to the same conclusion. "I am sorry if we have failed you," she said stiffly. "But that is not actually why we are here."

He smiled. "I didn't think you were. What can I do to help, ma'am?"

"You went to school with Cyrus Denton," Illana said,

returning the attention where it belonged. On her. "You were his friend. So now you're going to tell me everything you remember about the Abyssal Prince that came to Carrow Mill, and what really happened to it."

The man was quiet for a long time, still in a way that said he was somewhere else. There was a faint shimmer in his eyes when they focused again, and he nodded once. Sharply. "If you'd be so kind as to turn the sign and lock the front door," he said, looking towards me.

I went back to the entrance, turned the lock, and flipped the sign to Closed. When I came back to the counter, a crystal decanter was on the counter, and the man's hands shook as he poured himself a tumbler of courage.

"You're looking for the body," he said slow and clear. "Now let me convince you not to."

TWENTY-FIVE

Diana killed because it was fun. Sherrod killed
to send a message. Cy Denton? He was the worst.
Sherrod said "kill" and he did it, and never
asked why. People meant nothing to him.

....

Jack Wyatt (S)
Carrow Mill, New York—
From *Moonset: A Dark Legacy*

Matthew threw back his glass, swallowing down the amber liquor, then poured a second glass and repeated the gesture.

"I know the stories. Everyone says Moonset summoned that thing. But there's no way. Cyrus and I were close—maybe not so much after the Coven formed, but before that, definitely. I hung out with him and Charles—sorry, Charlie—all the time. Cy was the only kid who didn't make fun of me for my hearing aids. Back then I had to wear two, really ugly things.

"No one's seen an Abyssal Prince in a hundred years, so the adults in town, they never believed them. But Cy and the others, they wouldn't give up. They did all the research and investigating on their own. They monitored the rest of the school, trying to find a pattern. And eventually, they figured out who the Abyssal was.

"I don't know what happened when they fought it, but they came back different. They saw things, maybe did things, I don't know. What happened changed them all like they were soldiers coming back from war. I always thought that thing got in their heads. Maybe it didn't make them evil overnight, but it could have been the first step. Got them all mixed up on the path that ended ... " He scratched the back of his neck. "Well, we all know how that ended."

"This isn't relevant to my questions," Illana said coolly. She didn't like when people talked about *why* Moonset went dark. To Illana, all that mattered was that they *had*. Wondering why didn't make anything more clear. I was with her on that—I didn't want to speculate on where our parents had gone wrong. It wasn't my concern.

"It should be relevant, because they were always jumpy afterwards. I think that whatever happened, they didn't end it. Just stopped it for a while. And that someday it was going to come back to bite them in the ass ... only it's not their asses on the line anymore."

My father was already too real for me as it was.

"I don't know what I can tell you. There weren't any witnesses, and Cy was like a bank vault when he didn't want to talk. They crawled home to recover and meanwhile some hotshot guy came to town and took credit for everything, and they let him. But if there's a chance that thing could come back, you have to back off."

"The Abyssal needed a host," I said slowly, caught up on another thread.

"Yes?" Illana turned to me. I turned back to Matthew.

"Charlie's girlfriend. That's the weekend she disappeared, isn't it?"

"You mean Savannah?" Matthew shook his head. "I don't know who you've been talking to, but she's not dead. She took off. Left town and never looked back. Charlie ended things, said his brother was more important. She ran, but it was too late. Cy never forgave his brother for running her off."

"Charlie was quite clear. The girl is dead, not a runaway." Illana tapped a finger against the counter, a solid press and twist like there was something underneath she was trying to squash.

"You talked to Charlie already?" Matthew looked surprised. "Then I don't know why you're here talking to me. Didn't he tell you all this already?"

"If he had," Illana said witheringly, "do you really think we would be here now?"

The man scratched the back of his neck again and glanced towards the rear of the store. "I don't know what you want from me. This was all so long ago. I'm sorry I can't be more help, really, but I need to check on my dad. He gets antsy if he doesn't see *Wheel of Fortune.*"

Illana looked at me for a moment, then shrugged. "If something else comes up, we'll be back."

The man nodded immediately, and then realized his face

was blank and expressionless. The feigned smile slid back on with a practiced air. "Of course, ma'am. There's a stack of business cards by the door. Call any time."

Illana waited for his back to turn before she rolled her eyes. I stifled a snort at her irritation.

"Oh, hey," he called right before we left. "He never told me where it was, but him and the other Moonset guys had some sort of secret hideout. Some place they'd always go to get away from everything in town. I don't know if that helps or not, but there might be something there to help you figure out what happened."

———

Illana dropped me off back at Charlie's where I'd left my car. Adele was on the front porch, a pair of knitting needles in either hand though it didn't appear she was actually knitting anything. She smiled and waved one of them in the air. Illana didn't stay, pulling out of the driveway almost before I had fully exited the vehicle.

At home that night, everyone wanted to talk about Justin. How he was doing, when he was coming home. There were subtle comments about how lonely he'd been all afternoon, and how they'd tried calling to see where I was, but I never picked up.

Jenna raised her eyebrow in a question at one point, and I shook my head. Now wasn't the time to talk about it anyway.

Despite the way the week opened with excitement, the rest of it was a disappointment. There were no new leads on the dead Abyssal, no sightings of the current Prince, and no changes in the status of anything between. The school was running into a shortage of detention slips, though, as public displays of "inappropriateness" skyrocketed. There were at least half a dozen fights in the morning before school and at least one or two after.

Those among us with magic had taken to keeping to our own groups. Normally, Maddy had a group of girls around her, but with the violence in the halls, the witches had banded together. I used the opportunity to rope Kevin into helping me start the basics of set construction, although that was mostly me trying to keep him from severing a limb or stapling his foot to the floor. Set design was easy, the construction part was moderately difficult. The fact that my assistant could throw a perfect spiral pass on the field yet couldn't connect a hammer to nail without a body part in the way was disturbing.

But the worst part of all was that there was no sign of the Prince. I knew he had to be planning something, but had no idea what. The longer that his reappearance took, the more my nerves strained.

When I pulled back up to the school that evening, cutting around the back lane past the football field, which would put me right near the auditorium entrance, I didn't notice the flashing lights at first. But as I walked towards the door I couldn't help but notice the reflection of red and blue lights against the houses across the street from the school. Instead of heading inside, I walked around to the front of the building, past all the side entrances that were no doubt locked up by now.

There were three different police cars and an ambulance parked in front of the school, headlights blazing right at the front entrance. In addition, there were half a dozen bodies standing off to one side: teachers in their off time, administrators in yoga pants and ratty shirts. Only one or two students, really. A sobbing girl who couldn't seem to catch a breath for all of her shaking and gasping. And another girl, calm and big-eyed behind a pair of glasses, watching everything go down with perfect calm.

"What happened?" I asked. The eyeglasses girl looked at me and blinked several times. If possible, the crying girl started gasping even louder between sobs.

"He broke into the office, trying to change her grades." She nodded first towards one of the police cars, where a silhouette sat glumly in the backseat, slumped over and still. The second nod was for the crying girl, and I guess it made a little more sense now. Her Romeo had gotten busted trying to do her a solid. What could she do but weep?

"And the ambulance?"

"He couldn't figure out the password, so he put his hand through the monitor. They say he's lucky he didn't electrocute himself. I guess that's happened before."

"He-he-he." Each hysterical exhale was punctuated by a wheezing sound, and it took many of them strung together before I realized the crier was trying to say something, but she couldn't manage anything more than the first word.

He was doing it for me. He did it for love. He's my knight in shining handcuffs. It didn't really matter what she was going for, I knew where it ended.

"You should get her out of here. Unless the police are planning to interrogate her." Standing around while her boyfriend sat in the back of a cop car wasn't going to do anyone any good. Especially not with the current brand of crazy going around. She might decide that a jailbreak was the only acceptable alternative.

"I don't even know her," the girl said distastefully. "I just came over to see what all the crazy was about."

"Seriously?" I stared at the girl until she started to squirm, looking quickly towards me and then away. Then back again, to make sure I was still watching her. Finally she groaned, threw her hands out and grabbed the other girl by the arm and dragged her away.

People were really losing it. Or maybe that's how people actually were: come to watch the train wreck, but God forbid anyone ask you to grab some bandages for the wounded.

The auditorium was almost empty when I finally made my way back to the rear of the school and entered the building. Brice had it arranged with the janitorial staff that the auditorium doors would stay unlocked until eight or nine; after that, we could leave whenever we wanted, but we couldn't get back inside unless someone else was already there.

Almost empty. The Prince lounged on the edge of the stage, silver hair now streaked with black, like the photo negative of someone going gray. Golden skin was looking a little sallow, pink in some places, less human. And more makeup.

There were no crazy backdrops. No castles or asylums or creepy surroundings. Just him and me. His hands were braced on either side of him, ready to push off the stage at a moment's notice. He watched me warily as I approached, and even more carefully once I stopped. The Prince was the enemy. I couldn't forget that.

"I am very cross with you," he said clearly.

The lights in the building went out, and darkness consumed me.

————————

The lights came back on in a one-two clang. Not lights. Spotlights. One was trained on me, and I looked up into the stands to see who was manning the equipment, but it was too hard to see. The other, as I turned to look, was focused on the Prince, who now lounged in a hideously ornate throne, equal parts gold and human bones. Whoever designed the throne had a sense of humor: the legs were made from femurs, long and ashen, while the arms were made from tibias and fibulas and phalanges at the tips. And reigning above his head, a baker's dozen of human skulls, each far smaller than I would have expected.

Until I realized they were the skulls of children.

"Just for once can't you cut the theatrics?"

Puzzlement ran across the Prince's face unchecked. "But we are in a theater." To him, it made the most perfect kind of sense. That was what one did in a theater.

"This is an *auditorium*. A place where you go so people can hear you."

He appeared to think that over for a few seconds before tucking the whole conversation away. "Then hear me: I'm very cross with you, my champion," he said, retreating to a stern face that seemed hard to hold onto. The Prince was used to smiling, laughing. Levity. He could do anger and rage as well, but the emotions never sat so easily on his face. Then again, as he planned to slaughter three dozen Witchers, he was laughing and having a grand time.

"I'm doing what you told me to do. Trying to find out what happened. It takes time."

The Prince smiled slowly, but it wasn't the usual smile of joy that I saw. Now that smile carried *thoughtfulness, seething frustration,* and *calculation.* "I thought you might say that." He snapped his fingers, the sound almost immediately drowned out by a third clang of metal as yet another spotlight lit up.

I spun around, searching for it only to realize that it had come on just behind me and to the left. The far side of the auditorium: the only other entrance. Someone walked in slowly, barefoot and in thick black frames I'd never seen before. Brice, blue-eyed and sleep-rumpled.

He could have been a model, especially now, black hair sweeping into his eyes, his cheeks still stained red from where they'd pressed against a pillow.

"What's your name, pet?" The Prince was all smiles, welcoming like a sunny day.

"Brice," he said, and his voice was deep and gravely. The casual confidence I'd seen in him before was still there, but it was a skipping record: every so often, there was a jarring moment where his eyes unfocused and his eyes grew wide and worried.

"Hello, Brice," the Prince said formally. He extended a hand towards me. "Do you know Malcolm?"

"I know him," the other boy nodded. "He's new."

"He's seen you too," the Prince confided.

"Really?" The news made Brice happy, an easy smile ran across his face.

"What are you doing?" I could feel it like the heat of the spotlights against my face. "Stop it."

233

"But we haven't even gotten started." The Prince waved his hands with a flourish, then took a small bow. "The pleasure is all mine, Brice."

Brice smiled, the confidence now fully stripped from him, his aura of calm washed away. More than once he reached up to scratch his face, a nervous habit that I could now see for what it was.

"Do you love him?" The Prince continued. Dogged intent and a lilting *curiosity* framed the question, a thing that was both innocent and judgment at the same time.

"Who? Malcolm?" Brice scoffed. "I don't know him."

"Do you love him?" The Prince repeated. This time, there was more force to his words, a tangled cadence of words and thoughts and emotions and intent.

The quizzical look on Brice's face grew stronger.

"*Do you love him?*"

"Stop this!" I demanded.

"No," Brice said, but there was less resistance this time. "No, I ... I mean, I don't think ... "

"Think about it." The Prince focused his entire awareness around a boy who wasn't even supposed to be here tonight. A boy who was innocent of whatever dark designs the Prince had in mind.

Designs that were slow to take root, but quickly spread once they did. "I mean, I think I could ... " Brice kept trailing off, listening to something that was both above and below the audible words being spoken. Messages to the subconscious, placating the ego and the superego. Faintly, I could hear a trace of music in the air, notes I couldn't quite pick out.

"I…I think I do." The slack confusion began to fade, and the confidence returned. Brice smiled, all teeth and brilliant. "I *do* love him." My heart dropped into my stomach, because this wasn't a confession I wanted. Not like this. Not *ever* like this.

The Prince's lip twitched upward at the side, the most hideous attempt at a smile I'd ever seen.

"Stop it." I walked out of my spotlight, or at least I tried. It followed me as I ran and merged when I caught up with the Prince. Our lights together were twice as bright, but I turned my back to it. Facing him. "You don't have to do this."

"You think you can just send me away?" The Prince turned to face me, and the spotlights caught his irises, making them flare into brilliant yellow suns. His were the eyes of an animal, not the eyes of a human being. He carried a predator's feral rage and it smothered me. "You think you can just call on your Moonset magics and banish me like *I am some sort of bother!*" His voice rose to a shriek, and it battered my eardrums louder than any concert.

Around us the walls splintered, started to crack. A snowfall of plaster seeped from the ceiling. He would bring the whole room down around us. "*I am of the blood of the old Aos Si, the Court of Kingmakers. I am a Prince of the Abyss and the scourge of Hamelin. My songs make devils weep and quelled the rage of the Undying. You do not dismiss me! I will not be so humiliated!*"

His words were a thousand lashes of fire against my back, flagellation for every sin I'd ever committed against his name. Agony awoke inside of me, and I fought for the breath to scream.

I took a step back, nearly stumbling to the ground. I managed to land on my knees, to press my hands against the floor and kept myself upright. Somewhat. Sounds ratcheted through my head, clawing apart my eardrums. His fury hollowed me out on the inside, and I almost wept in the face of it. Every muscle, every tendon in my body quelled under the fire of the Prince's wrath.

And then it was over. Above me, I could hear the Prince's breathing grow faster as he struggled to push down his feelings.

"Yes," he said, "that was quite unbecoming." The Prince reached down, grabbed my arm, and hauled me back up to my feet. Only he pulled too far, and my feet dangled inches above the ground. "Oh," he said, as if realizing for the first time that he was taller than I. "Bother." And then he dropped me back to my feet.

This time I remained standing.

"Brice, my darling," the Prince said, taking care to smooth out any wrinkles to his shirt that the tantrum might have caused.

"Yes, my Prince?"

The Prince looked slyly at me and then that hideous smile returned, slow at the corners like it could somehow trick me into ignoring it. "Malcolm loves you too."

Brice's entire face brightened, the rush of joy filling him so full he could barely stand still and contain it. He moved tiny little movements, jerks of hands and feet and shifting weight back and forth between legs. He looked about a second away from fist pumping the sky in triumph.

"But ... " and here the Prince let his word hang in the air, thick like the noose I knew it to be.

"But?" Brice was guileless, unaware of where things were heading.

"Please," I whispered, because that was all that was left of me. "Don't."

"Did you bring the knife like I asked?"

Shaky hands pulled the knife out of a back pocket. It was a big knife, something straight out of a restaurant kitchen. In the light trained upon him, it glowed like a forest fire.

"Malcolm would like it so much if you were to bleed for him."

"No he wouldn't," I shouted immediately, but all protests died once the Prince clasped his hand around my shoulder. At the simplest touch, every muscle in my body contracted, flexed and tensed and surged to impulses that didn't come from me. I tried to move my mouth, my hands, my anything, but they were under the Prince's control. I was his puppet.

Brice looked down at the knife, and then back up at the Prince. He nodded slowly. "You're sure?"

The Prince's smile was warm and his words carried *contented* and *proud* across the room. The feelings swept over Brice and his smile became less strained. More easy. "Wherever you think is best," the Prince added. "Though Malcolm loves danger. He enjoys a threat. So be sure to give him a show."

No, I wanted to scream. *Don't do this.* But Brice stripped off his pajama pants and his tee shirt, leaving him clad in only a pair of black and blue designer briefs.

I could feel the Prince's avid interest as his breath swept past my ear. Brice studied his body, piece by piece, looking for the best place to start. Eventually, his arm dropped down at his side, and he nodded to the Prince.

"Malcolm is scared for you," the Prince murmured.

"Don't worry." Brice gave me a small, trusting smile. The

kind of smile I might have wanted once, but I'd never earned it. I wanted to *earn* it. "I bust the curve in AP Anatomy." For a moment, I was a fool, convinced everything was going to be okay. That Brice could defy the Prince in the same way I'd managed. That he was too smart, too studious, to be in danger. Because he might have to cut himself, but he knew the anatomy. He knew where to cut, and where to avoid, in order to not bleed out in seconds.

For a moment, my heart was so full of hope and relief that I strained to bursting. If even one person could resist the Prince's song, then it wasn't all for nothing. We could fight him together.

Brice didn't flinch as the knife sliced across his skin. There was nothing but a pleasant gasp as the femoral artery released a spray of blood that carried all the way to the tips of my shoes, staining them crimson.

I'd never worked up the courage to get to know Brice outside of the play. And now I never would. He dropped to the floor. The smile didn't fade from his face even though the light from his eyes did.

"Draw the curtain on the second act," the Prince said coldly, snapping his fingers.

The throne vanished. The lights returned. The Prince was gone.

The body was not.

TWENTY-SIX

*Sensitive witches can read things in the Coven
bond and know when trouble is happening. But
seeing the future before it happens is dangerous,
rare, and deadly. Almost always there is a dark
origin to that power, a pact made and bound
in the bloodlines. It never ends well.*

....

From a lecture series on
rare gifts among witches

Quinn beat the cops to the scene, despite the fact that the
police station was only a few blocks away. "The Prince?" he
asked quietly, even though it wasn't a question.

"The Prince," I agreed.

There was drama once the officers arrived. A boy dead
and bled out before they'd arrived, me with the blood-soaked

skin and clothes. Quinn, who was *obviously* not a student, yet hanging around like he had every right to be there. But it was drama that the Witchers made disappear, with a few pointed looks and a lot of magic.

It wasn't the first time they'd interfered in a police investigation. It wasn't even the first time they'd interfered in a *homicide* investigation. There was the trail of bodies back in Kentucky, and several since we'd come to New York.

"If you've got any more tricks up your sleeve," Quinn said quietly while his eyes focused on the investigation around us, "now would be the time to pull them out."

"If it was that easy, don't you think I would have?"

I knew Illana would tell Quinn everything that I'd confided in her. More than anyone, he was the one she trusted. They weren't even technically related—he was Robert Cooper's grandson, and she was Robert's second wife. At best, she was his step-grandmother. But it didn't seem like either one of them acknowledged the difference.

"And what about him?" Quinn asked, nodding his head towards Brice. "What's the story there?"

"He was just…a friend or something," I said. I was dubious about Brice. I didn't really know him all that well, and he was either conveniently intrusive or just dogged in latching onto new people. "The Prince wanted his message personalized."

There was a disconnect as Quinn's eyebrows shifted in one direction with his mouth turned in another, a salsa dance or a tango of movement as he tried to pull together a response. "That's fine," he managed a second later. He looked a little constipated, but then treading the love lives of people only a few years younger than him was probably incredibly awkward. "Did you find any leads on what really happened to Kore?"

"Not as such." I wiped my hands on my jeans, but the only thing it did was smear the colors into my skin. "The Abyssal has a host, though, I know that much. I think he might be using Luca somehow. That's why no one can get him to wake up, because the Prince is holding him captive. The Abyssals *did* protect him when the farmhouse started coming down."

"So what do you want to do?" Quinn asked.

Why was he asking me? I wasn't an expert. I was the least educated of my siblings and probably the least talented witch in the entire town. I was the last person who should be making the decisions.

They say Cyrus liked to take orders too. The thought spurred me to say something, anything. "Isn't there a test? Something you can do to see if he's the Prince's butt monkey?"

Quinn spread his hands out in front of him. "You saw what happened the last time I went against that thing."

I was too tired to glare at him. "I like you better when you're monosyllabic."

"Funny, I was just going to say the same thing." Quinn's expression grew serious. "I'll have someone head to the hospital to check Luca over again. But we should keep looking at alternatives. The Abyssal could be anyone, and they might not even know it. They could be walking around, completely unaware that there's a demon in their head."

———

Jenna was on the end of the bed when I woke up the next morning. "Huh?" I sat halfway up, trying to see through the haze of a glorious sleep and then being unceremoniously ripped from it. At first she was just a pale, black blob, a gargoyle someone had left by accident.

At least that seemed far more likely than Jenna herself being in my room. Voluntarily.

"Whuzzat?" My head dropped back to the pillow and I yanked the comforter over my head. Blessed warmth started to return, seeping back into my skin.

It didn't last long. The covers were yanked off, and now the gargoyle was perched above me, scowling.

"Something's wrong with Cole," the gargoyle said. "Again."

I slapped my hand against the nightstand three different times before I managed to smack against my phone. With the treasure in hand, I burrowed back down under my covers and winced at the light.

"It's only eight thirty," I muttered. "Can't something be wrong with Cole after eleven?"

"He's been up since five."

Oh, Christ. It was supposed to be Saturday. After getting home last night, I'd laid awake for hours staring at the ceiling, trying to think of anything other than Brice in that auditorium, and how callous the Prince had been. The questions had been the fuel that kept everything running. *How long until he comes after someone else? Will he keep killing people if I don't solve this fast enough?*

"Coffee."

The sound of a cup settled just to my right. "Black like

your heart," Jenna confirmed with an understated smile. Her hair was down and in her face, fresh from sleep and just a little poofy. It must have been serious if she came over without putting on any makeup first.

"What happened?"

"There's a girl in his gym class. I'm not sure about the details. I don't know if there *are* any details."

I stared at her for a moment, then sipped at the coffee. Once I realized it wasn't scalding hot, I downed the whole thing in a single motion. There wasn't enough coffee in the world. "You think it's the Abyssal's spell?"

"I think he got up and left sometime this morning before anyone else was awake," Jenna said simply. "They did the last bed check around five. He disappeared sometime after that."

I climbed out of bed, all thoughts of sleep faded like my dreams. "Let's go," I grumbled.

We went through Cole's room and the rest of the house, even asked Bailey for information, but there was no sign of where he headed. No clue as to what he had planned.

"You're *sure* he's about to do something bad?" I asked for about the thirtieth time.

"It's Cole," Jenna fired back, and really that was all she had to say.

"Has he been acting weird?"

Jenna favored me with a dark look, while Bailey coughed her way into the conversation. We both turned toward her.

"He keeps talking about some teacher. But he wouldn't tell me anything about her. Just kept saying I wouldn't understand."

"We can handle this," Jenna said a moment later, forehead wrinkled in thought. "Malcolm and I tapped into the Coven bond when the Witchers were getting beat down. If the three of us work together, we should be able to find him."

I scrubbed a hand over my face. *More magic.* "Have you ever done that before?"

She pointed a finger in my direction with a very firm, "Don't start." And then, "Bailey, help me move the coffee table." Together, the two girls cleared a space in the living room. We sat in a circle, close enough that our knees were touching, Jenna to my left, and Bailey to my right.

"Close your eyes. Concentrate." Once again, Jenna was taking the lead. I think she liked it, the chance to be the one in charge, the one who made the decisions. Ever since Justin's attack, she had thrived. As horrible as it was to think, maybe the distance between them would do her some good. Force her to grow up and stand on her own.

"In class, they talked about finding your common ground. But we lose more of it every day," Jenna spoke quietly, each word slow and smooth. "You can feel it, can't you? We're falling apart, and *things* are coming between us. Luca. The Abyssal. We have to trust each other. All we have is each other."

Unlike the last time, when it had taken a confession of things I didn't want to dwell upon, this time I fell into the space Jenna's words carved out easily. The Coven bond was there, light and elastic and wrapping around the three of us like a cocoon. And above it, around it, were the other rings. The other layers.

Now that I knew they were there, I could feel them, feel the way they interacted with each of us and with each other. The circle of tar and chains was a counterpoint for a circle of ozone force, kept active and in motion by their repelling forces.

Moonset hadn't just crafted one bond to keep us together. There were many of them. And there, in the space between them, was the darkbond. I could feel it pulsing, and through it, I could see each of the others.

The Coven bond made it so that we could always find each other in a crisis, like now, but the darkbond made that access more personal. I could feel what the others felt: Justin in the hospital, bored with a nagging darkness in his gut that was just waiting for the chance to break out; Jenna worried and exhilarated: managing something Justin never could. Bailey, quiet and terrified. And Cole: Cole was planning. Determined. His focus was startling, he was committed to what he was planning. I'd never known him to be that serious about anything. But whatever it was, it was going to be bad.

"I feel him," Jenna said, at just the moment I was going to open my mouth.

"He's in town," Bailey added a moment later.

The picture in my head clarified by degrees until I could *see* him. Books, and the smell of dust and tannin soaked into the woodwork. Stale air, recycled a thousand times over until it was nearly as old as the oldest volumes on the shelves. "He's in the library."

"He wants to..." Bailey hesitated. "I think he wants to burn it down. Why would he want to burn down the library?"

Because someone must have told him it was a good idea.

Maybe they complained about a miniscule library fine, or how much they hated writing research papers. Who knew how flimsy the reason was. People all over town were overreacting off the slightest trigger. The Prince's curse had spread to Cole, and now he was acting on some sort of sociopathic instinct. The library was the enemy, therefore the library must be burned down.

"Illana said that sometimes you can communicate with them. People in your coven. Even from long distances." Jenna's presence in my head grew troubled and sluggish. "But there's something blocking him. He's resistant."

I could feel the two of them in my head, pulsing, and close and real. But I could also feel all the layers of the bond around us, and before we lost this, I had to know for certain. "What's the bond feel like to you? Do you feel all that?"

"It's warm like summer," Bailey said, and I could feel her wrapping herself in it. "I know you're all out there and it makes me smile."

"I know I can find you no matter where you go," Jenna followed up the moment Bailey started speaking. "I know if we're ever separated you'll still be there. In my head."

"But what about the rest?" I pushed. "What about the chains, and the weird gravity, and the bones?"

Twin sources of silence made my words an empty echo. "You don't feel it?" I asked. Was I really the only one?

"There's just the bond, Mal," Jenna said, but now her words were slow and soothing. I could feel *things* passing between the two girls, the equivalent of guarded looks and pointed gestures. Psychic, nonverbal communication. "Don't panic, okay? They didn't *actually* do anything to us. We're just a normal coven."

They really couldn't feel it. That meant they couldn't sense the mental grimoire that existed somewhere in the ether all around us. I couldn't tell if I was more worried or relieved. *Any* of the others would have abused the power at the first chance. But it was more than just a happy coincidence that I was the only one who could tap into it. I would never be free of them, regardless of what I wanted. Whatever Moonset had planned, I was an integral part of the equation.

How much had they known? Did they know one of us would grow up to despise where we came from? That we'd turn away from the magic entirely. Was that why they did it? Maybe they knew the only person that could be trusted with true power was the one who didn't want it in the first place.

Had they known, even then, that it would be me?

I pulled away from them first and let the connection between us sever, a rubber band snap that put me back in the living room. I looked up to find Quinn leaning against the wall, arms crossed in front of him. "Well?"

"Library," Jenna and I said at the same time. It was such an unexpected moment that the pair of us stopped and stared at each other. We never had moments of synchronicity like that. Maybe her and Justin, but never the pair of us.

"Bailey, will you go tell Nick and Kelly what's going on?" Quinn asked, leaning forward to stare down at her.

She climbed to her feet and walked towards the front door. But she stopped by the table and turned back towards us. "I can do that, but I—I don't think I should go with you. I think I should stick around where someone can keep an eye on me."

Jenna realized what that was all about just a few seconds

before me. Bailey still carried the guilt from her part in Luca's crimes. She wasn't able to move on. "That wasn't your fault," Jenna said firmly. "You got hurt trying to help save people. No one blames you for what happened."

Bailey could be stubborn when she wanted to, though. "I still think I should stay home. It's safer. Kelly's been trying to show me some defensive stuff. I think I'd rather be here and be watched. Just in case."

"Sure," I said, summoning up a smile. Jenna stared at me. "If she's that worried, she'll be safer here. You and I can handle Cole."

I hoped that was true. I'd already almost lost one brother. I couldn't handle losing another.

TWENTY-SEVEN

*Some Covens have to struggle to find an
equilibrium, the members jockeying for position.
But Moonset, they were flawless from the
first day. Almost like they were meant to be.*

....

Adele Roman
From the forward of *Moonset: A Dark Legacy*

The three of us took Quinn's car into the city. The library
was just off of Main Street, set back from the curb and surrounded by a multitude of trees so thick that it was barely
visible from the street.

"Closed on Saturdays," Jenna noted, as we pulled in past
the sign with the hours of operation.

"Not like that would stop Cole. You've been teaching
him lock-picking spells, haven't you?" Quinn asked from the
driver's seat.

I preferred to stay in the back and keep my thoughts to myself. The number of people walking around the city like it wasn't under a surreptitious siege surprised me. Hadn't anyone noticed that business trips, vacations, and reasons to leave the city of Carrow Mill were flitting by without a care? The Witchers had managed to brainwash the entire town, but they couldn't manage to take down an Abyssal Prince.

How exactly was that possible, then? How powerful was he, if they couldn't stop him, and how was I supposed to do anything that they couldn't?

When Quinn pulled around to the rear of the building, the back door was swinging widely. I inhaled as soon as I got out of the car, but there wasn't any trace of smoke in the air. It hadn't gotten that far, at least. But if Cole had packed some sort of accelerant (and he was just enough of a troublemaker to know that an accelerant was necessary), there could already be a lot of property damage inside.

Quinn stopped us at the door. "Listen, try to talk him down. Try to reason with him. But don't let him know that I'm with you. I'll stay behind, keep an eye on things. I'll step in if things escalate."

"I don't understand—" Jenna started.

"Because of Justin," I said softly. "Because reasoning with him didn't work, and he got hurt because I thought it would."

Quinn clasped a hand on my shoulder and I immediately shrugged it off. Jenna glanced between the two of us and rolled her eyes. "Fine, whatever," she said, stomping down the steps. "Cole Sutter, I *swear to God* if you so much as strike a match I'm going to stuff you into a trash can and roll you down a hill!" Jenna hollered her threat into the dark library, and the words echoed and bounced off of all the walls, so unused to loud voices. "Again!"

There was silence from the rest of the building.

The library interior was divided into two parts. To the left of us was the hallway leading to the children's and teen section, and to the right, the adult and reference sections. Each were about the same size, and there were literally dozens of stacks for him to hide behind.

"Do we split up?" I whispered.

"Have you ever *seen* a horror movie? Just don't go far. I'm throwing you in his way if he's all rage-zombie feral." Jenna motioned me forward, and taking a hunch, I headed for the reference area.

We didn't have to go far. All of the reference shelves were half as high as the regular stacks, which meant an unobstructed view all the way to the rear of the library. I didn't see any sign of Cole, but I saw a stack of books that was most definitely out of place.

Jenna followed behind me, her footsteps slow and cautious. I don't know what happened to Quinn, he'd disappeared the moment we came inside. The lights were out, and none of us had bothered to turn them on: it was probably better if the lights stayed off for this.

There was a serpentine path of reference books—thick, heavy monstrosities—lined up against one another like a row of dominoes that had already fallen to the ground. They cut across one of the stacks, disappeared underneath a work table, and then emerged out the other side to circle around the interior wall.

I followed the stack, and Jenna followed me. We passed through Astrology and Religion, cut across to American History and the Civil War, and then into Biographies (Local) and then Biographies (Non-local).

The stack continued to run along the perimeter of the library, and once or twice I noticed other lines of books, other tentacles of this design Cole had come up with. And finally, I found *him*. Just outside the Cooking aisle, right next to a shelf filled with books like *Pastries for Beginners*, and *How to Bake the Perfect Bundt Cake*.

Cole was surrounded by a ring of books, of which there wasn't just one line spilling out like a tentacle, there were several. And it looked like we caught him in the middle of planning for a few more.

He didn't even look up at us as we approached. "You're not supposed to be here yet," he said. He looked down at his watch, eyes thoughtful. "I still have ten minutes more."

Jenna strode past me and stepped easily over the spilled books. "'Not supposed to be here?' What do you think you're doing, Cole?"

His jaw was set, his hair a sleep-spiked road map of flatlands and mountains. "You wouldn't understand."

"Try me." I stepped forward, and when Cole flinched, I held up my arms quickly. "It's okay, Cole. Just tell us what's going on."

Jenna snatched the lighter out of Cole's hand, a long-stemmed red and black thing used for fireplaces and outdoor fires.

"I don't need that," Cole told her quietly. There was none

of the crazy, animated energy that Cole usually possessed. There wasn't even any of the sour, huffy scowling that he sometimes fell into. This was scary Cole. Calm, collected, and absolutely determined in what he was doing Cole. "I know spells for fire."

"Just tell us what's going on," I said, raising my voice before Jenna snapped and lost it. I continued questioning Cole. "Did someone tell you to burn down the library? Did they talk about a book they hated or something?"

Jenna looked my way and I waved her back towards me. Just as carefully as she'd stepped into the ring of books, she stepped back out. Her steps were careful in a way that Jenna was *never* careful. Cole's weirdly blank expression wasn't just freaking *me* out.

He stood taller, straining for every inch. "This is the best alternative. I see that now. I didn't always see it, but now it's clear." His conviction wavered for a moment, his words uncertain. "If—if there aren't any books, then there won't be any English class. And if we don't have English class, then no one has to fail."

It sounded like it made sense, but I didn't buy it. Maybe someone had vented to him about their grade in English, and Cole took it too far to eliminate the problem. At least he wasn't trying to kill someone, or proving his self-inflicted love. But in the hesitations and moments between his words, I saw something else. Something I couldn't understand.

"I'm sure she's a nice girl," I ventured, "but I've got a better idea. A way that you can get rid of that English class entirely without having to set anything on fire."

His response was pure petulance, shades of the old Cole. "But I *want* to set it on fire."

"And then what happens to you?" Jenna demanded. "Not exactly the time to be a ringleader, Cole."

"This is the best alternative!" Cole insisted. "Why don't you see that? There has to be a fire!"

I looked around, trying to be as subtle as possible. *Where was Quinn?* There were any number of spells that Cole could invoke that would snap to life before we even had a chance to stop it. Spells to create fire were a dime a dozen, and all he would need was a candle's worth of flame to set the whole thing in motion.

"We're just trying to understand, buddy. Just explain it so the rest of us understand," I said, but I wondered if being rational was exactly the wrong approach to take. Maybe it had nothing to do with being logical at all.

"I'm in love!" Cole shouted, his frustration escalating. I spotted Quinn as he blurred into visibility from behind Cole, approaching at a still, slow walk. Each step was chosen with care, and he hesitated with every one, making sure it made as little noise as possible.

"This is not the kind of awkward burning sensation you're supposed to have when you're in love!" I fired back.

Jenna just *looked* at me. Even Quinn's eyebrows judged me.

Cole's eyes narrowed and he just *stopped*. And the gut feeling I had—the feeling that for whatever reason, Cole was lying to us and setting this fire for some other reason altogether, screamed out a warning. His mouth opened in anger—

Quinn was on him instantly, one gloved hand covering his mouth and the other across the forehead. He whispered spells under his breath, and shifted his hold when Cole's eyes rolled up in his head and he started to slump.

That was all it took. A few whispered words and Cole was incapacitated.

I looked at the design of books and crouched down to run my fingers along one of them. I expected my fingers to come away wet, evidence of gasoline or whatever else Cole was going to use to ignite the building, but there was nothing. When I tried to kick some of the books aside, they hung together, latched together like magnets.

I tried to pry them apart by hand. They gave, eventually, and with a significant amount of force, but as soon as I waved them closer together, they would snap back into place.

"Impressive," Jenna said, kneeling down beside me. "I wouldn't have expected something like this out of Cole." She looked up and studied the line of books, her lips moving slightly as she worked through something in her head.

Quinn had him in a fireman carry, easily thrown over one shoulder. "Come on, I want to get him out of here. I'll have the library locked down until we can get someone in here to undo whatever it was that Cole was working towards."

"It's some sort of resonance spell, but they usually only amplify sound," Jenna said, her voice coming from far away. She reached out, ran her fingers along one of the books. "This is *complicated.* I can't even follow it all. It might be making his spell ... bigger? Where'd Cole learn how to do something like this?"

"That's not important now," Quinn said, either from impatience or the strain of holding up our little brother.

Jenna looked forlorn as I dragged her away from the books, her forehead still furrowed in thought even after we'd left the building. "Yeah, you wouldn't think so," she said in an aside to herself.

Quinn drove us straight to the hospital, which was now completely under the Congress's control.

"How many kids are in here already?" Jenna asked.

"About a hundred and thirty." There were only five hundred kids in our school. In just a couple of weeks, the Prince had infected nearly a quarter of the school.

We had to pull around the rear because of all the construction. I grabbed Cole and we headed back into the hospital. A pair of older women dressed like nurses waited for us inside with a gurney. Once I set him down, one of the women brushed the fringe off his forehead and murmured spells into his skin.

"Put him in with Justin, please," Quinn said from behind us. One of the women smiled slightly and nodded, and then they pushed their way further into the hospital. "Give them a few minutes to get him settled and then you can probably go visit with both of them."

Quinn and I went to get coffee while Jenna took a seat in the waiting room. She kept wringing her hands, but whatever it was she tried to wipe away, it never gave up its hold.

"That's two," I said quietly. "Three to go."

"Bailey's here too," Quinn said after a momentary pause, looking over my shoulder. "She had Kelly drive her here right after we left. I got the call after we went into the library. Cole freaked her out more than I thought. She's worried she'll do something again."

I closed my eyes. No wonder she wanted us to go on

without her. I knew the things that Luca had done to her had left a mark, but I thought that with time she'd start to recover. But now I had to wonder if she'd ever have the chance.

All of us were close in different ways. Some of us weren't close at all, but Cole and Bailey had their own particular bond. Being the youngest, being the "kids," they were often pushed to the side while we tried to protect them. They bickered and fought as much as anyone else, but they were probably the most realistic pair of siblings among us.

That meant that Jenna and I were the only ones left. I hated to admit it, but I was surprised and a little impressed that Jenna had lasted this long.

I touched Quinn on the shoulder before he could walk away, and then just as quickly snatched my hand back. He turned, looking down at his shoulder before he met my eyes. "I'm going to stop in to Luca's room first."

His eyebrows furrowed. "What are you thinking?"

I wasn't thinking anything, to be honest. But I still couldn't let go of the idea that Luca was somehow involved. That he was the one who was hosting the Prince. It made sense, if the Prince was attached to his life energy, then keeping Luca in a coma meant he had free rein of the town.

"I just want to check in. Who knows, maybe crazy uncle Charlie will be there and I can ask him a few more questions."

I made my way back up to Luca's floor, only this time it was more active. All the doors were still propped open, but now there were witches walking up and down the halls. When I went to his room and found it empty, I had to trail my way back to the nurse's station. The nurse had given me the creepy wide eyes that said she knew exactly who I was, and would I please refrain from killing her horribly?

"Far end of the hall," she squeaked. "Last room on the left."

Even in the middle of a crisis, some people couldn't forget how much they hated or feared us.

I didn't expect to learn anything new from Luca. But maybe staring at him would somehow make things make more sense. Was that how Moonset had killed the last Abyssal Prince? Did they kill the girl, and the demon along with her? Was that really all I would have to do to stop the Prince from hurting Justin and the others?

But what if I was wrong?

I stopped short of Luca's door, stilled by the sound of someone's voice. Someone vaguely familiar.

"Almost time, now, little Luca. Just a few more hours and everything will fall into place just the way it was meant to. All you have to do is just keep sleeping, and I'll wait for your cousin."

I knew that voice. Masculine, but not too masculine. Beaten down and weathered.

"Are you coming in, Malcolm? Or just going to lurk in the hallways all night?"

I stepped into the doorway, and saw Matthew Dugard, the curio shop owner, sitting on the edge of Luca's bed, a small book in his lap.

"Nice to see you again, son," Matthew said pleasantly. "I was just telling Luca why I sold him this little ditty." He waved the book in my face. "When you think about it, it's impressive. He almost broke the town, and all it took was a couple of pages from *Twenty-three*."

"What is that?"

Matthew looked surprised. "It's a primer to the black arts, obviously. The very volume that young Luca Denton turned to in an hour of crisis."

"And why do you have it? Where did it come from?"

"Two very good questions," Matthew said. He lacked the amiable presence he had in his store, behind the mask there was nothing but a bitter weariness. "The answer to the first question is that I'm taking it back. But haven't you figured out the answer to the second already?"

"You sold it to him."

"I *gave* it to him." Matthew peeled the hearing aid from his ear and now his smile was cold and cruel. "Close the door, son. Let's have a chat."

TWENTY-EIGHT

*The most insidious part of Moonset was the way
they preyed upon the weak minded. So many
soldiers recruited to their cause were hurting
and damaged. They made the perfect
sleeper agents, hidden in plain sight.*

....

Moonset: A Dark Legacy

"You gave Luca the book." I didn't close the door. I wasn't an idiot.

"It was a gift," Matthew demurred. "Given to me to hand over to just the *right* individual."

The hearing aid was a tiny worm of plastic on the ground between us. "And that?" I asked. "Some sort of game?"

Matthew set to adjusting the blankets around Luca, pulling them snug and tight up against his skin, and tucking them in around the sides. "A test. The great and powerful Illana Bryer barely had a second thought for me. You know, I hoped to be caught by now. I never thought it would take this many years. But I was faithful. So very faithful."

I'd heard fervor like that before. The ecstasy in the words, the chaotic light in the eyes. Moonset had been many things, but one of the worst parts was the cult that grew up around them. An army of lunatics who lived and died for them. I took a step back. "I'm getting Quinn."

"Do you even know what it's like? To be smarter than everyone around you? I've waited for *years* to be discovered. And for what? Nothing. I gave Luca the book, blatant as sin, and *still* they didn't find me."

"He's in a coma."

Matthew nodded sadly, and set the book carefully where Luca's lap would be, if he were awake. It was almost like he'd been reading just before he fell asleep, and the book had been left forgotten in his lap. "After all I did for him, and he couldn't do this one little thing for me."

"Why is it so important that you get caught?"

"What good is a movement without a martyr?" Matthew walked away from the bed. "I could have gone to my glory with my head held high—taken down with him and killed without ever admitting everything. But he had to go to sleep and ruin everything." He shook his head, hands constantly in motion, brushing his pants, touching his shirt, scratching his face. "He's never going to wake up, you know."

"I figured." He wouldn't wake up as long as the Abyssal Prince was up and moving.

A faint smile, one that might have been filled with shades of mockery, crossed his lips. There was a crank for the window, which he spun around until it wouldn't spin any further. Hospital windows didn't open very far, most likely so that patients couldn't hurt themselves. A tiny whisper of air escaped into the room. The humor in his voice intensified. "Did you?" Whatever the joke was, I wasn't in on it.

"It was you, wasn't it? You were the one who summoned the Abyssal Prince last time. You were the one that started all of this."

He pushed his fingers between the slats of the shades and spread himself a little window, peeking out into the afternoon light. "You *would* think that, wouldn't you? Oh, no, I was a late recruit. They asked me to stay behind. Told me they'd be in touch. And for *years* I kept my beliefs to myself. Prayed every night for your father to make me strong, and to Sherrod for wisdom. Ten *years*. And then *he* showed up on my doorstep and told me what had to happen. God, he was magnificent. Their living heir. He made me a true disciple."

"Cullen Bridger." The terrorist trained by Moonset. The one who had hunted us our entire lives. He'd sent a wraith to kidnap us back in Kentucky. And all the while, he'd had someone working for him here in Carrow Mill.

Matthew inhaled at the sound of his name, sighing like he'd smelled the sweetest fragrance. "I know his true name. He told me. The name you know is just a mask. He is so much more than that."

A breeze worked its way into the room from the crack in the window, and with it, the smell of something sharp and harsh carried to my nose. Gasoline. Not a lot, but enough.

"You think if you kill Luca, that it will send the Abyssal back to his prison?" The man's smile was slow, beaming, and utterly unhinged. "Let's test that theory out," he said, producing a packet of matches like a magician coaxing a dove from a hat. And with just as practiced a motion, he struck one against the back, and when it caught fire he held it up to the rest so that the entire packet started to burn. All that, in the time it took me to process what was happening.

He threw the packet onto Luca's bed. The blankets caught fire easily.

I pressed further into the room, but Matthew was there to block me before I got more than two feet inside. He was stronger than he looked. Or I was weaker than I thought. He had no problem pinning my arms behind me and shoving me against the wall.

"Come on, Malcolm. Don't you see?" He pulled my chin to the right, forcing me to see the fire growing thicker, the smoke billowing up darker and darker.

"You have to be *tested*, Malcolm. You have to *earn it*. Come on. Use your magic. Save the boy. This is your chance to be everything that fate has designed for you. Take up the mantle."

"I'm not a hero," I growled. I knew spells to start little fires, same as Cole, but I didn't know anything that would help put them *out*. If Justin were here, he could have stopped it. Jenna too.

But I wasn't entirely helpless. I reached deep down inside, to the place where the Coven bond attached to me, and reached for the magic that wasn't quite magic. It was faster than instinct, I reached for it at the same time as it reached for me, two missed connections that finally came together in a ray of light.

I opened my mouth as wide as I could, and a sound deeper than anything inside of me emerged, a sound more real than anything I'd ever said before. The word was a hazy rush in my ears, I couldn't even say for sure what it was that I'd spoken. My body reacted on autopilot, trembling as the word tried to force its way out.

Whatever the curio shop guy had done to me, the spell sliced right through it. Cut through his magic and scattered the shreds into the air. My strength returned even as his vanished, and I pushed him off me easily. He stumbled to the ground, collapsed into a puddle of himself.

A wind like a hurricane swept through the room, snuffing the flames and throwing the blankets clear from Luca's body. The curtains ripped away from their rods, the other hospital bed crashed against the window, and Matthew shot against the far wall. Somewhere out in the hall there was the sound of sirens, screeching noises that were dull to my ears compared to the roaring inside. It tore away the scent of burning cotton and cooked meat, but not fast enough.

Energy buzzed through me, a surge of endorphins and adrenaline that could have made anything possible. But before I could do anything, before I could try to find help for Luca—oh god, his legs!—there was a new sound. The angry clash of bells, vibrating the air itself.

"Thank you," Matthew whispered from the floor as the Abyssal Prince strode into the room. The sounds from the hallway dwindled and muted in his wake, and the view of the hallway became flat and acrylic, a painting instead of a door. There were tears in Matthew's eyes, and he prostrated himself down on hands and knees. Worshipful.

Luca still slept, despite the fact that his legs were ravaged. But the fire had been caught before it spread too far, and the equipment breathing for him continued to do its job.

"Do not thank me, mule. You put your hands on my human." The Prince's lips drew back in a sneer. *Contempt* and *fury* boiled the room alive. "*Beg.*"

"Forgive me!"

The hollow cry didn't do anything to appease the Prince. The sneer widened so much that it exposed the silver teeth inside his mouth. "Weakness." The disgust in his tone forced Matthew down onto his belly. The man mewled, a pitiful sound full of keening and despair. The Prince's words crippled him. They never crippled me, and I was just a bystander.

The Prince cocked his head to the side, then glanced over a shoulder. "Alas, they come. The boring ones." His mouth opened wider, a piercing vibrato that ripped through me and dragged the three of us from the room. A prism of light swept over my vision as we were ripped out of the world.

We emerged in the curio shop, dim and full of shadows. Afternoon had just barely started at the hospital, but now the world was full-on dark. Normally, when the Prince moved me from place to place, it was instantaneous. This was the first time there was a disconnect. Why?

From somewhere deeper in the building came the sound of canned laughter, a laugh track to an old comedy. The Prince stood next to me, hand on my shoulder. "Be calm," he whispered in my ear, and *calm* washed through my body, a pleasant drug that eased my worries.

Without the lights, everything inside the shop seemed

more insidious and macabre. Masks on the walls glared with frenzied hunger, statues on the floor seemed to move and jump at will. There were movements out of the corner of my eye, but stillness wherever I turned.

"Now then," the Prince straightened beside me. He leapt onto one of the display cases and crossed one leg over the other. "You were about to expose your every squirming thought about my dear, departed sister. And of course your role in her murder."

"It was me. I killed Kore." Matthew smiled as the confession slid past his lips. He still had that same look of worship on his face, despite being humbled on the ground only seconds ago. "I cast the invocations to the Abyss. I cleared the path so she could escape. I brought her here." And then his smile grew wider. *Hopeful.* "She died because of me, and now you've come. My reward is at hand."

The Prince at my shoulder was a silent creature, for so long that the ticking of a dozen grandfather clocks stacked along the walls started to drive me crazy. Each was just a fraction of a section off of the rest, so it was a constant buzzing of ticks. A stopwatch without any end.

"Lies," the Prince said finally. "You are a stained spirit, a worm indeed. But you are *lying*. Haven't I said how much I despise a liar, dear Malcolm?"

He patted me on the shoulder, and the touch sent a thrilling electricity running across my skin. Excitement poured through my every vein. I would listen to his voice forever if I could. He could read to me from Adele Roman's book, all about my father's crimes, and I would not mind. "You…don't?"

He beamed down at me and my heart thudded in my chest. He was pleased. I'd given him the right answer. My heart leapt in my chest and I couldn't stop smiling.

"Not a question, pet," he whispered out of the corner of his mouth.

Matthew looked between us, and I saw something unpleasant in his expression. I made a sound, something that must have been worrying enough that my Prince turned away and looked back at the man sprawled over his own floor.

"No," the Prince continued, "I'm not looking for *you*. I'm looking for the crawling things in your head. Secrets. Worms oozing all over themselves. Dirty minds. Not like my Malcolm's. Rigid and sparkling like a diamond. At least it was," and again, the fury in his voice was a tangible thing. It caused all the lamps and candles in the building to catch and bathe the store in light.

I was protected from the onslaught by the hand on my shoulder. Only the emotions he wanted me to feel dripped from his fingers into my skin, and all others washed over me without leaving a trace of moisture.

Part of me knew I was under his spell as much as any of his victims, but I just didn't *care*. I would be under his spell forever if I could. Why would anyone want to exist otherwise? When he touched me, spoke to me, his love consumed me. I never worried to know what he felt for me. It ran through my veins.

Just like a drug, the hateful part of my mind offered, the part that worried and dwelled.

"No," Matthew insisted, and now I could hear it. The discordant notes when he lied. "It was me. I was responsible. You have to punish me." Everything a lie but the prayer at the end.

"Curious," the Prince murmured to me. "Men who seek punishments they haven't earned."

"I made this possible," Matthew interjected, suddenly hostile. His face grew dark and he stabbed a finger forward, pointing to my Prince. "If it wasn't for me, you'd still be wallowing at the bottom of the Abyss!"

The Prince's fingers tangled in my hair and I sighed. "He wants to be punished. He begs for it." He looked past me towards the other man. "Why?" The Prince released his hold on me, and pushed me forward a bit. "Make him explain, my champion. Humans are so horribly complex."

With the release of his hold on me, the fog in my head lifted. It took a moment to sift through the last several minutes, to put everything into context. The Prince had never subsumed my will under his own so effortlessly before. Typically the emotions swept over me and influenced me for a moment, but this had been more pervasive.

He could suppress my will entirely if that's what he wanted. I really would be nothing more than his puppet then.

My stomach roiled, and I spent another moment trying to keep from vomiting everywhere. The Prince might forgive me many things, but vomit on his person would probably not be one of those things.

As I got myself under control, I made an immediate decision. I had to play along. That was the only way.

"He wants to know why you're lying." I turned around, trying to orient myself, and walked towards the exit looking for the light switch. Not that candlelight wasn't effective, but I wanted to be able to actually look the man in the eyes.

"I'm not lying," the man lied. Without the Prince's influence over me, I couldn't hear the lies in the way I had before. But he was just so obvious about it, now that he wasn't hiding behind his mask of mundanity.

"But see, there's the problem," I replied with mock severity. "You want to be punished, so the only way to really punish you is to not do anything at all. To leave you here." I turned towards the Prince and nodded at the door. "Come on, let's go."

"Wait!" The man scrambled to his feet, his desperation so great that his fingers clawed into the wood flooring underneath. "Please! You have to. Or—or I'll tell everyone. I'll tell the Congress exactly what I did!"

I smiled. "And they'll never believe a word of it. Remember? You're an invalid. That's the way you wanted it. To be overlooked and forgotten." It was seriously creepy, trying to talk to someone who was clearly so far gone on their Moonset propaganda that they'd do anything to fulfill their directions.

The Prince looked between us like we were the most fascinating game of tennis he had ever seen. His head constantly flicked from the left to the right as he followed the verbal volley.

Matthew stared up at me, and I could tell he was weighing his options. Was I right? Would the Congress completely ignore him? Or would they throw the book at him just to have a scapegoat.

"Just tell the truth," I said quietly. "And then you'll get everything that Bridger promised you."

The stillness in the curio shop was interrupted by a heaving breath, a whimper of nerves. "I didn't summon your sister," he admitted. "I was barely friends with them. Once Cy found his Coven, he didn't have time for anything or anyone else. They went off to their secret clubhouse and never told anyone what they were up to. Sherrod didn't come to me until later, until the day before it all started. He said there would be a sign, and I would know what to do. And then the Congress was destroyed, and the witches went to war."

Went off to their secret clubhouse... "Do you know where they went? The place they always disappeared to during high school, right? Do you know where it is?"

He shook his head and just before he opened his mouth, the Prince's voice cut through the air with a terse, "Lies."

"I'm not lying!"

"Do you really think I should leave him be, my human?" The Prince turned to me for answers, and I remembered the momentary thrill when that had happened before, when I'd been *eager* to gain his praise. It made my skin crawl now.

I didn't want to help the Prince, but it was the only way I knew to save the others. And maybe, if I found out what happened to Kore, I could use that as a way to leverage the Prince into leaving *all* the children behind. Or else I would have to kill him too. "Tell me where they went."

The man began blubbering. "I don't know. I don't know. I don't *know*."

"Tell me where they went!"

"It was some kind of park!" he finally howled. "I don't *know* where. All I knew was that it was isolated. They *made* it isolated. Cy always had this gold thing he would flip—a dollar coin or something. Whenever I asked, he'd always pull it out and start playing with it."

No. Not a gold coin at all. A gold *token*. Just like the one on Charlie's bathroom counter, the only thing that hadn't fallen to the floor.

"I think I know where they put her," I said, surprised at the revelation as much as anyone. I turned to the Prince. "Send me back. Let the witches deal with him. You said it yourself. He's not the one you're looking for."

The Prince made a small pout of a face. "I was going to have fun with him." A wave of *hopefulness* and *need* washed over me, but I tried hard to hold onto my thoughts. To keep myself under control.

Even still, I hesitated. "But … are you sure?"

The Prince stared at me with lantern eyes. They swallowed up my vision, made me smaller and more insignificant.

No, I had to look away. Had to break the connection, whatever it was that the Prince was doing to my head, making my thoughts not as sharp, stealing my mind and replacing it with complacency.

It took an eternity to turn my eyes down, but once I did, warmth spread into my chest. My heart was a gentle roar in my ears, and I realized I was breathing heavily, like there would never be enough air. I'd sweated through my shirt and swallowed down dust in my mouth.

"Let the Witchers deal with him. Matthew *wants* you to kill him. Don't give him what he wants. He's been standing in the way all this time. He could have told you where Kore was buried weeks ago, but he didn't. He still wouldn't have, if we hadn't pressed him."

"No, you have to!" Matthew scrambled to his feet, his face darkening from red into a purple rage. "It was promised!"

The Prince weighed his options for only a moment before he turned back to me. "I want answers, my Malcolm." And then the creature screamed, and Matthew and I were ripped back out of the world and deposited back into an almost-empty hospital room.

Empty except for the handful of Witchers who weren't expecting intruders. Nick and Kelly were both standing near the door, talking to guards from the hallway.

Something was different this time around. Maybe it was the Prince's renewed fury, or maybe his irritation with me for wanting Matthew left unharmed. But the travel between spaces was rough on my body, a deep muscle ache flaring to life from my neck all the way down to my toes. My ears rung with the sound of his scream, and even my teeth ached.

"*Bad guy,*" I said urgently, right before I dropped to my knees. Nick was at my side in an instant, helping me back up to my feet. My head swam and my blood sped through my veins like whitewater rapids. The other three Witchers had surrounded Matthew Dugard, though they waited until a nod from Nick before they began hauling him up.

Nick held me steady when my legs kept dropping out from under me. "What the hell happened? The alarms go off, and we find Luca's been sautéed, the room's trashed, and there's no sign of you."

"Who else?" I said glumly. "The Prince showed up after Matthew put his hands on me. He…*wanted* the Prince to kill him. I think that's the only reason why he's still alive. The Prince barely does what I ask, but he definitely won't want to do something if he's been manipulated into it."

"Sounds like you know the Abyssal pretty well." There was a dangerous tone in Nick's voice. One that made me stop and look at him, stoic faced and all.

"I'm not on his side or anything," I pointed out, irritated that I even *had* to do that. "But he won't take the curse off of Justin if I don't get him the answers he's after."

"But it's still helping one of them, Mal. Just because you're doing it for the right reasons doesn't make it right. It doesn't mean you can trust it."

"I don't trust him. Do you think I'm some kind of idiot?"

Nick spent a long time staring at me. "I think you're the only one who calls it 'him.' There's a reason we call it the Abyssal. Because when you think of it like a prince, you forget that he's a monster."

I took a step back, eyes wide. "I don't… I'm not… "

"We have to get him out of here, Mal." Nick gave me an apologetic look and took charge of the other Witchers. They surrounded Matthew and pulled him to his feet. Once he was up, they started to escort him from the room, one of them reciting a steady stream of spells that had the same kind of cadence as the Miranda rights.

Kelly stayed by the door when the rest of them left. I walked up to her, my head a messy jumble of thoughts. Maybe I was giving the Prince—no, the Abyssal—too much influence in my head. Maybe that was why he found it so easy to manipulate me.

"Is there any word on Luca? Did the fire get put out in time?"

Kelly had her fist over her mouth, touching her thumb to

her upper lip in a steady rhythm. It took her a second to recognize that someone was talking to her, and another moment to turn my way. "Oh, hey, what?"

"Luca," I repeated. "Any news?"

Her worried expression intensified. "Too early to tell. The fire definitely did some damage, but we won't know more until later. You put it out, right?" I nodded. "You did good. There were some resistance spells cast into the bed. It must have been pretty hard to make it go out, huh?" I didn't say anything and she continued. "They're afraid to try any healing spells on Luca, in case there's more on him. They could end up doing more damage than the fire. And by the time the spells would fade, any help the healing spells can do will be almost nonexistent."

"So even if he wakes up, his legs are . . ." But I couldn't finish the thought.

Kelly exhaled, low and slow. "Pretty much."

I nodded. "Can you find Illana? Tell her I'm gonna be . . . do—"

"Mal!" Kelly was at my side in a moment, catching my weight and helping me brace against the wall. I tried to right myself, to make my feet do what they were supposed to, but there was a delay somewhere in my body.

She helped me into a chair, and I collapsed gratefully into it. Whatever energy surge had hit me after tapping into the darkbond magic, there was a time limit on it, obviously.

"Just . . . stay here. I'll get Illana."

She left me in the room, and all I could smell was the faint smell of burnt cotton and flesh. Cole's words came back to me there at the end. "*This is the best alternative. There has to be a fire.*"

I chewed on my thumbnail while I waited for Illana, worrying.

TWENTY-NINE

It's a thing that Covens do. Go off by themselves.
So no one ever wondered where Moonset
disappeared to every day, not until after.
There are those who still wonder.

....

Simon Meers
Case Report on *The Moonset Legacy*

"And he said you're all to be tested?"

Illana found an empty doctor's office for us to use, and we sat on either end of a rather large leather couch. Despite the fact that we were two floors away, I still kept catching traces of smoke and char in the air. It was hard to tell if it was actually there, or just the memory of the scent burned into my head.

She was in the elevator when Kelly and I approached, silent and severe. Today she wore a dark-green business suit.

I got in, Kelly stayed behind, and Illana took me upstairs in order to debrief me.

I lowered my hands very carefully into my lap and studied the fingers. "I never believed in destiny, you know. I mean, I knew I was going to be tied to the others for the rest of my life, but I never believed it *meant* anything."

"Fate is just a guide, a choice, like any other." Illana smiled at me, a little soft and a little tired. "I think out of all of them, you might understand the best. Headstrong, like me. But you know when to run and when to stand tall."

I nodded. The cuff of my jeans was faded and torn at the bottom. I dragged my fingers along it, tugged at the loose threads. "I know you think Moonset had a grand design for us. And I know there's magic in my head that would agree with you. But these tests. These games, or whatever they're supposed to be. I don't think that was Moonset at all."

"What makes you say that?"

It was hard to put it into words. The spells in my head were ephemeral things—only real for a moment, and then vaporized as if they'd never existed. "The curse protects us. It forces us to stay together. It forces us to *rely* on each other. But this magic they left us. The magic they left *me*, it doesn't fit. If they wanted us weaponized, we would all have access to it. It would be hard-wired into all of us. But it doesn't work like that. The spells burn out as soon as I use them."

"You think it's more self-defense," Illana asked, her voice musing as she let the words roll over her lips and through her mind.

"Maybe. Or maybe they knew the kind of world we'd

grow up in. That we'd know there were going to be times where we'd need something more to protect us. So rather than give us something easily abused, they gave us … this."

She mused over that as she reached for the coffee table and that damned teacup she dragged everywhere with her. There'd been no offer of drinks for me.

"It doesn't work, just so you know."

She raised her eyebrows.

"The teacup," I explained. "You bring it out when you want people to think you're not as intimidating as you really are. You want to remind them you're just a little old lady who drinks tea. It doesn't work."

She touched one hand to her heart, smiled, and set the cup back on its saucer. "You think I'm intimidating? You're a sweet boy."

I exhaled at the same time that my stomach rebelled and growled so loudly it overtook Illana's laugh.

"When's the last time you ate, Malcolm?"

I shrugged.

"I want you to go home, eat, and let us handle the rest. Tell me what you figured out about the Abyssal, and we'll take it from there."

I'd *seen* the Witchers try to take out the Abyssal once before. I saw them fail. Spectacularly, but it was still a failure. "I don't really know anything." I forced myself to stop playing with the fringe on my jeans and to just look at her. She didn't have any more power over me than anyone else, no matter what she might want me to think. "He admitted that he gave Luca the book, but he said his ties to Moonset didn't really come until later. All he said was that Bridger, or whoever, wanted us here. That our ... trials started here."

"And what else?"

Was this how Justin felt when he held things back? Did he know that the next words out of his mouth could get someone killed? Maybe a lot of someones? I stopped the Prince once, but the Witchers were outgunned in almost every way. If they came after him again, I wouldn't be able to make him disappear the way I had last time.

"I'm not sure," I said slowly. It was easier to pretend ignorance than I thought. "Did Quinn tell you about what Cole said?"

I'd thought the change of subject was somewhat slick, but Illana's eyebrows said otherwise. "He mentioned there was an incident."

"Cole kept talking about how it was important that there be a fire. That his fire would be the best alternative." I let my words hang in the air, trailing off into worries I couldn't let cross my lips.

"Are you saying you think he knew somehow? Do you think Cole is still under the influence of the Abyss."

My response was immediate and vehement. "No! No, that's not what I meant at all. But I think he *knew* something. He wasn't weird like Justin was." And then the worry clawed its way into my head and gave words to my fear. My voice dropped low. "I think he faked it."

"And why would he do something like that?"

Because he knew something we didn't. Because somehow, for some reason, Cole knew there was going to be a fire. "Bailey freaked out, right? She committed herself because of Cole. And then the fire with Luca. I think Cole knew what was going to happen today. And I think he was trying to stop it in his own way."

"You think he knew there was going to be a fire? That Luca would be assaulted?"

I shook my head. It didn't add up. *Bailey* was the one who sensed things sometimes, who was too in tune with her senses that she sometimes knew things that she had no way of knowing. But Cole had never been like that. Had he? Would any of us have noticed if he was?

Justin would know what to do. He might not have trusted Illana with everything that I had, but he'd know what to do about Cole. He'd know how to keep Bailey's spirits up.

"Excuse me, Illana," Kelly ducked her head into the room. "I apologize for interrupting."

"Don't be. Come in." Illana climbed to her feet, looking between us. "I doubt the two of you have cleared the air about what transpired between you." She huffed out a breath, letting her sleeves swallow up her hands. "We've all been victims of a magical prank once or twice in our lives. And the boy is not exactly hard on the eyes."

"Hey, I'm sitting right here!"

"It's fine, Illana," Kelly said kindly.

I shook my head, and offered a grin. "Like she said, it was a stupid prank. I'm just sorry if it got you in any trouble. Jenna doesn't think before she acts sometimes."

Illana looked between the pair of us with shrewd eyes. "Excellent. I want the pair of you to start working together.

You have some things in common," she mentioned. "Kelly is as close to a savant in ancient magic as anyone I've ever met."

"Ancient magic?"

"Symbols, Malcolm. The written element of magic. All covens have a symbol: you've seen Moonset's for yourself. There are many magics that lack a verbal correspondence. Things we can't put into words. Sound familiar?"

The spells that were hidden into the darkbond. When I used them, *something* came out of my mouth, but it wasn't in words. It was something else entirely. And when I flipped through all the spells, I'd seen dozens of symbols, more complicated and intense than anything I'd ever seen before.

I got up without another word and hurried behind the doctor's desk. There was a stack of papers in one corner. I flipped them over and started to sketch out the whirlpool symbol I'd seen when the Prince summoned me.

"This is what he—" I stopped and cleared my throat. "This is what the Abyssal uses to summon me. It makes the world shift around me until I'm somewhere completely crazy. I think it uses the symbol to manipulate me." I held the paper out to her, even though it was a crude drawing it was still as close as I could get. "It moves. Clockwise, like a whirlpool, it's not static."

Kelly took the paper and bit at her lower lip. "It's definitely old. So it doesn't take you anywhere, it just makes everything look different?"

I nodded. "I think he creates a world that he wants to live in, and forces me to see it too. But if there's someone else there, the world changes. I think everyone sees something different."

She brushed her fingers around the wake of the whirlpool,

but never let them actually touch the ink itself. "You want to know how to stop seeing what it wants you to see?"

"Or how to break the spell once I'm inside it."

Kelly hmmed. "It's a filter. Instead of bending space and time to move you to somewhere else, the Abyssal bends reality, creating a world it can more comfortably inhabit. The more of a hold it has on our reality, the more powerful it becomes." She tapped her finger against the edge of the paper and looked to Illana. "A clear heart spell might work, don't you think?"

Illana's response was surprising, to say the least. "Absolutely not! I will not put that kind of magic out into the hands of a child." She glowered at Kelly as though she had very purposefully disobeyed her.

"How about someone explain what a clear heart spell is?" I offered, raising my hand a little bit. "If it'll keep the Abyssal Prince from getting in my head, I'm all for it."

Illana's eyes flashed fire when Kelly opened her mouth, and the younger girl closed it just as quickly. Illana turned to me. "It's a very dangerous kind of magic for those who haven't prepared fully. It clears the heart of any stray emotions, making it an empty platform."

"That doesn't sound so bad."

"If the spell lasts too long or is cast improperly," Illana continued, "it remains empty. No one can manipulate them, but they stop feeling. Anything. As long as the spell remains, they won't feel anything at all. The damage to the mind can be...incalculable."

Kelly ducked her head down at the silent rebuke. "Illana's right," she said, her voice now less animated than it had been before. "Think about how behaviors have changed with the Abyssal's influence. If you never felt anything at all, it would be just as bad. You'd lose your empathy, your morals, your judgment. It would put a lot of people in danger."

"There *is* no discussion. Malcolm will have an appropriate guard at all times. We will not allow the Abyssal to come after you at his leisure. Not any longer." Illana's eyes honed in on me, cutting me down in an instant. "This is not your battle. Whatever the Moonset fanatic seemed to believe, we will not put you in harm's way. Your trials, whatever they may be, are at an end." She sank down into the doctor's chair behind the desk and let her hands brush against her forehead. I couldn't tell if she was exhausted or sick, but the sudden bit of frailty didn't sit right across her shoulders. "Take him home, Kelly. Make sure the boy eats."

My stomach, traitor that it was, rumbled its approval.

––––––––––

There were two women sitting in a parked car out front, and a convenient number of black-clad, athame-armed dog walkers on the sidewalks of my neighborhood. I took a minute to get my bearings while Kelly went inside. Despite the fact that it only *felt* like I'd gotten up a few hours ago, an entire day had passed, and somehow my body knew it. The fatigue had continued to grow the further we got from the hospital until I was yawning almost constantly.

Jenna was on the couch by herself, leaning against an arm

tucked under her hair, and fast asleep. Nick, Quinn, and Kelly were huddled around the table, talking in low tones.

"I know it's a conundrum," I said, slipping off my jacket. "Three guards for two kids. That kind of math always gives me a headache. Tell you what. Double up on Jenna. She's the troublemaker."

"Bite me, Zoolander," Jenna said without opening her eyes.

"Aren't you the one with a demon boyfriend?" Quinn looked skeptically towards me. Jenna smirked and settled back in on the couch.

I scowled and walked up the stairs to my room. It hadn't surprised me that everyone was waiting for me. Ever since Justin had been hospitalized, their house had stopped being base camp. And now that Jenna and I were the only two left, of course they would all migrate here. They knew how much I hated having to share my space with too many people.

But if Jenna thought she was crashing in my room, she had another thing coming.

I managed to get a shower and scrub the smell of smoke and hospital off of me without interruption. I was tense, though, expecting someone to start banging on the door at any second. But I got out and into a fresh pair of sweats and a tee shirt before Jenna appeared, walking right in like she knew I was decent.

"They know you're holding back," was all she said as she curled up on a corner of my bed.

"No," I said firmly. I wasn't giving up, or worse, *sharing* my bed with her. It didn't matter that she was my sister in all the ways that mattered. I was not dealing with a night full of elbows and cover hogging.

"Relax, I'm not here to ruin your beauty sleep." She craned her head back towards the door and whispered, "*Audos fet.*"

On a list of a thousand things I wanted to deal with, Jenna using magic in my room was pretty close to the bottom. "What was that?" I asked tiredly.

"They're down there eavesdropping. You know they are." Jenna patted the other side of the bed, like all I was waiting on was an invitation. However long she'd been pretending to sleep downstairs, there wasn't a trace of it on her now. "So are you going to tell me what's happening or not?"

It wasn't just Jenna asking me to catch her up; it was deeper than that. It was a question about whether or not I trusted her. For years we'd had our ups and downs, but she would still be there five years from now, and ten after that, assuming we lived that long. Without Jenna, my life might have been easier. Simpler. But it was also Jenna that helped me stop the Abyssal Prince before he killed the Witchers. Without her, there wouldn't be any sort of resistance at all.

"School's canceled tomorrow. Too many absences. I think they're hoping that if everyone stays home, it'll limit how many outbursts there are."

"Okay." I climbed onto the bed next to her, still baffled that we were the last two remaining. "Maddy and Kevin?" I asked suddenly. "What's going on with them?"

"Both normal. At least as of today. Why?"

"See if they want to come over tomorrow."

"What are you thinking?"

I wasn't thinking anything. But I wanted some extra hands on deck in case Quinn decided he didn't like what I was going to propose in the morning. Too many Witchers might provoke the Prince into another fight he couldn't possibly lose.

———————

Of course, that morning conversation never came. Jenna and I woke up to the same roar of fire engines surging down the street at a little past six in the morning. I climbed off the bed and over to the window, stretching out my arms as I walked, trying to work out some of the kinks.

The fading red tails of the fire trucks were quickly followed by a pair of white police cars, a black sheriff's car, an ambulance, another police car, and then another ambulance.

"Someone brought a parade to town and didn't tell us?" Jenna snarked, but both of us hurried downstairs immediately. Quinn was in the kitchen, wrapping up a sheath across his forearm, dressed in the all-black paramilitary uniform of the Witchers.

He didn't look pleased. "The Abyssal's turning the volume up to eleven. Nick will be here. I need to get downtown. There's already been two fires started, and a fifteen-year-old stole a van and drove it through the front of the bank."

He wants all the adults distracted. I knew without being told that this was the Abyssal's plan all along. Now that I had some kind of idea about where Kore was buried, and who had been responsible all along, that must have meant the Prince knew too. We were connected in some way, even still. And he didn't want interference when it came to the end.

I was okay with that.

"Fine," I said flippantly. "Have they shut down the roads yet?"

Quinn shook his head, and then strapped a second knife around his calf. It still amused me that Witchers didn't need guns, but they still used all the same tricks to conceal them.

Once he was gone, and Nick outside to see him off, I nodded to Jenna. "Call Maddy and Kevin, and plan to get dirty."

"You know where we're heading?"

I nodded. "Unhappiest place on Earth."

THIRTY

"Robert Cooper is the worst kind of snake:
the kind that pretends he is anything but.
I can't wait to meet him again. I want to
watch him slither before I slit his throat."

....

Cyrus Denton
From notes recovered from
the Moonset compound

With Nick in charge, the house became a central hub of comings and goings. The furniture was removed from the dining room and a map of Carrow Mill was tacked onto one of the walls, with a growing mass of red dots for every incident. Within an hour, the city was lost in a haze of crimson. Witchers pushed their pins into the wall, studying the growing chaos, and left wearier than they'd entered.

The teenagers of Carrow Mill, almost to a man, had lost their minds.

None of the younger witches had been affected, aside from Justin. Cole had played at it, and Bailey locked herself away just in case, but the rest of us were untouched. I wasn't sure why the Prince had done me the favor. Or if it even *was* a favor.

Everyone was so busy around us that they didn't even notice when we walked right out the garage door. The air outside was a thing of sirens and smoke in the air. The city was still quarantined, and every sound and smell justified it now.

The streets could have stood in for a zombie apocalypse. There were cars overturned, six-car pileups. Once, on the way to Maddy's, we had to back up and circle through an entire development to find a working road.

Kevin and Maddy waited inside the house, but came out before we'd even pulled into the driveway. On the far end of the street, a trio of dark shapes pulled themselves out of the shadows like the first wave of zombies in a movie.

Now, with the four of us, we were ready for what was probably the stupidest call I'd ever made in my life. Four teenagers against a killer and a demon.

"So you think Moonset's super secret lair has been in the Enchanted Forest all along?" Maddy was of course skeptical.

"Remember how you said that kids used to break in, but there wasn't much to see?" I said, raising my voice against the howl of sirens as two cop cars sped past us in the other lane. Once they were gone, I took my foot off the brake and started rolling forward again. "I think there might be more to see than you think."

"There's no magic there," Maddy said waspishly. I think she was more annoyed about the fact that she was a local, and she'd never thought to look there herself. How dare anyone else figure out something before her. "Everyone would know."

"Moonset dabbled in a lot of different kinds of magic," Jenna said. "Who knows what's there. It could be masked from humans and witches both. Or it could be that only the six of them could get past their wards."

"I still think we need some of the Witchers. We can't go up against that thing by ourselves," Maddy added.

Jenna was all confidence, and I didn't like it. She'd pinned her hair back and thrown a black skull cap on, like we were some sort of teenage crew planning a heist. "Malcolm banished it once. He can do it again."

I didn't have the nerve to tell her how wrong she was.

———

The rust-covered, battered, and practically decrepit gate surrounding the entrance to the Enchanted Forest was probably imposing once. It was, in places, almost ten feet high, and the tips were the kinds of spikes that looked naked without a skull to skewer. But over the years, the gates had bent, bowed, or in places been shoved out of alignment, and then someone came along and put up chain-link fencing. Only five feet high, but still new and in good repair. And in front of both gates were a variety of actual chains with an overcompensatingly large shackle and faceplate.

There was even a wooden sign above the gate, although it dangled from only one of the lines that had held it up before, and the only part that was still legible was the *chant* of Enchanted.

"How long has this place been closed?" I asked.

Maddy walked right up to the lock and shrugged. "Dunno. Back when my parents were kids? Maybe earlier than that. It was open for almost a hundred years, I guess. People wanted *real* amusement parks with *real* roller coasters. Not some spinning teacups and giant pumpkins."

She had the locks opened in a matter of seconds. Even Jenna was impressed.

It was obvious that the park had been closed forever, and the forest had started its reclamation. Concrete slabs that had probably once been impressive and orderly were now broken and overturned and had cracks shot through with darkened greenery. The ticket office to our right was now a hollow shell with only two and a half walls, and a trio of pine trees growing up through the middle.

Everywhere we looked it was a blend of old and new, a real-life version of those TV shows about a world after people were gone. Garbage spread in all directions, there were remnants of chairs and ladders scattered on the ground, and evidence of ancient graffiti on every available surface.

"What's the plan?" Jenna asked. "How are we taking this thing down?"

Oh Jesus. She thought I'd brought them here for some sort of epic beatdown. Of course that was the conclusion she'd come to. It was exactly what she and Justin were hard-wired to do. Run *towards* the danger. Stop the bad guy. Justin had done his part stopping Luca, and now it was her turn. It didn't matter that three dozen Witchers couldn't defeat the Abyssal. What were two-fifths of a rag-tag coven and a pair of idealistic Solitaires going to do?

"We're not taking down anything," I said. "If it shows up, don't go after it."

Her lips pressed inwards, but she huffed out an attempt at agreement. "Okay, fine."

"I mean it, Jenna. He got Justin to fillet himself for no good reason, and when I pissed him off, he talked a kid into severing his femoral artery. He did that by *talking*."

We crept around something that looked remarkably like a tar pit, but had probably been a pond or a fountain. There was a wheelchair half-submerged in the muck, and a decrepit clown statue missing half its head. The mud was settled and thick, but it looked more like the middle of some spring showers instead of deep winter.

"I don't think there's anything here." Kevin had pulled up short by the ruined fountain, and when I turned back, Maddy had stopped with him. Neither one looked like they were willing to take so much as another step. But Jenna was still at my side.

"There's probably a spell somewhere," Jenna said, abruptly taking charge. "You go take the left side, I'll take over here."

Jenna on a power trip was something I should have been prepared for. But we'd been getting along decently well in recent days, so I thought maybe I'd lucked out, and she'd turned over a completely new leaf.

I walked back the way we'd come, around our stalled companions, and circled around the far side of the tar pond.

Here there were trees from outside the park that had become heavy and overgrown, dipping down into the park space like streamers. A rusted, broken-down snack truck sat against one the fences, almost completely obscured by the trees.

I don't even know what I'm supposed to be looking for. After a moment, I shouted that very thought over my shoulder.

"Look for spells," Jenna called back helpfully. "Anything out of place. Maybe something carved into the ground, or on an object or something."

That was certainly helpful. I crouched down on the ground, try looking under the snack truck. I could already smell something foul and sickly sweet from here, and if Jenna thought I was going to climb through the truck, she was out of her mind. There was no telling what kind of nastiness was in there, percolating over the last thirty years. I had no intention of finding mutant ice cream that had evolved itself a brain because someone forgot to turn the freezer on.

There was nothing else nearby that screamed *magic* to me. Just a lot of weeds, renegade grass growing up between the slabs of concrete, and general din and decay. I covered my eyes with a hand and looked for Jenna, but she'd disappeared back inside the ticket office.

She was definitely braver than I was.

So much braver that she emerged from inside the office, up to where the roof would have been if the building hadn't already started falling down. Jenna braced both her hands on the side of the wall, and looked over the surrounding area. Then with a triumphant laugh, she vanished out of sight. For a second, I thought I'd heard the laugh wrong, and she'd tumbled down twelve feet to the ground, but before I could even make it halfway to the ticket office, she emerged with a "Whoo!" and ran back towards the pond.

Jenna was a girl on a mission, and she hopped right up to the edge of the pond where the fences still blocked the way. "Mal, help me move that."

"Are you okay?" I asked, ignoring her and checking her for injuries. Other than a few layers of dust caked to her clothes, she looked unhurt.

"*Help me with that,*" she repeated through her teeth. I guess it was too much to hope that her good mood would have lasted until we were done.

Since I had literally no idea what the *that* was that she wanted me to help move, all I did was to cup my hands low and give her a boost when she tried to climb up over the fence. She perched at the top long enough for me to return my attention to the pond to figure out what in the hell she was after. But just in case something bad was about to happen, I grabbed the top bar and vaulted myself over and behind her.

If one of us was going to get in the mud, it was only fair if we both did. Even though the idea of ruining my running shoes made me want to just turn around entirely. But it wasn't the pond she was interested in. It was the clown head. The creepy, broken clown head.

"I have . . . no idea where you're going with this." Still, this was almost worth it just to watch Jenna spend precious seconds trying to find the best spot to step in to keep her shoes as mud-free as possible.

I wiped my sleeve across my forehead, surprised at the

trail of moisture it absorbed. I was sweating, and not only that it was *hot* over here. Not like a warm thaw in the middle of a harsh winter. Like actual heat. I could strip down to just a pair of shorts and it would still be too hot.

"That's what ... I'm trying ... to tell you," she grunted, reaching one side of the clown head. Of course she took the side that was clean and free of gunk. I got the muddy hepatitis side. "Come on. Help me pull this out."

We counted down from three together, and at one we both started to pull. The clown head was heavy, bogged down underneath an unknown amount of mud, and had probably settled in there three decades ago. It barely moved an inch except for right there at the end.

We counted down again, and this time, we found some leverage. The clown head was mired in the muck, but once we started, it began to rise inch by inch. We managed to roll it over onto its face and out of the pond, darting out from under it at the last second before it rolled over our shoes.

"Now what?" I wiped at my face again with the back of my hand, but I was more careful now that my hands were spackled with mud.

"Over the fence," Jenna directed as I groaned.

Together, we heaved the thing up over our heads and tossed it onto the concrete. I turned to the pond, trying to figure out whatever it was that Jenna had seen that made the clown so interesting. Only when I turned back around, she'd hopped the gate again and had gone back to Kevin and Maddy.

I followed suit, confused as I watched her reach down and yank up a handful of weeds, tearing them all along one of the cracks and making it stand out against the faded gray stone.

"It's the Moonset symbol," Jenna said, gesturing with her hand. "Dark pond, a fiberglass head broken in half for the crescent, and then these." I stepped back to see what she'd seen.

The Moonset symbol was something we'd learned about after coming to Carrow Mill. The symbol that defined Moonset, that they left behind after every one of their crimes. Luca haunted us with it: carving into lockers, infecting our phones, even burning it into doorways. It was a message to the Congress demanding our presence, and a warning to us of what was to come.

The symbol itself was fairly simple. A circle shaded in darkness except for a crescent moon of white at the side, and rays like the sun extending from all around it. Six of them, one for each of the six members of Moonset.

"You think it's the spell?" I squinted, feeling like the day was suddenly a whole lot brighter. The temperature hadn't eased up since leaving the pond. In fact, it was nearly sweltering now.

Kevin tugged on his hoodie a couple of times, like getting some extra air flow was going to solve the problem. Maddy, on the other hand, adapted quickly. After seeing how Jenna and I had stripped out of our layers, she did the same. She had on a dark-red camisole that was almost identical to Jenna's in every way but color. And before anyone could interject, she started walking forward, past the pond that barred her way.

"Seems like it," she said to me, shrugging.

Now that I was looking for it, I saw the trailing black and green breaks between the concrete, and the way they arced around the pond like waves. Just like the rays in Moonset's symbol.

"Now we know they were here," Jenna said. There was a waver in her voice that didn't match the hard light in her eyes. Our parents had walked this same path. It was something to think about. If Moonset really had set up shop here, there had to be something in the park that would pinpoint exactly what they'd done with Kore.

The problem was that the Enchanted Forest was no small park. For as many attractions as were still standing—there was still a Haunted House of Mirrors though it looked to be sadly lacking mirrors—there were empty spaces where the earth had overtaken what had once been there.

The decapitated body of the clown slumped against the Tunnel of Love, hunched over and posed like he was taking a leak. Only one of the swan-shaped cars was still on the track. "I'm *not* going in there," Maddy announced, a sentiment that was unanimous. The water was brackish or possibly even solid, thick like sludge that had time to settle.

Past the tunnel was a junkyard's worth of garbage strewn in a line, a barricade against intruders. Jenna and I shared a look. If the symbol at the pond wasn't enough, the blockade was a definite sign. It seemed like the exact sort of thing an adolescent group of know-it-all punks would have conjured up. I bet Jenna was just pissed they thought of it first.

"Here, grab that board," Kevin directed. He and I started shifting around some of the salvage, creating a gangplank up one side. He went first, turning back long enough for a simple, "There's a bench!" before he leaped out of sight.

The rest of us followed, climbing to the top of the mound and then jumping down to a bench that was still standing upright. Once we were at the bottom, Maddy surged ahead, only to scream and fall back. The three of us surged forward, only to be confronted with ... a giant, plastic spider the size of a VW Bug.

Jenna looked down at Maddy, hands on her hips. "Oh, calm down, Little Miss Muffet, I'm pretty sure it's non-violent." I don't know how Jenna managed a straight face, because once Kevin started laughing I lost it. Maddy, on the other hand, just got redder and redder.

"I just hate bugs," she muttered.

The temperature continued to rise until it was rainforest hot. "Maybe we should have tried this at night." I used the sweatshirt over my face and hair like a towel, trying to soak up at least some of it. Not that it would do much good. None of us had brought supplies. This was supposed to be a simple "sneak into the park and see what we find" mission. Not one requiring snacks and hydration.

And then things took a turn on the creepy side. It wasn't just the spider. Along the wrought iron gate, someone had skewered baby doll heads at regular intervals. Sometimes the dolls were in decent, if weathered, condition, and sometimes they were mutilated: heavy makeup, hair now a faded gray but obviously had once been black. But all of them, from the perfect blond-haired child to the dark devil-spawn versions a few rows away, had completely black eyes.

And every so often, just in case we still weren't sure which way we were headed, someone had glued or melted some of those dolls' arms onto the horizontal bar of the fence, pointing their way towards the carousel.

Wings rustled, and once in a while I heard the faded caw of a crow, but every time I looked, I couldn't find any sign of it, or them. Definitely more than one bird, and yet the skies were clear. This part of the park was clear of trash and debris, and looked like it could have been abandoned only yesterday. There were no wayward plants, no weeds growing up through the ground. As a matter of fact, there wasn't anything growing at all.

There wasn't much of anything as we approached the carousel. Up near the top of it, there was a symbol drawn in spray paint. It clawed at my eyes, something that sent my chest yearning for something it couldn't have. Some spells could be boiled down to their basest parts, a sigil of intent and force. This one was like that, a metaphoric punch to the spirit. How could a few lines of spray paint *want* so much? It burned against the metal frame of the carousel with barely repressed need. I tore my eyes away before the pull got any stronger. There were enough things trying to work their way into my head.

Beneath our feet, the bricks and concrete crumbled down into dirt. The fences fell away, twisted and deformed like plastic brought too close to the flame.

"What is this?" Kevin was the first to voice his concern, but we were all feeling it. None of us were stupid. The setting around us had every indication of *bad mojo* and it would be the smart thing to do to back away and let the adults handle it.

I was ready to do that, to call it a day and convince everyone to leave with me, when I saw it. Right there at the edge of the metal circle holding up a variety of real and imagined equine breeds, some with horns and others with painted black eyes, was a very human intrusion. A dark-blue sleeping bag, recently used. A lantern. Empty beer bottles, and a bigger bottle, clear and nondescript that housed barely an inch of clear liquid. I doubted it was water.

"'Bout time, you little shit-stain. Been out here for days."

I sighed and straightened my back. "Charlie Denton, ladies and gentlemen. The drunk and only."

How long has he been here?

"Thought you'd come alone." Charlie spat out a hunk of something brown and vile.

"*This* is your long-lost uncle?" Jenna's skepticism was well deserved. Charlie looked more like someone's long-lost homeless person than family.

"I'm calling the Witchers," Kevin, the boy scout, said immediately. But he barely had his phone out and in his hand before Charlie snarled a drunken word and the phone went flying. He made a gun with his hand and fired, and the phone exploded into a ball of green fireworks.

Jenna and Maddy were a half second away from starting a fight they wouldn't win. I stepped in front of the others and held out my hands to either side, fingers spread and pointed towards the ground. Everyone hesitated, like they expected some great big magic show of force. I probably could have done something, tapped into the darkbond and pulled out a bit of fancy ubermagic to knock everyone in line.

But that wasn't who I was.

"How long before Illana figures it out?" I asked him.

Charlie squinted at me. He still had the finger pistol formed, only now it was halfway towards me. "Not long. Never really thought it would last as long as it did, though."

Seeing the token in his house, finding out that Moonset had ties to the amusement park, knowing what I did about Luca's mother. Charlie had even told me the truth from the first time I met him. *Bad blood is bad, no matter how hard you pray.*

Charlie had been the one who summoned the Abyssal Prince to Carrow Mill. *Charlie* got his girlfriend possessed. Killed, really. *Charlie* who hated his brother beyond all reason. Not because Cy joined Moonset and became a monster, but because even as a monster, he'd protected his brother. I had no doubt that Cyrus knew what his brother had done, and yet he'd covered it up. No one had ever questioned what really happened to the Abyssal Prince, or one insignificant girl.

"She's still down there, waiting for a Prince to wake her up again. Even dead's better than the Abyss," Charlie said. "Sometimes, when I'm here, she talks to me in my dreams. Roots around my head and makes me suffer." His lips widened in a smile, and I saw the crazy up front for once. Charlie *liked* it. Whatever happened to him here, whatever the Abyssal Prince could still do in death, whatever torture she put him through was a relief to him. She was like maggots to the poison in his head.

"I thought Moonset killed the last one," Jenna whispered at my side. "If she's alive, then what's she still doing here?"

Charlie heard, though, and he laughed. "You think it's that easy? That there's only two kinds of people: living and worm-meat? Some things don't die the same way you will, little girl. Oh yeah, I see you, Diana's little demon. The dead don't do *quiet.* They scream, and shout, and rattle their chains. Ain't nothing left but a need to be heard. You'd best remember that."

"I'd text myself a reminder," she said sweetly, "but you nuked my friend's phone."

Charlie lifted up the bottle of clear fluid. Vodka or gin, I was pretty sure. He only got really talkative when there were a few drinks in him. "Ain't that the truth," Charlie crowed, lifting the bottle towards her in a salute. "You dig her up, you'll see what I mean. Bitch ain't dead. Clawed her way into my baby and won't give it up no matter what. Savannah always loved horses. Best place for her."

"They buried her alive," Jenna said slowly. "Jesus."

"*He* ain't got nothing to do with it." Charlie drained the rest of the bottle and then tossed it away. It clattered and spun on the dirt after bouncing off the ground, but managed not to break.

"So what are you doing?" Maddy called out. "Why wait out here? You think she's going to come back?"

It was the question I should have asked myself from the moment I realized Charlie was involved. There was only one reason Charlie would come back here. He summoned the Abyssal Prince, and in some way, he was responsible for what had happened to his girlfriend. Whether he gave her to Kore, or Kore took her because of who she was to Charlie, either way it was his fault.

"Moonset didn't stop her," I realized. "*Charlie* did. All Moonset did was cover it up. That's why they let Cooper take all the credit. They didn't want anyone asking questions, and the best way to do that was to make someone else responsible."

Kevin walked up next to me, opposite of Jenna. "Is that true?" There was something strange in his voice. Maybe the boy scout needed to hear him confess for it to stick.

"Damned anyway. What's it matter?" Charlie's surly attitude wasn't exactly an admission of guilt.

"Is it *true*?"

I reached out and put a hand on Kevin's shoulder. It was cold to the touch, so much so that I snatched my hand away as soon as the feeling stretched up my arm. It tingled like an electric shock, my skin hissing from *too cold* and spasming from *stun gun*. I looked to him in horror, my thought processes dulled by the sensations running up my arm. My jaw was locked. I couldn't speak.

Charlie didn't notice, though. Charlie never knew when to shut his mouth, and I couldn't stop him from barreling on. "Thought I was the smarter one. Thought I'd found something that would show Cy he wasn't so great. But then it took her, and they came to me for help." There was a haze of sadness in his eyes. "You have to bury the body beneath a circle of iron, y'know. Lucky for them, we got one big one right here."

One second Kevin was next to me, the next he was twenty feet away. Charlie was on the edge of the carousel, and Kevin in front of him, standing solid with nothing but air beneath his feet. Charlie flailed, Kevin's hand gripped around his throat. The sound of the old man's gasp brought me back to myself.

The sound of his neck snapping, though, was something else entirely.

THIRTY-ONE

Not all creatures die a mortal death.
Sometimes death is cunning: a caress instead
of a slap. Even death can fall in love.
Even death can dare to break the rules.

....

The Princes of Hell

Kevin let the body drop, and Charlie flopped onto the ground the way that corpses do. Silver light spilled out of his eyes, spotlights that washed the expression out of his face. He stared at the three of us, head cocked to the side like an animal studying prey. Looking for weaknesses and patterns to exploit.

"Kevin?" Maddy's whisper fell to the dirt around us and crawled forward.

"He hasn't been Kevin for a while," I said dully. How long? When had Kevin stopped being Kevin, and when had he started to be the monster?

"I asked you to name me," the Abyssal Prince said, using Kevin's mouth. "You refused. I was forced to take a name for myself."

"You didn't take a name," I spat. "You stole Kevin's!"

Jenna and Maddy came up on either side of me, and for a second, I thought they were *protecting* me, like they were somehow going to shield me from whatever it was that the Abyssal was going to do.

"*Borrowed.*" The Prince held up his pointer finger. "Though quite a bit more permanent. He's still in here, alive and well. Only we've become something more. It's really a beautiful thing, Malcolm. I am him and he is me. We are one. My spirit, his soul, one inspired blend of creation."

"He's not going to let us go," Maddy said, even as she was busy tying up her hair to keep it out of the way.

"He will." I stepped forward, because everything was okay. Charlie was the reason we were all here. He was the one who invoked Maleficia, summoned up an Abyssal Prince, then found a way to kill it. He was the one who took all those repressed loathings about his own past and his brother's crimes, and spat out a kid to repeat the same cycle of darkness.

Bad blood indeed.

That was all good news, though. Because Charlie was dead, and that was the deal. I stared the Prince dead in the eyes, letting the light blind me. I didn't have anything to fear from him. "You got what you wanted. Charlie's dead. You know where Kore's buried. Now you promised you'd fix Justin and the others, and leave. Let the kids go. You've got your vengeance."

Kevin stepped off the carousel, ignoring me as he started

to circle it. There was a frown of concentration on his features, not a look I'd normally ever seen before. Kevin didn't have to work for anything, and he definitely didn't struggle for answers. But the Prince was.

Something was wrong.

"You haven't delivered my sister's body. Not completely. Not yet."

Had to bury her beneath a circle of iron. Charlie had said as much. That meant... "You can't get under there. That's why she's buried here. She can't get out. And you can't get in." The words slipped out without meaning to, and Kevin's head whipped around. He didn't like me knowing one of their weaknesses. Even less that I spoke it out loud.

I might have just signed all of our death warrants.

"If you think we're going to help you, then you're not listening to the human you've got hostage up in there." Jenna would pick now of all times to really push her luck. "If there's a hole in the ground big enough for one dead Abyssal, there's room for two."

The Abyssal *laughed.* Kevin's face twisted in ways I didn't even think were possible, rictus extremes of a Joker's grin that made my jaws hurt. "Stupid little girl. You're trying to anger me. So transparent. There is nothing I fear in your darkbond. I can't harm you, but..." He reached out a hand, and a three-part harmony slid out of his mouth like the call of a snake-oil salesman.

I'd seen the kind of damage his songs could do. Whatever magic the Abyssal had, it was wrapped up in his voice. But the song wasn't meant for me, and Jenna wasn't reacting either.

We both turned towards Maddy, the only one of us not protected by the Moonset curse.

She took a halting step forward, and then another, her forehead a giant knot of confusion. She looked to be struggling, which was good, but I knew it couldn't last forever.

"Leave her alone! She's got no part in this!"

The Prince's silver eyes slammed into me with a physical force, and I took a step back in surprise. "She came along for the ride. She knew the risks." The words echoed all around us, as his mouth was busy with the sonata call. His torchlight eyes turned to Maddy. "You've always loved me, haven't you, my dear?"

Jenna ran to block Maddy's path, and with a wave of his hand like a maestro's flourish, the Prince threw her to the side. Jenna crumpled to the ground and found my eyes. For a moment, we both hesitated, waiting. *Praying* for the curse to activate. But there was no intent to kill us in his motivations. Our greatest defense—the Coven bond that was supposed to kill anything that tried to kill us—was useless.

"You don't have to do this!" I didn't try to stop Maddy, instead I made a beeline for Kevin himself. "What happened to not wanting to be a monster? What happened to all that talk about wanting to be human? About wanting to escape what you were?"

But my pleas fell on deaf ears. "Did you really believe that I would want to debase myself that way? That I would become anything less than what I am now?" He sounded surprised by my questions.

I gritted my teeth. "Yes." Ten feet away. I kept walking forward, refusing to be intimidated by the song and dance.

But Maddy was still walking forward too. And she was going to reach him first, unless I picked up my speed, or did something to distract him.

"I thought you loved me. Is this how you show your love? By showing off and hurting some stupid girl because you're afraid of what happens if you hurt one of us? Afraid that all your power is nothing compared to the curse cocktail my daddy whipped up?"

The song stopped, and the Prince held up his hand to halt her. Maddy jerked to a step as he stormed towards me, literally stormed. He kicked up clouds of dirt around him with every step, and thunderclaps struck every time his heel stomped down. The heavens above us became a hell as the clouds turned tornado-drill black in a span of moments. The sky could barely contain his rage.

I never stopped, though. I wasn't afraid of him. Despite everything he'd done. Everything he'd set into motion. He'd killed in front of me. Twice. And yet, he was a bully. And the first thing I ever taught Justin and Cole was the most important rule in life: you never, *ever* back down to a bully.

So he stormed into my space and I shoved him back. Got in his face, pressed my forehead against his and used my larger size to my advantage. "Fight it, Kevin. You're stronger than this."

"Oh, Malcolm." He reached up to run his hand down the side of my face, but I slapped it away. "Do you really believe everything that fairy tales say? They are wonderful lies, masterful even, but what do you expect? They are named for my kind, and we are the most beautiful lies you will ever swallow whole. Kevin is *gone*. I am everything he was and more."

"Kevin's my friend. And I'm going to find a way to free him from you if it's the last thing I do."

He mulled that one over. "It could be. Malcolm, don't you see? This isn't an invasion, with my spirit pushing his soul aside. This is a *merger*. Even if you could find a way to force me from this body, Kevin is *me* now. You'll leave nothing but an empty shell behind."

"No."

"That's why they buried them together," Jenna said in a whisper behind me. "Because they couldn't get Kore out of the girl."

"There is no *together*. Only the Prince, and the shell."

I took a step back. Kevin's fate had the power to do what the Prince could not. Hurt me. Wound me. He'd been the first person who actually seemed like he *got* it. He was a witch, but he was also a decent person. Something that I'd always thought was about as rare as unicorns. To know that he was … that there was no fixing this. Not for him.

Kevin was dead.

Was this how Charlie felt, once upon a time? When he'd come to stop his girlfriend from killing his classmates, and she pleaded with him? When she professed her love and made him promises?

In my moment of distraction, Maddy and the Prince came together like two magnets. He ran fingers through her hair, and crooned to her, soft and quiet. "I can kill her quick, or I can make you watch. It's your choice, Malcolm. Or you can choose how she hurts herself first. My song cannot be ignored. She will do anything I ask, because I ask it of her. Because she *loves* me. Don't you, pet?"

Maddy tipped her head to one side, exposing her neck. There was a quiet, dreamy smile on her face. "Hey, Kevin?"

The Prince leaned in towards her, Kevin's hair falling rebelliously into his eyes. "Yes?"

"I'm into girls, asshole." The knife came out of nowhere. Maddy shoved it under and up, one smooth plunge through the skin. But that wasn't all she had up her sleeve. She used the momentum to shove herself backwards and shouted, "*Lex divok!*"

The Prince hurtled backwards almost a dozen feet, the fury in Maddy's voice matching the extra punch in the spell. He stumbled off the ground for a moment and flailed, but just as he should have toppled to the ground, preternatural grace kicked in and he landed as carefully and as easily as if he'd planned the attack himself.

"You should have been more specific," Maddy called out. "Because Kevin's been my best friend for years, and I already love him like a brother. But not like what you're going for."

A blossom of red crept out from underneath Kevin's hoodie, but the Prince plucked the knife from his skin like it was little more than a scratch.

"Calm down," I shouted, stepping in front of Maddy before the Prince could retaliate. "We'll move the carousel. You can have your sister's body, or whatever is left, and *no one has to be filleted in the process.*"

I put my hand on Maddy's shoulder and pointed her backwards. "Stay behind Jenna."

"I'm not scared of that thing!" she replied, indignant.

"Good for you," I said, my words short. "But if he tries

attacking you again, he has to go through Jenna first. And she's got the curse on her side. This is the only way to keep him from using you."

The Prince eyed the three of us as we gathered together, but he didn't move from his perch. He crouched down, playing with the knife that Maddy had left in his gut, flipping it around his hands like he was some kind of badass. Was that something *Kevin* knew how to do? Or something the Prince had picked up?

I turned my back on him, because worrying about what the Prince could or could not do wasn't getting me anywhere. Jenna was biting her lip, but she still looked ready to fight. "We can't beat him," she said softly. Too softly for the Prince to overhear. Hopefully.

"We don't have to beat him. We just have to ..." but I didn't know what we just had to do. Nevermind that. I switched tactics. "Back in Coven class, they said you can share knowledge through the Coven bond." Jenna nodded slowly. "So you could theoretically use spells that you'd never been taught, right?"

"What are you thinking?" she asked slowly.

"Cole knows a hell of a lot of illusions." It was convenient that that was his talent, because he had a habit of making even the most innocuous spells destructive by accident. Illusions couldn't set things on fire or knock walls down. "When the Witchers fought the Prince, they used force. Attack spells, violent spells. Maybe you can't kill it with fire, but maybe we can trick it."

A slow, vindictive smile started to spread across Jenna's

face, the kind of smile that made principals tremble behind their desks. There was no one better suited for driving someone crazy. "What are you going to do?"

"I'm going to figure out a way to move the merry-go-round."

"Mal, this isn't an extra set of reps at the gym. I don't care how strong you are, you can't move the whole thing. It has to weigh tons."

In such a short amount of time, I'd come to rely on the spells hidden in the darkbond. Spells that our parents had left for us. Why, I still didn't know. I should be worried that by tapping into their secret magic, I was somehow playing into their hands. But at the same time, this magic was the only thing I'd seen slow the Prince down even a little.

I didn't dare keep my eyes closed for more than a moment. I didn't trust him not to strike out at the others the moment my attention was turned away. So I had to concentrate on the bond between us, on the things that kept us together. The fights. The wars. Jenna and I on the roof of the hospital, the two of us against the world. Cole on my nerves and Justin on my back, and Bailey, scared little Bailey who I sometimes thought was the most like me. She *wanted* things she couldn't have so badly.

Maybe we were chained together, and maybe that meant that there were things I wouldn't be able to do. But that didn't mean I stopped fighting.

We all had our battles. Maybe mine weren't the mountains I'd thought they were. A month ago, I never would have thought I'd have given in to our heritage and actively pursued the magic that might save all of us. But here I was.

The Coven bond opened around me, and I could feel us like the five points of a star. Equal points. Their lives swarmed around me, and I felt the four of them rallying together. The Prince could do a lot of things, but he couldn't do what he'd once promised me. He couldn't break this down.

No one knew how the Coven bond formed, or what caused it to form. But I did. The five of us together were a perfect circle, balanced in ways I couldn't entirely understand, and some that I did. When it came to our hunger for power, Jenna and I were opposite points, and Justin the fulcrum in between. But in other ways, Justin and Jenna made up one side to themselves, and I was the fulcrum between them, and our younger siblings.

Moonset's magic spun around me like a halo, and I knew somewhere deep in my head that *this* was why I was the one who could use it. Because I was the only one who would hesitate before pressing the button. I was the last line of defense.

I didn't have the slightest idea what half of the magic inside me did. But I knew it was dangerous. It was powerful, and though it didn't *feel* dark, it came from Moonset. And they weren't the good guys, no matter the good deeds they'd done along the way.

Both times before, when I needed something to happen, the selection was done by instinct. I reached out, and grabbed whichever symbol or spell felt the most *right*. But just as I reached out this time, my eyes slipped up, and I saw the symbol painted onto the roof of the carousel.

Once when we were younger, Cole had been obsessed with the idea of camping. He wouldn't shut up about it until Justin and I took him out back to camp in the yard. But once we got out there, he realized how dark it got at night, and he freaked. Flashlights wouldn't cut it. And so Justin and I had to drag out every extension cord we had just to reach all the way back into the kitchen and plug in the tiny lamp from Cole's bedside table.

Looking at the symbol was like plugging in that last extension cord, and the sudden explosion of light caused by the connection.

I could hear Jenna and Maddy moving around me, but I couldn't look away. I heard the Prince snarl, and prayed they were still safe. Because I didn't know what was about to happen. But it was going to be big.

The thousands of spells spinning around me in the aether cycloned around me and stopped on a symbol like an arrow, careening into the darkness. My mouth opened reflexively and the arrow exploded out of me. The symbol beat against my skin, hummed in time with my heartbeat. This was *mine*. Something that wasn't meant for the others.

The last of the symbol forced its way out of me and left me gasping for air, my lungs screaming from drought. How long had I been locked like that, mouth opened but not a single sound to be heard? Sweat dripped down my face, down my sides and back.

My ears started to buzz, the way they did around electronics. The slight hum to the air, a hint of something about to happen. The air around me stilled. My eyes cleared only to see that *everything* had stilled. The words I'd heard Jenna using were in the air all around me, a dazzling mix of fireworks and shadow. Rainbows refracted around miniature prisms, darkness collected like fog.

The pattern of it was breathtaking, but it was the frozen rictus of Jenna's grin that made my heart skip in my throat.

Something was wrong. Jenna, Maddy, the light and the dark. Somehow it was stuck. Time was frozen. Or maybe not frozen, but split right down the middle between moments. And there was the Prince, only now I could see the two trapped in one. Kevin's body, his insides squashed by trying to contain something that was so compressed that the Prince had been right: there was no room left inside for something as gossamer as a soul.

I touched one of the lights, one of Jenna's illusions. It rippled in the air like still water. The only sound was my breathing. The terrified staccato rhythm of my heart. Sweat dropping from my hair to the ground beneath me. I was the only sound in this temporally free world I'd created.

The buzzing in my ears came and went, the pitch of it changing by degrees. It was like being a radio, and having the frequency slightly changed. And even that was erased, until I really was the only thing I could hear.

Until the voice in my ear. The voice I'd never heard before and yet would know anywhere.

"Hello, son."

THIRTY-TWO

*"We've often asked why. Why was it so important
for Moonset to have children? I sometimes wonder
if they wanted to leave something good behind.
Their chance to make amends."*

....

Illana Bryer

"Each of us is recording one of these, because we're not sure
which of you will hear it." Cyrus Denton's voice in my ears,
as calm and as even as if we were having Sunday breakfast
around the table. "Brandon can pinpoint a lot of things, but
not this." Brandon Sutter. Cole's dad. Was he some kind
of seer? There was no record of that anywhere. But then I
remembered Cole's insistence on the fire.

"Oh well," he continued as though this was just another
insipid conversation. Not like he was reaching across the years

from his cage in Hell. Not like he was at least as much of a monster as the Prince himself. "I'm sure you know the stories about the Abyssal. Listen to me, Malcolm. Whatever you do, you *must* kill it. If you're hearing this, you're the one that can access the Codex. You must not tell anyone that it exists. The Congress will destroy you the minute they learn of it."

The Congress. This was Cyrus towards the end. He must have known that the Congress would rebuild itself, that Moonset would not be successful in their attempt to eradicate the world they came from.

"There are many things we've learned over the years. Magicks that would blind you with their beauty. The Codex is our fail-safe for you. It is of the oldest kinds of magic, the kind that came before all others. There is little that can stand against it. But be careful, you may already know that the power is finite. Each spell will only work once."

This needs to stop. I can't be hearing this. It didn't matter what he said. Because no, no, this was exactly what I needed to avoid. It was easy to be the son of Cyrus Denton when he wasn't real. When he was a monster at the end of the picture book. Not a voice in my head. Not the kind of memory with hooks and barbs. Not something that would stick to my thoughts like tar.

I screamed, but there was nothing to do for it. His voice was a recording in my head and I could tear myself apart, but it would continue until it was done. Until he was done with me.

"If you hear this, you've met one. We always knew another Abyssal Prince would come. These creatures don't die the way all things do. Their bodies fall, but their spirits do not depart. And should one escape, this town is a beacon that will draw it in. It will want the sibling it lost. Only he knows how to bring his sister back to life. One Abyssal can be stopped. But two...I do not know that the world could recover.

"Kill it, and bury it here. The merry-go-round is made of iron, and that will be enough to contain it. Forever."

There were other sounds. Background noises. Voices. Cyrus's voice changed. I heard him exhale, so real in my ear I almost thought I could feel it against my skin. "Malcolm, I just—"

But I would never find out what he'd meant to say next. The sound cut out with a jarring whine of feedback in my ears. I writhed around, the sound so loud it felt like my brain was liquefying. More than that, though, I was desperate to restore the connection. To find out what he'd been about to say.

Time started up again around me, knocking me to my knees with the force of it. Things in my head were upended, a computer with too many things to process. I could still feel the halo of magic spiraling around me. Only now it was like there was something else at play, seeking out particular entries.

There was movement around me. Explosions. But with the slurry in my head, coating everything in a thick, slow molasses, I couldn't summon up even the smallest amount of focus. It was like the night of the farmhouse, when the four of us had been seated in church pews, mindless puppets waiting for Luca to invoke the Maleficia and bridge the way for the Abyssals to possess us.

I'd been there, that night. But also not. It wasn't easy, like being asleep or not being aware. I was aware. We all were. Aware, and trapped inside our bodies unable to control anything, *do* anything. It was a waking coma, knowing every moment that the cage you were in was perfect, and you were never getting out. And no one would ever know you were still there, because you couldn't *do* anything.

When I had nightmares, they were about that night. About what it felt like when the Abyssals and Luca had wrapped us up tight and barely left an air hole in the box.

I screamed, and this time it had the power to do what it couldn't before. Every infraction, every argument, every conflict boiled up in my chest until I opened my mouth and *roared*. It was nothing more than all of my frustrations, fears, and rages given a voice, but three sets of eyes turned towards me.

The three of them, two humans and an infernal faerie, stared at me like I was the one who'd lost my mind. Spells tumbled down due to lack of concentration, fireworks fizzled out, and illusions turned to mirages turned to shimmers.

I looked to the carousel and *wanted* to see it move. The spells in my head scurried to obey. I could picture the spell in my head as it slithered and danced along my teeth like jungle vines and flew from my mouth. The carousel, the entire structure, began sliding toward me with all the speed of a Big Wheel tricycle. But as it gained momentum it picked up speed, until it rolled through what had once been the battlefield with the Prince.

The others scurried backwards and out of the way, but as it approached I hopped on and wove my way through the army of horses, grabbing onto the poles to keep my balance. I wasn't the only one. On the other side, the Prince was also slipping through the aisles, but he jumped and bounced from the horses' saddles. His balance never faltered.

We both approached the other side. The ground beneath

the carousel was hollow and deep, a pit that a normal-sized person couldn't have climbed out of. At the bottom there was a gray and blue sheet spread out, and a girl no older than seventeen on top of it.

She was casually pretty, blond hair swept away from her face. Despite the fact that she'd been dead for at least twenty years, it looked like less than twenty minutes had passed. There was no decomposure. No rot. She was as healthy looking as she must have been on the day she died.

Except that her skin was tinged the faintest, yet most inhuman blue.

Was that the Prince's influence? Or was it simply the lack of oxygen in her blood? Did she even *have* blood anymore?

"Oh my God," Jenna breathed, as she and Maddy appeared after running the long way around.

"Kore," the Prince breathed. A curl of *relief* wrapped around me, the kind that settled in the bones.

"Mal!" Jenna's warning tone ended in a shriek when the body in the grave *twitched.*

Maddy fell backwards, with not even a hint of her normal poise. "She's still alive?"

The Prince looked both sullen and amused at the same time. "Do you think a single mortal death can snuff something that was forged in the chaos of Creation? Always, we endure."

We were closer than he must have realized. His need to be closer to the sister he'd lost brought him right up next to me. And when he looked up at me, there was such *joy* in Kevin's eyes. He thought I would fail. He'd expected it.

"You have been a valiant champion, my Malcolm," the

Prince started, but before he could say anything more, I grabbed him by the front of Kevin's hoodie.

My heart clutched, but even as the nerves in my body spiked, I smiled. Cocked my head to the side. "Do you hear that?" He stared at me, giving away nothing. But I saw his eyes flicker, just for a moment. "That little thread of fear, tangling up in my heart and growing." I shook my head, smiled. "You made a mistake, Kevin. You thought I was afraid that I would grow up to be just like my father. That's not it at all. Not quite.

"I'm not afraid of becoming my father someday," I said. Even though I was separated from the others, I could still feel the swarm of symbols in my head, the rush of thousands of pages flipping along the Coven bond.

"I'm afraid, because I already am."

A grave big enough for one was big enough for two. There was nothing I wanted more right now than to put him down where his sister was. Forever.

I opened my mouth, summoning the spell that would stop him. The one that Moonset had set aside for just this very purpose. That was the point of the conversation with Cyrus, and the confusion afterwards. Subconsciously extracting the proper spells, the ones that would stop him. Three of them bounced through the back of my mind, flaring like tension headaches waiting to be born.

The Prince *screamed* before I could get the spell out, and the world rocked apart around me.

We were torn out of reality and stitched back in somewhere else. The transport was rough and hard on my body, and

I slammed down against the ground after what had to have been a ten-foot fall. The tiles around us cracked and spider-webbed, in some places ripped out of the floor entirely.

The fall had the bad luck of separating me from my hold on the Prince. I looked up from the tile to see him stumbling backwards, all his preternatural grace gone in the face of his fear.

He *knew*. Maybe the spells I'd used before had clued him in, or maybe he saw it in my eyes. I don't know. But he ran from me like he knew I was going to kill him. And worse, like he knew that I *could*.

The hospital lobby was still boarded up after the attack, windows covered by sheets of plywood and everything else moved into corners from where it had been. The hospital? Why would he bring us to the hospital. And then I looked up and swore.

The Prince had systemically stolen the hearts of half the student body. As the infections got dangerous, the Congress had been locking the kids up for their own good, turning the entire hospital into a mental ward to keep them docile.

"Throw off your shackles, my children," the Prince screamed from the far side of the room, never taking his eyes from me. There was something *more* to his voice, a reverberation in the air that I couldn't explain until I realized it was coming from the speakers. He spoke, and his words echoed throughout the building.

"Your Prince has finally come for you," he continued. "Break the chains that bind you. Come to me. Be free, children. Be my hands. Be mine."

He brought us to the hospital because he had a ready-made army just waiting in the wings.

"Kill anyone who threatens me," the Prince screamed, wide eyed as he stumbled into a stairwell and slammed the door shut behind him.

A psychotic army he'd just set against *me*.

Perfect.

THIRTY-THREE

*Upon their surrender, Moonset offered up the
location of the compound where we found
the children. What was once a finishing school for
southern girls a century ago was filled with plans,
schematics, hit lists, and incendiary devices.
And five babies, sleeping sound.*

Moonset: A Dark Legacy

Chaos descended upon the hospital quickly, a wave of psychotic rage tangible in the air. There were lights and electricity for another thirty seconds before the building went dark.
Screams and other sounds of fury rumbled through the floor.
I had no idea what was happening inside. Had everyone gone
feral? Were the Witchers holding them back? I had no clue
what I was stepping into.

"Why are you doing this? You know me. You know what it is I want. That hasn't changed." His voice continued to haunt me while I planned my next move. "*I* haven't changed. I am the same as I was that first day."

"Lesson number one about humans, then," I muttered under my breath, wiping my face down with my shirt. "Monsters might stay the same, but people change every second."

"Yes, you did," Kevin replied over the speaker system. "Changed. Who taught you hoard starfire? I hoped I was wrong, that the way you banished me was a fluke. You've been keeping secrets, Malcolm. I do not like it."

Starfire? *The power inside me, the one that doesn't have a name.* It was woven into the darkbond. But the Prince, who was more perceptive than most, couldn't see it. And he'd acted like he knew so much about what Moonset had done to us! It had been a lie all along.

I crept down the hall and past the gift shop. There was another stairway towards the back, and it wouldn't come out right by the elevators. If anyone was going to be waiting for me, I was sure they would be there. But if I could sneak up through a side hallway, maybe I could get away without catching any of his darkbound minions in a bad mood.

But where did I even start? Where would the Prince go? There had to be hundreds of rooms in the hospital, and he could be hiding anywhere. And it wasn't like I knew the kind of magic that could track him down.

But maybe one of the others did.

The more I reached for the Coven bond, the easier it was to find, becoming like a second awareness in my head.

There was something comforting about it, feeling four pulses of light all around me, knowing that they were still alive without a shadow of a doubt. That they were okay.

Malcolm? Malcolm, can you hear me? Jenna in my head. *Mal, you'd better still be okay, I swear to God I will kill you myself if you're not.*

I tried to send something back, some confirmation that I was okay, only to hear silence in my head. Maybe if I hadn't blown off all the Coven bond classes, I would know *how* to communicate with them now. I kept trying for a few seconds before I finally broke and texted her.

This was just great. Here I was, trying to kill something older than the dinosaurs and I could barely use enough magic to light up the stairwell so that I could see.

My fingers slipped over the keys when I heard gunfire coming from the floor above. I froze and crept towards the wall and out of the way, just in case. Who thought that guns were a smart idea to bring into the hospital? Did the Witchers even use guns?

Above me, the fired shots grew louder when I snuck into the pitch-black stairwell. I grabbed for the handrail before the light disappeared and took a few deep breaths. Acclimating myself. But I didn't have long. A shaft of light appeared a few floors above me as someone opened the stairwell door. The sound of the next shot recoiled into the stairwell and intensified it a thousand times over. I staggered back towards my own door, barely able to hear anything.

But when I got back out into the hall and ducked around the corner, nothing happened. My ears continued to ring for a few minutes, and the only bright side was that I missed the specifics of Kevin over the loudspeaker. I could hear him talking, but couldn't make out the words.

Finally, the ringing quieted, and I crept back the way I'd come.

With all the noise, I lost my connection to the Coven bond. Connecting a second time was more of a struggle. Every time I reached for it, I found myself recoiling again, anticipating more shots ripping through the hospital, and maybe me.

The stairwell door flew open before I could grab it. I fell back as bodies flew past me. They didn't pay any attention to me. All of them were rough and ragged, dressed in hospital gowns over pants and shirts. All of them teenagers. Kids I knew on sight.

"You cannot stop me. And you cannot stop your children, can you? The way your spells fall past them. My words are all they hear now." Kevin laughed over the loudspeaker. He'd stopped talking to me. Now he was talking to someone else, and the rest of us were in on the call. One of the adults, maybe? One of the Witchers?

"I told you they belong to me. Only my magic speaks to them." His voice sharpened and grew louder. "The adults don't trust you. But you are my children, and you are *strong*. They seek to lock you up, afraid of what they see in your eyes. I want you to show them. Let your passions catch flame and show them who you are!"

The Prince wasn't just mobilizing a personal guard, he was deploying an army. "What are you doing?" I didn't have to raise my voice, but I did anyway. "Why are you doing this?"

"They continue to resist. I won't let them hurt my children."

"They're not *your children*," I broke in hotly. "Children shouldn't be sent to *war!*"

"Your parents certainly didn't think so," the Prince said slyly. Hearing Cyrus's voice might have thrown me off balance, but there were a solid dozen years of walls in place. The Prince seemed to think he could use my parents against me, but I wasn't the one who crumbled under their pressure.

"The adults are going to stop you. They're smarter than you are."

"No they aren't," he singsonged like this was a game. "They need something more concrete to worry about."

I needed to stop talking to him. The more I talked, the longer he was in control. And the longer he was in control, the more people were going to get hurt. So he continued talking, continued trying to seduce me with his words and his own particular brand of righteous carnage.

And I focused on my family instead.

Jenna's words preceded the bond this time—*just concentrate on your heartbeat and hold this in your mind*—but the pulse points of the others followed, everyone but hers and mine were accelerating, fueled by fear.

The image she sent was of three closing parentheses, an image of something broadcasting. Simple, but I followed her directions even as she was chiding me—*I swear to God you'd better be listening to me. Damnit, Mal, where are you? Please be okay*—and felt something click inside my head.

Jenna? I tested.

Her relief washed through the bond. *Mal! Where are you? We'll come find you.*

Whatever you do, don't let anyone near the grave, I said. *You have to make sure no one else finds it.*

Mal? Bailey. Bailey was okay. *The lights went out. People in the hallway keep screaming.* Hearing her voice in my head was a relief. I *knew* they were okay, but it was something else to hear her voice. The more I focused on her, the more I could see the things she was seeing. It wasn't the Coven bond that flared around me, though. It was the darkbond.

Bailey and Cole had barricaded themselves in with Justin, who was still out of it. I could *feel* Bailey's exhaustion through her words. They'd been smart, and jammed the other hospital bed up in the small alcove by the door, trapping it between the wall and the open bathroom.

Bailey was curled up on the bed next to Justin, her hand on his forehead. And she was doing everything she could to keep him docile, but she was scared, and weak, and the Prince's sway was stronger than she was. Bailey's gift for controlling people was stronger than anyone gave her credit for, and making Justin resist the Prince's commands was taking a toll on her.

Cole had a baseball bat in his hands, and he was on guard. *Where the hell did you get a baseball bat?* Of *course* Cole would have a baseball bat.

Found it. Took it. Cole kept himself casually innocent. I remembered what the Prince had said about only infecting Justin. Cole had said there had to be a fire, but we'd stopped him before he could start one, and then Luca.

But now wasn't the time to worry about all of that. That would have to come later, after I'd stopped the Prince.

How has he got a bat? Jenna asked. *Are you there with them?*

No, I sent back. *But I am at the hospital. Can't you feel along the Coven bond, see where they're at?*

No, she replied dubiously. *They haven't shown us the spells to access that yet. How are* you *doing it?*

Of course, because it was the darkbond, not the Coven bond that gave me access. *That's a very long story for later. But I promise I'll tell you,* I hurriedly added, before Jenna could voice the growing frustration I could feel from her.

You guys stay where you are. Cole, you have to keep an eye on Bailey. The Prince is strong. Really strong.

I'm fine, Bailey sent, even as Cole added, *I always watch out for Bailey.* There was an undercurrent of "how do you not know this by now" to his message.

He's hiding behind the kids he infected. How can I stop them without hurting them, Jen? Because when it came to magic, Jenna knew more than any of the rest of us. Bailey had a gift for mind control, but she could barely keep Justin down, which meant that was out for me. And Cole could use illusions, but I didn't know how much good they'd do.

The Prince said he's making them resistant to magic. The Witchers can't contain them, I added. *So I need alternatives.*

Chloroform, Cole suggested.

Hospitals don't have a ready supply of chloroform, I don't think. Even if they did, it would be locked up. Jenna was thoughtful. *I have a few ideas. You guys, pool together anything you think might help.*

That was how I came to find a handful of spells I'd never bothered to learn myself. Magical cheat sheets in my brain. Three of them. Justin was the lone holdout, but then Justin was off in his own little world. But I could feel Jenna skimming through the spells that Cole and Bailey knew, and I saw the moment she crept into Justin's head.

And the shock that struck her when she did.

Most of the magic we knew was similar. Each of us, in theory, got taught a few unique things. Spells geared towards our skill sets. So Bailey knew spells that Cole didn't, and vice versa. Justin and Jenna, as the most capable out of all of us, knew the most. I, by choice, knew the least. That wasn't the problem.

The problem was everything *else* Justin had in his head. There was a whole compendium of magic that not only didn't look familiar to me, but to none of the others, as well. Spell after spell. Dozens of them.

Justin's been hoarding magic. Jenna voiced the betrayal that cut her the deepest, but it cut the rest of us all in different ways. For Bailey, it was the advent of more secrets. For Cole, it was a renewed, and broken, trust. For me, it was just the same gnawing worry as always. Each of them thought magic was the solution. Not the problem. But at least Jenna was honest about her power cravings.

I brushed up against the part of us all that connected to Justin, and caught nothing more than flashes. A book. Something about a postcard. And a gnawing terror that woke him up every night.

This can be what you're looking for, Jenna said, having choked down her own feelings. For a moment, our connection became more than just words, as she showed me spells and pieced different ones together. A cobbled-together arsenal of magic that none of us knew the origin for.

Jenna was diligent, handing me almost a dozen different spells, and explaining the ways to use them. The only flaw to the plan was that I had to keep my concentration on the Coven bond, because the knowledge I was using wasn't mine. And the moment I lost them, I lost all of it.

The Witchers couldn't stop the Prince. They tried. The Prince was going to burn the town down and take the children as an added insult. There was only me. Only me, and the magic.

Good luck, Bailey said quietly.

I didn't tell them how much I was worried luck wouldn't be enough.

————

"You don't want to do this," Kevin whispered over the speakers as I came out onto the fourth floor. Part of me just *knew* that he was in Luca's room.

Emergency lights led a murky atmosphere to the hallway. I thought all hospitals were supposed to come equipped with backup generators, but then again, I didn't know that it was the Prince or his followers who'd cut the power. Maybe the adults thought it would give them the tactical advantage. Or maybe they just wanted to hedge their bets. It was harder to tell you were losing in the dark.

Waves of regret curled up in me, and my steps stopped. *Why was I doing this? Why was I the one who had to fight?* I shook my head. The adults should be the ones to deal with all of this. Not me. My conviction wavered.

When I tried to figure out what changed my mind, I couldn't latch onto anything. Those weren't my feelings. It was the Prince. His passions swept over me and blotted out everything but the jangly adrenaline locked in my limbs. Manipulating me without even trying.

There had been three symbols that had flared in my mind when Cyrus was talking. Three of the spells in the darkbond grimoire that had been pulled from the shuffle. One to open the grave. One to kill. And the last, to protect myself.

Warning bells rang with nerves that were all mine. Instincts told me not to use it, warned me against the cost. But I had to. I pulled the symbol down from my head and into my mouth, but even as it scurried over my teeth and out into the world, my body erupted with pain. Burns flared across my collarbones, and I screamed as the world burst into hues of red and white agony.

Just below my neck, an invisible knife carved along my skin, swayed and curved lines like a figure skater's dance of swirls and loops. I pulled my shirt away from my skin, dizzy when I realized what it was sticking to was blood. I dropped to my knees, howling, but the wounds continued to grow along my skin.

This was my protection? This was my defense? I was *killing myself,* and I didn't know why. I struggled with the tee shirt, pulled it down just enough for my skin to breathe, and saw the black and red lines on my skin. My skin split beneath the knife, cauterized by the heat, and healed over again. At first the bleeding was heavy, but it dissipated quickly, vanished until I thought I might have imagined it.

In minutes, the skin all along my collarbones was scarred and puffy. I panted, trying to figure out what I'd done to myself, when the scars started to darken—taking the shapes of the spell I'd unleashed.

The darker they grew, the more my thoughts cooled. Calmed. The adrenaline was still there, because adrenaline was physiological, not emotional, and it was crucial to survival. The Prince's voice continued to echo all around me, but his feelings couldn't touch me. But my thoughts were clear enough to realize I wasn't feeling *anything*. No more anger, no more guilt.

"Don't make me do this, Malcolm." Kevin's voice was a plea, carried through the floors and ceilings by the hospital's address system. "I don't want to hurt you."

"Stop this. You're making it harder than it has to be."

"I offered you everything," he spat in a violent surge of feedback.

"I offered you something too," I replied. "A quick death."

The walls shook with the wail that came next, *rage* and *melancholy* and *hurt* rocketing through the hospital like the emotional bomb that it was. For the first time since I'd first stumbled into the Prince's realm, I felt nothing in his wake. But immunity had its price, and I felt nothing at all.

"If you love me—" the words choked out, bolstered by the Prince's supernatural presence. *Regret* turned to *resolve* as it swept past me. "If you love me, you will *kill* him. Bring me his flesh. Bring me his eyes. Come to me cloaked in his blood, and you shall have all of my love. Forever."

The second time the walls of the hospital shook, it had nothing to do with the Prince himself. It was the combined berserker rage and fervor that he had stoked all throughout his darkbound. Was this what Moonset had planned for us—foot soldiers who would do everything they commanded? Those who remained roared in triumph and acquiescence.

They started to pour into the hallway. First came a lanky red-haired giant and a blond girl who'd been one of the first to approach me after Jenna's spell took effect and the school fell in love with me.

He swung at me, and as I dropped down to duck out of the path of his fist, the girl went for one of my legs. My balance was off, and I went tumbling down easily. She jumped onto my chest and reached for my face, her nails looking long and sharp. *Just like I told you,* Jenna said calmly in my head.

"*Aavis ul vacus. Din renardi.*" I shouted, clawing my own hand as I faced it towards her. As I climbed to my feet, I repeated it, this time clawing my right hand as I held it towards the red-headed kid. Both of them gaped, confusion painting their faces as their mouths moved, swallowed, and tried to understand what was happening to them.

You're depriving them of oxygen, but once they drop, let the spell go. It shouldn't take long. It sounds like it's a sleeper-hold spell. Like she said, they dropped a few seconds later. I let my hands drop and walked over to them. I touched each of them on the forehead with my fingertips. "*Dormic daia.*" *To keep them unconscious,* Jenna had explained.

Hands grabbed me from behind, spun me around, and tossed me. The guy who'd snuck up on me wasn't much bigger than Cole, and once I realized what was happening, I caught my stride and reversed myself as I grabbed at his arm and turned his own momentum against him. Even one-handed, I was strong enough to spin him into the wall he'd been planning to throw me into.

The kid had the wind knocked out of him, but it didn't stop him for long. He charged forward, sliding on pajama pants that were just a bit too long for him. By the time he reached me he'd almost sprawled into a pile at my feet, but I grabbed him before he could fall. *"Corous ven manus,"* I whispered, palm against his forehead.

Maybe you can turn them against each other, Jenna had said. *That spell will cross the wires in his mind. Fair is foul, and all that.*

I didn't expect it to work, despite what Jenna had said, but all the fight dropped out of the kid and he looked up at me and shrugged, then turned back and started walking the way I'd already come.

I hurried after him, turned him back around and sent him off as a scout. When a dark-haired girl came around the corner and snarled when she caught sight of me, the tiny kid snarled right back and went after her.

Picking the kid was the right choice. He was small but fast, and the more he blocked the dark-haired girl, the more confused she got. Because she only had one purpose, one objective. Give the Prince the gore he savored. She swung, and the kid darted around her and leapt onto her back like a monkey, tumbling both of them to the ground.

While they wrestled on the floor, I hurried past the pair of them and turned down the next hallway. There were almost a dozen more, all spaced out between here and the end of the hall. It looked like a mix of all the best athletes in school too. Kevin had chosen well.

It confirmed what I'd guessed, though. The Prince was hiding out in Luca's room. I still wasn't sure why, or what their connection was, but maybe he thought of Luca like the only safe port in a storm. Luca had set all of this into motion. It was only fitting he be there at the end.

The first of the guys charged at me, dropped his head like a bull, and thundered down the hall.

I can help, too, Cole said, supplying a handful of illusions. Some of the same ones that Jenna had utilized earlier. Seriously, first with the Prince and now with his minions, Cole was becoming indispensable. I made a mental note to tell him later.

"*Phantous nic.*" I took a giant step to the left, grinning when my body split into two and a duplicate Malcolm stood where I'd been. The guy charged right through the illusion and crashed into one of the walls. Okay, maybe now I saw a little of what Cole did when he messed around with illusions.

When the next one charged me—one of the guys who'd helped beat on Brice—I shifted position and wound up like a pitcher, only instead of a ball, at the apex of my throw I whispered, "*Luxic dai.*" A ball of light flew from my hand and smacked him right in the face, exploding a shower of light into his eyes.

He dropped to the ground, hands pressed against his eyes as more surged up from behind him. And then it was a good old-fashioned street brawl. I went on the offensive immediately, punching the guy at the front in the face and grabbing him by the arm. I swung him around and used him like a shield, and the next wave of attackers clocked him instead of me. I winced in sympathy when one of the punches slammed his head back into my shoulder, and he slumped in my grip.

One of them came in at the side while I was distracted and a foot slammed into my ribs, and down I went. My head smacked against the concrete wall, and for a moment there was nothing but swimming anarchy. But I shrugged off the pain, not because it didn't hurt, but because it didn't matter.

I climbed back to my feet and this time, when one of the basketball horde charged me, I kicked him in the stomach before he closed the gap. Then, while he was hunched over, I shoved him into his friends. Down they went like bowling pins, and I crossed the hall and walked into Luca's room.

"You might as well call them off now," I said, casually closing the door behind me. "It's over."

"Why are you making this so difficult? I would have taken you with me. Showed you this world, as much a fresh start for me as for you. All you had to do was give me this one thing."

"I'm not smarter than my father."

There was a startled pause from inside the room, but I still wouldn't look at him. Wouldn't give him the power. I couldn't hear the breathing devices. Luca must be somewhere else. Or else they'd evacuated him when the kids started to rampage.

"I know you think you are, Kevin. You think you can save me from my fate, unravel the Coven bond and free me from the rest. Maybe even take the magic out of me." I rested my head against the cool metal of the door. Closed my eyes. "But did you really think you were smarter than Moonset?"

"Why do you keep trying to hurt me, Malcolm? Why do you insist on fighting me at every turn? Why can't you see things the way they truly are? The chains that shackle you are unnecessary. I can show you how to cast them off."

"And what happens then? They had an entire contingency plan in place for the minute you showed up here. Because they always knew one of you would find a way out. And they made sure I had what I needed to put you back down where you belong."

"You have no idea the forces you're tampering with, Malcolm. Please, I'm begging you. I know it feels good," his voice drifted, "I know it feels *so good,* but that is a power better left buried. I don't know where they unearthed it, or how they manipulated the darkbond the way they did, but you have to let it go. It is not meant for you, my human. Nor for any other human."

His concern washed over me and then fell away. I didn't need him to tell me. "The oldest magic. The primal voice. I know."

A long pause. Elsewhere in the hospital, I heard shouts. Screams. But the room around me was quiet. My heartbeat was slowing down to even, now that the threats from the hallway were gone. Now that we were alone.

"I can take you away from here. Still. All you have to do is ask." Kevin's voice lost the throbbing hypnotic lilt that made the Prince's words so potent. "Please, Malcolm. Don't do this."

"I can't let you bring her back."

"Then take me," a second voice, rough and raspy. I looked up and saw Kevin on one of the beds, but in the other was

Luca, his eyes were open and aware. "You promised," he continued, holding out a hand across the aisle between them.

Kevin looked between the two of us like he was weighing his options.

"Luca? What are you doing?" Luca was awake. This changed... something. Had this always been part of the Prince's plan? For Luca to wake up right before the end?

Kevin climbed off the bed, and held a glass of water up to Luca's face. As the boy eagerly sipped and swallowed, Kevin looked over at me. "I truly don't understand you," he whispered. "I did everything right. Everything a human is meant to do. I was kind. I gave you my favor. I wooed you. Spared you. Protected you. And still you deny me with every word."

"You're right," I said simply. "You don't understand. How can you think to love me, when you don't even know what it is? You think the madness you unleashed is love? Love isn't decimation. And that is why you'll *be* human. Never be real."

"Don't listen to him," Luca said, voice more clear now. "You're as real as any of us. You can do better. I can show you how."

"Luca, don't." I frowned, trying to understand where he was coming from. "He's not Kevin anymore, no matter what he looks like."

"I know who he is," Luca said sharply, pale green eyes that were twins of the ones I saw in the mirror every morning. "Do you think I don't know that? I rescued him. And now he's going to return the favor."

"He has to be sent back. You got mixed up with the Maleficia before, but it's not your fault. You were targeted. The man who sold you the book—"

"The man who sold you the book is dead," Kevin replied smoothly, brushing the fringe out of Luca's face. He looked to me. "I know you thought you were saving him. Matthew screamed for me before they killed him."

The Congress had him put to death already? No, I thought, shaking my head. That wasn't right. They would have wanted to extract all the information they could have first. He'd lived in Carrow Mill in secret for decades. They would want to know everything he had done. That was the only thing that made sense.

"That's what they'll do to me too," Luca said. "I'm not ready to die yet."

"It's not your time," Kevin agreed.

"Stay out of this," I said, crossing the room and shoving Kevin back to the other bed. Trying to deal with Luca directly, without the creature in between us, whispering in his ear. "Luca, you were a victim in all this. They'll understand. We'll *make* them understand."

"And what," he said dismissively, his lips curled, "live the rest of my life like you? If he wants to drag them all down to hell with him, who am I to stop him? This town's done nothing to earn my trust."

"I always gave you a fair shake, Luca. I never held it against you," Kevin supplied.

"No, you didn't," Luca said slowly.

"I won't let you leave with him," I said, turning back to Kevin. He'd taken to lounging on the bed, hands tucked behind his arms.

"Why, because you're *family*? I offered you everything, Malcolm. You're the one choosing to be nothing."

Cold logic only took me so far. I *knew* the Congress. Doing the smart thing wasn't always their way. Luca was right; he would be eliminated. They thought it was better to kill an infection before it could spread. And even if he'd been duped into becoming the warlock who'd summoned the Maleficia, he was still a warlock. The black arts were a contamination.

My hesitation was all they needed. Kevin moved like a blur, shoving me as he lunged for Luca's bed. I flew back, across the room and into the wall. My shoulder hit it hard, a jolt of fire shooting down my arm as I cried out, dizzy with sudden pain. To make matters worse, as I landed, my foot twisted wrong and my ankle spasmed beneath me as I dropped. This wasn't happening. Not now. I gritted my teeth, focused my breath, and tried to use my good arm and my good foot to come back up. The pain faded, quickly, but the throbbing was heavy and hard. Even thinking about moving was a bad idea.

My shoulder was dislocated, or maybe something had torn. The ankle was definitely sprained. But I wouldn't stop. I had to protect them. There was pain, but it didn't seem important.

Kevin had his hand over the top of Luca's head, palming it like a basketball. "You don't even know what they locked away inside of you."

I surged forward, dropping when my arm hit the side of the bed and the pain overtook all my senses. I crumpled to my knees, my head swimming. "What do you mean?"

"Oh, their plans for you make me tingle, my champion," he whispered. "You were right. They planned for *so many* things. I can see them now. You have no idea what they have in store for you. Even now, they must be laughing."

"Kevin…" I grunted, trying to force my body to comply with my wishes, but it was hard. "Don't do this."

"We'll meet again, my prince," Kevin whispered.

"Release them," I demanded. "Kore's not coming back. You don't need them."

He inclined his head. The longest minute of my life. Finally, he exhaled. "Do you think they'll be happier? Now that they have nothing to believe in? Now that they've torn apart the worlds they knew? It sounds horrible."

"Horrible is just a word," I said.

Kevin smiled. The next moment they were gone.

THIRTY-FOUR

Initial reports suggest that the parents of the Denton and Sutter boys, and the Spencer girl were Moonset followers, fanatics chosen by the leaders for this one purpose. No names were recorded, though we are not hopeful to find survivors. They served their purpose.

....

Simon Meers
Case Report on *The Moonset Legacy*

Quinn stayed in the room with me while the doctors took a look. I was pretty sure both of the women who'd looked after my injuries were witches, but they bandaged my wounds like medical professionals. "I need to show you something," I said to Quinn, once I'd hijacked a pair of crutches. They'd set my shoulder, but that was as far as I'd let them go. Quinn could have stopped me, but he didn't.

I let him drive. By the time we arrived at the Enchanted Forest, the cold numbness had extended to my extremities, and though my ankle still hurt, I found I could tune out the pain and walk almost normally.

Jenna and Maddy were still waiting by the carousel, but by that point, they'd sat down on the edge of it and let their feet swing into the open air of the grave. The bottle of Charlie's moonshine was now empty, I noticed.

"Kevin?" Maddy asked, resigned like she already knew the answer. I hesitated. No matter what else happened, Maddy was still the loser tonight. She'd been friends with Kevin longer than any of us. He was the reason she and I were even a little friendly.

I grimaced and shook my head.

"But you stopped him?" Jenna asked, her voice just as tremulous. "Right? You stopped him, Mal."

"Justin's okay," Quinn said gently, because the sight of Jenna wavering shook me. I felt something flutter in my chest, but before the bundle of nerves could knit itself up into a boulder in my stomach, the lines across my collarbone flared up, devouring the barbed-wire emotions before they could feed.

"He took Luca and ran before I could kill him," I said. "He'll come back. I don't know when, but he won't give up on what he wants. He'll come back."

"For Kore?" Jenna shook her head.

Quinn was staring at me, a frown on his face. I turned away, disliking the knowing light in his eyes. "Yeah," I said to Jenna. "Yeah, he wants his sister back."

And if I was lying, then only Quinn and I had to know.

It took two days for the smoke to clear and for the city to catch its breath. Carrow Mill certainly wasn't prepared for a riot, especially not one that fizzled out right at the zenith as cars burned and buildings were looted. Over a hundred high school students "woke up" and wandered away, despite the fact that ten seconds before they'd been filled with murderous rage.

The plus side, as Quinn explained, was the highly suggestible state the teenagers were in. Rational thought was hard to come by, and they believed the cover story of a new strain of flu, the kind that raised the body temperature and left them irrational and out of control.

The Witchers had their hands full trying to put out the literal fires as well as the more parental ones in the aftermath. Parents wanted answers, doctors wanted explanations, officials demanded scapegoats. I didn't envy any of them.

But cleanup wasn't my job. At least not the cleanup of the town itself.

It wasn't like any of the other moves. There were two days of methodical packing, of cherry picking the parts of Carrow Mill that we wanted to hold on to. We had *time* when we never had before. Always it was being rushed out of town before dawn, hoping against hope that if something was going to follow us, the dark would slow it down.

But now we knew it was coming. Now we had time to prepare. Cole didn't have to choose between his Xbox or his PlayStation, he was able to take both. Bailey could take any and all the clothes she wanted.

Justin slept a lot—apparently being the love monkey of a monster meant you lost a lot of your strength—and Jenna didn't leave his side. Cole lasted a day before being brought down by another migraine. We'd taken to living in the same house again, Justin's by default. He and Jenna shared his room, Cole and Bailey took hers, and I stayed on the couch. It was fine. I didn't sleep much.

No one interrogated us. No one asked any questions at all, in fact. It was weird. After Luca had been captured, there'd been days and days of questions. The Congress had met in the school office while Robert Cooper tried to throw us under the bus. But this time...it was like no one cared. Like we'd suddenly stopped mattering.

Everyone left me alone. I didn't pack anything at all, and no one came looking for me. The drapes in the living room were shut, I kept all the lights off, and it was a suitable den for two days. I flipped through shows on Netflix and drifted for two days as one episode played after another. Comedies, always comedies. But I never laughed. Not even once.

Quinn came in eventually, the door softly clicking into place behind him. The rest of the house was still. Was it early? Or late? I wasn't exactly sure. I climbed up out of the sprawl I'd found myself in. He nodded his head back towards the door, and I followed him back out into the sunshine. Morning, then. Early morning, at that.

"We'll leave in a couple of hours," he said, standing at the edge of the porch, looking across the street where a small U-Haul was already parked. We didn't have a lot, but more than would fit in a couple of SUVs.

"Guess it's the detention center for us after all, right?" That had been the threat once. Kids called it the Priory—the juvenile detention center for witches. Where the most bitter and broken kids were sent. At least the ones that could be salvaged. Luca never would have made it there.

We'd been circling the drain for years, but the threat had become more real thanks to Illana. But that was before Carrow Mill. We'd been meant to stay here. Permanently. No matter what prank Jenna pulled, they wouldn't move us. We were done.

Guess I managed to do something even Jenna couldn't do.

"It's only for a little while," Quinn said. "The Priory's not as bad as you think. It's the safest place for you. Maleficia and Abyssals ... you're too exposed out in the world."

I nodded. It occurred to me that this was the first time I'd spoken in days. Ever since the park, and putting the carousel back where it belonged. Quinn had taken the initiative to cover up the drag marks in the dirt, any and all evidence that we'd even been there in the first place. We'd wrecked the Moonset symbol that had been set into the ground near the entrance, which meant that anyone could break into the park now if they wanted.

Quinn and Illana ducked their heads together once the Prince was buried again. The two of them were plotting something, but I wasn't interested in figuring out what. All I knew was that everyone left me alone afterwards, and no one asked any questions. Another Abyssal Prince had attacked Carrow Mill, and once again, it had been covered up.

"No one wants to press, because you look ... " Quinn trailed off. "Well, you look like hell. They just want to know that you're okay."

I shrugged. That wasn't an answer, even I knew that wasn't an answer, but it felt like I barely had the energy to stand there. Listening was hard, but actually holding a conversation? That might exhaust the meager bit of energy I had. I was running on empty.

"I know a thing or two about fate," he said, ducking his head down. It had been a few days since Quinn had shaved. Since he wasn't looking at me, I took the rare opportunity to study his face without him noticing. His cheeks were rough with stubble, but it was a good look. "One of the first things you learn when you sign up to become a Witcher is that fate gets to have a bit of fun with you. You're not your own master anymore. You go where you're needed unless you're either very skilled, or very special."

"Which one are you?" The words were rusty, crumbling and eroding in my throat. But I managed them.

"Which one am I?" He shook his head. "Some days both. Some days neither. Most days I can't sleep for hearing fate's mocking laughter in my ears. No one's ever expected more from me than I do. But sometimes you get what you want and then you realize there was something more. Something you just lost out on, because you made the wrong call."

Somewhere during Quinn's speech, he decided to meet my eyes again. His voice grew softer and softer, and I had to lean in to hear it.

It was just the two of us, and despite the fact that I'd made an active business out of never crossing the wrong lines, of never getting too close to Quinn, or letting myself *think* about Quinn, or to consider him as anything other than a means to an end—a conduit to his grandmother—I leaned closer. His eyes dropped down to my lips, and there was fragileness there, to that moment.

"You're still a kid," Quinn said. Just as casual. Just as matter-of-factly.

"I'm eighteen."

"Doesn't mean you're not still a kid," Quinn said slowly. "When you grow up…" he seemed to be at a loss for words. "It's not your fault. Most kids get to be kids. You've always been a POW. All of you. And I mean, I get it. You've done an admirable job, shielding Bailey and Cole the way you have, but the three of you… it surprises me sometimes, how well-adjusted you are."

"My brother stabbed himself in the stomach for the girl he loved, and my sister and I just dug up a dead body," I replied. "Well-adjusted is a little much."

"It's not… appropriate." Quinn seemed flustered. Struggling with his words. He wouldn't meet my eyes anymore. His breathing was a little more shallow, his movements shaky.

Maybe a week ago, I would have pushed the issue. Leaned forward and called Quinn out on his sudden cowardice. The tattoo against my skin burned like an electric blanket turned up just a bit too high. Uncomfortable, but not exactly painful.

I hadn't felt much of anything since the spell I'd used to inure myself against the Prince's influence. The spell that worked too well. Before this had started, before the Prince had come for me, Jenna sat in a classroom and announced, "Malcolm hates everything." And maybe it was true at the time. Partly true, but still truth to be found inside, like treasure inside a cave.

But now it wasn't. Because even hating something meant there were feelings there. And I didn't feel much of anything. The Prince was gone, and I should have felt happy, or relieved, or anything other than empty. It wasn't depression, because I didn't hate my life or my family or my situation. Not anymore. I had accepted it.

I was one of the children of Moonset. My father was a bad guy. He killed people, but he also tried to save me. Good people could do bad things, but the reverse was just as true. That didn't mean they were misjudged, or there was more to the story. Just because Cyrus Denton put a voice mail in the ether didn't take away from the thousands of people he'd killed, or the terror he'd helped to create. But he'd been a good guy, once, and helped stop a monster before it killed his friends. But somewhere along the way he'd gotten lost, and he wound up walking down a road to a bad end.

"Come on," I said, turning back towards the door. "I'll go wake the others. It's time to go."

Carrow Mill wasn't our home anymore. But I knew I'd have to come back someday. To finish what Moonset had started. To finish what the Abyssal Prince had started.

My road to Hell had only just begun.

THE END

About the Author

Scott Tracey (Avon Lake, Ohio) lived on a Greyhound bus for a month, wrote his illustrated autobiography at the age of six, and barely survived Catholic school. His gifts can be used for good or evil, and he strives for both for his own amusement. *Witch Eyes* was his debut YA novel.